★ A clarification about my modus operandi: even when I resist the temptation of censorship or when I don't dilate the original prose as I please, I am an indelicate transporter, a clumsy mover, a seedy trafficker. I dispatch fragile and labeled objects from one edge of the ocean to the other, and although I certainly do my best, I bang them and drop them, I damage and dent them, scuff them and scrape them, I destroy them despite myself . . .

Revenge of the Translator

Brice Matthieussent

Deep Vellum Publishing
Dallas, Texas

Deep Vellum Publishing
3000 Commerce St., Dallas, Texas 75226
deepvellum.org · @deepvellum

Deep Vellum Publishing is a 501C3
nonprofit literary arts organization founded in 2013.

ISBN
978-1-941920-69-5 (paperback) • 978-1-941920-70-1 (ebook)
Library of Congress Control Number: 2018936731

This work received the French Voices Award for excellence in publication and translation. French Voices is a program created and funded by the French Embassy in the United States and FACE (French American Cultural Exchange).

Cover design by Anna Zylicz · annazylicz.com
Typesetting by Kirby Gann · kirbygann.net

Text set in Bembo, a typeface modeled on typefaces cut by Francesco Griffo for Aldo Manuzio's printing of *De Aetna* in 1495 in Venice.

Distributed by Consortium Book Sales & Distribution.

Printed in the United States of America on acid-free paper.

Revenge of the Translator

...I, who am not even the pawn of a pawn in the great chess game, far from it, now want to take the place of the queen... —I, the pawn of a pawn, a piece which doesn't even exist, which isn't even in the game—and next I may want to take the king's place as well or even the whole board...

—Franz Kafka
Letter to Milena Jesenská,
about the *Letter to His Father*

The machine works with words.
—Jean Suquet

for Maeva A.

Chapter 1

THE TRANSLATOR TAKES THE STAGE

★

★ I reside here below this thin black bar. This is my place, my living room, my den. The walls are painted white and covered with several lines of thin black characters, like an uneven frieze, a changing wallpaper. Welcome to you, dear reader, who has crossed the threshold of my lair. It's not as spacious as that of my upstairs neighbor, but in his absence I welcome his visitors who have been rerouted by his inexplicable desertion. I know it's him that you came to see, and you've stumbled upon me instead. You will have to make do. I rub elbows in this modest space. I pile up these lines to keep my cave from becoming a coffin, my bunker from becoming a tomb.

Make yourself at home, relax, and, please, check at the door your flattery and formulaic smiles typical of visitors to the proprietor, the seigneur and master, who lives and receives guests on the floor above. I hope that you will not feel too out of place, even if I have a few surprises in store for you. Just be careful not to hit your head on the ceiling. As you'll see, the height changes from one room to the next. Know also that in my home all the spaces are adjoined, like the maids' rooms that are sometimes lumped in a row alongside each other on the top floor of a building: each leads into the next and you must cross all of them to reach the last. It's not very practical, but there's no way around it.

Normally, I don't host anyone, I remain invisible and silent, allocated to my cramped residence, relegated beneath the earth.

There, above, in the open air, above the bar, that airtight, insurmountable lid, I am certainly omnipresent, but in a way that even I don't really understand, in a bizarre form, ectoplasmic and constrained. I maneuver around incognito, disembodied, an obedient and faithful phantom like a shadow fastened to a body, since the beginning of time existing in the mold of the other, of my noisy neighbor who struts in the spotlight, that tall beanpole you came to visit, but who has suddenly disappeared without leaving a forwarding address.

This is not a life; it's barely existing. My notes? Apparitions as fleeting as those of a ferret or a mole, of a shooting star or a green flash: the servile explications of the exegete fear-stricken by faith. (*Translator's Night*)

★

★ *Mon père, ce géant au regard si doux*. In French in the original English text, as are all the passages in italics followed by an asterisk.

Each time I appear it's after this little typographical star, the humble asterisk. Here I write like the tail of a black comet, zooming from left to right in the white margin of the page. But I'm tied down, I'm a comet not only relegated to the negative space, but also on a leash, a pet star: far from roaming as I would like through the firmament and doing as I please, I am steered, radio-controlled by the upper asterisk that summons the note, that hails me like a master calls its dog and orders: "Fetch." Stick in my mouth, gaze full of gratitude and tail wagging to show the measure of my admiration, I present myself before my superior and exist only in relation with him, in relation to him. Held up to his measuring stick, I am but a millimeter tall. Nevertheless, on both sides of the black bar exists a curious symmetry: the two asterisks are the same size, as if the star in the firmament were reflected in the sea of my text. And then, dear reader, all you have to do is pivot the book you're currently holding in your hands 180° and everything flips: now it's me who's up in the sky, level with the horizon and the clouds and the layers of pollution looming on top; my pretty star dominates that of the other, flyspeck floating in an insipid bowl of milk.

Enough.

5

This French quotation in the text is erroneous. June 18, 1850, Victor Hugo actually writes in *La Légende des siecles (Après la bataille):* "*Mon père, ce héros au sourire si doux.*" The two errors—*géant* instead of *héros*, *regard* instead of *sourire*—can potentially be explained by faulty memory.

Regardless, according to the testimonies of his close friends, the author's father was, in reality, an authoritarian, sometimes brutal, man, subject to sudden and spectacular fits of rage. From the first pages of his novel the author evokes the paternal figure: this is surely not insignificant.

Have I gone too far? Am I being too much of a chatterbox? (*Tapir's Nose*)

★

★ This time it's Racine who is maimed. Instead of express-
ing his resentment toward Rome, he writes (in French in the
American text): "*L'homme, unique objet de mon ressentiment.*" I wonder whether this blunder, this lapse that takes us from romanthro-
phy to misanthropy, from Rome to homme and from pillar to
post, whether this violent translation★★ doesn't make us reflect on
the act of translation itself, this Tarzan's jump from above into the
unfathomable abyss of a dense jungle. (*Tarzan's Nosedive*)

★★ *In English in my French text.*

★

★The crowbar that here allows the stranger dressed in a large black cape to force his way, by night, into the restored Normandy cottage owned by the French writer Abel Prote, to break into, collect, or erase the data on his computer, this crowbar slipped under Prote's white door, is running through my mind. This crowbar titillates my birdbrain. For all you need is a solid pull on the handle of this tool so that the lever raises itself at the same time, and that's all there is to it, the door vanished, the path clear.

Thus, it would perhaps suffice for me to accumulate enough of these lines here at the bottom of the page for the white door, the thin black bar signifying the bottom, to violently swing off its hinges. My inferior remarks, my commentaries and other digressions would act, then, as my crowbar. What would I see next, after the fall of the white panel? What unknown space would we discover together? Is the asterisk the peephole permitting me to scrutinize what lies beyond, the secret passage behind the mirror?

But, until then, a doormat I remain. (*Notion's End*)

＊

＊ *Antique père océan:* this phrase refers to Proteus in the *Odyssey*. He's the god of the sea who watches over the grazing of herds of seals and other marine animals that belong to Poseidon. Gifted with the power of metamorphosis, Proteus can become not only an animal, but also an element, such as water or fire, to escape from inquiring minds. He lives on the island of Pharos, not far from the Nile Delta.

In the book that I'm translating, *Translator's Revenge* (in French it should be, if the publisher agrees, *Vengeance du Traducteur,* but the publishers of course consult the managing editors as well as the sales representatives who in their turn consult the booksellers who then ... Anyway, the jury is still out on the French title, it could just as easily become *Panique à New York* or *La Séductrice de Saint-Germain-des-Prés*, or worse). Where was I? Oh yes, Proteus. This Greek god often reappears in the text under various forms as the tutelary divinity of the young American translator David Grey. (*Translator's Rote*)

★ Hide-behind. In French: *le Se-cache-derrière*. The author, whom I questioned about this neologism, immediately responded to me by email that he discovered this bizarre term in the *The Book of Imaginary Beings* by Jorge Luis Borges and Margarita Guerrero, in the chapter entitled "Fauna of the United States." I quote: "The *Hide-behind* is always hiding behind something. Whichever way a man turns, it's always behind him, which is why nobody has ever satisfactorily described one, though it has killed and eaten many a lumberjack."

That the author is comparing his hero David Grey, American translator of French novels,★★ to a Hide-behind, a furtive and voracious assassin, serves as proof of the nebulousness of his prose. I, for example, have never killed or devoured even one lumberjack, no character or any author of the numerous American novels that I've translated into French. One could nevertheless make the claim that I have masticated their texts, but discreetly, on the sly: not only the delicious flesh, the choice and daring cuts, the tasty tendons and crunchy passages, but also the bones, the cartilage, the tough nerves, the descriptive tunnels, the clogged arteries, the indigestible joints, the nails, the repugnant hairs, the contrived dialogues, the misplaced voices, the twisted prose … All of that cannibalized, digested, absorbed, then vomited back up in my own language. Sometimes you have to have good teeth and a solid stomach.

★★ There are so many passages, even entire pages, that I have redacted in my translation that I have to give a bit of explanation of the novel's plot.

This Hide-behind, invisible because he is always hidden behind the back of another, makes me think of the Courbet painting *La Source*. In a pastoral setting, we see, in fact we devour with our eyes, a young nude woman with sumptuous curves, depicted from behind. Nonchalantly resting on a large rock, she is absorbed in the contemplation of a little spring into which she has plunged her hand. Standing before this painting and behind that engrossing beauty in which I, without her knowing, admire her large hips, her fine waist, her shapely back, her languid posture, I am Borges's Hide-behind. Ready to jump on my prey. Like a good translator. Not seen, not caught, but carnivorous.

Little by little, I climb. (*Trickster's Nook*)

★

★ The bar, the lid under which I marinate in my gravy, this lifeless slab, reminds me sometimes of the fish sleeping at the bottom of the *turbotiere*, hermetically sealed before being cooked, cut, and savored. Meanwhile the other man strutting on the floors above plays the charlatan, the street peddler, luring customers in with his stentorian voice and turnstile arms, gathering visitors onto whom he offloads his glass beads and multicolored strings, to swindle them and convince them on top of it all that they have taken part in a grand affair . . . I'm thrilled to shut him up.

But I am no longer within the confines of my role, I overstep my duties, I forget my place, as they say. Frankly, what's the point of losing my temper? Am I jealous? Claustrophobic? Probably a bit of both. I must bring myself back to task, curb my delirium, rediscover the lucid, the serious, rigor and sobriety, precision and concision, discreet and efficient erudition, etc., etc., etc. For I am—as we all know—a humble artisan, the man behind the scenes, the coal miner digging in the darkness of his tunnel, his dictionaries serving as his only light, his wisdom his only tool, fidelity and drudgery his only objectives, even though infidelity and laziness are the two mammary glands of the novel!

The mole digs his underground tunnels, the other above parades and struts before his audience of admirers and flatterers.

Enough. (*Delirium's Mainspring*)

★

★ Dumbwaiter, *le serviteur muet.* Here, once again, the author misleads his reader with a web of prejudices, all humiliating to my profession. In fact, the dumbwaiter, *le serviteur muet,* is a goods elevator that, in certain old New York buildings, is at the disposition of its tenants. It's also a vertical pass-through that you sometimes find in a restaurant. In Great Britain it's a dessert stand. Comparing a translator to a dumbwaiter, a goods elevator, a serving hatch, or a dessert stand makes my blood boil. For, in the end, without this pass-through, the author wouldn't have any say in the matter. And if I serve him soup, it's only this poor substitute that allows him to stay, somehow, above the bar: not the solid, rustic, homemade broth, but the sachets of freeze-dried powder whose exact composition we would rather not know.

Or else, kind reader, my author is a poor stage actor who doesn't know a single word of his text. And I, hidden from all gazes except his in the prompter's hole, whisper his lines to him one by one; I read his text in a drone, I feed him beakfuls. From my lips he takes his sonorous nutrients and immediately spits them out for the delighted public who, nine times out of ten, see nothing but fire. Invisible, I brood at the bottom of my obscure opening while in the spotlight he brims with pride.

The following comparison the author makes is even more unpleasant. He equivocates the translator David Grey with a lazy Susan, *une Susan parasseuse.* A lazy Susan is a rotating tray installed in the middle of the table in certain restaurants, especially Asian establishments! (*Toiler's Nausea*)

★

★ I notice with stupefaction that I, the humble goods elevator, the pass-through, the rotating tray, etc., have succeeded in sliding, insinuating myself into the bottom of each of the novel's pages
thus far. A bit unusual, isn't it, a bit audacious, for the translator is
ordinarily a discreet, self-effacing being who knows how to behave
himself. But why shouldn't I? In any case, what's the point of bury-
ing my head in the sand? This novel is utter nonsense and the
author a scoundrel. In my opinion, I should never have agreed
to translate this book... I should delete these sentences, the publisher will not allow them. Then again, no, I'll leave them. Like the
driver stretching his legs when he finally reaches the rest stop on
the highway, I feel better and better: I no longer have pins and needles in my limbs, my aches are fading, my cramps dispersing. When
translating nonstop, one gets stiff, atrophies, fades. And I notice that
this escapade is oxygenating my blood, that this improvised stop is
doing me a great deal of good.

Where was I? Oh yes, this novel is utter nonsense. Imagine,
dear reader, that the hero of *Translator's Revenge*, the young and
sympathetic David Grey, a professional translator (from French to
English), a native New Yorker, whom you don't know very well
yet, sometimes mistakes himself for Zorro, the masked avenger
dressed all in black who always appears without warning, where
no one expects him. In fact, a bit like me, I'm suddenly realizing... Sometimes, Grey also disguises himself as the enigmatic
character you find on the labels of certain bottles of port: a man
dressed in a long cape and a big hat that plunges his face into
darkness. All of this is of course ridiculous, for as soon as a translator feels even the slightest desire for vengeance, his work suffers

for it: his head is elsewhere, he becomes absentminded, or worse, dishonest. As for David Grey's absorption of the man in black on the bottle of Sandeman port, it's teeming with perfidious double entendres: is the translator drinking? Is he plotting against the creator of the book? Is he an assassin? A mercenary ready to sell his services to the highest bidder? A saboteur secretly slipping grains of sand into the well-oiled machinery of the novel to make it skid out of control or even flip over, bringing a full halt to the mechanism? Or else a coward, a shameful, timid man who constantly hides his face and shows only his back? And so returns the specter of the Hide-behind...

Instead of accumulating humiliating images and insidious allusions, the author would do better to restore the profession's coat of arms, one that should depict a chameleon. (*Translator's No*)

★

★ Concerning the coat of arms: "I must have a sinistral line in my coat of arms," David Grey says to the beautiful Doris. Here he is citing William Faulkner's *Soldiers' Pay*. The sinistral line is the distinctive sign of the illegitimate branch in a coat of arms. Subtle, no? And, incidentally, the text informs us that David Grey is left-handed. (*T.N.*)

★

★ *Fragments épars.* This is a reference to my author's second novel (*Scattered Figments*, Janus Press, New York, 1995), in which the character Abel Prote, the French writer, appears again. I won't say any more. Mum's the word. Let's remain civil. (*T.N.*)

I'll simply add that the French translation (Éditions du Marais, Paris, 1997) is horribly botched: words, sentences, even entire paragraphs forgotten or deliberately deleted, misinterpretations, mistranslations, Anglicisms, solecisms, appalling blunders, and clumsiness. One laughable detail: a confusion of the American volume measurements makes it so that, according to the vile translator whose name I won't mention, the characters apparently guzzle liters of whiskey, while at the same time the author explicitly describes their desire for drink to be very moderate, "similar," he clarifies, "to a piece of old blotting paper riddled with colored stains that can no longer absorb anything except the rare drop of ink." The French translator, distracted or intoxicated—was he drinking?—took no notice of this lovely image. Thus, he proposes a nearly-empty bottle of whiskey that, as if it were a miraculous spring, continuously refills large glasses to the brim numerous times as soon as they are knocked back, as if the protagonists of *Scattered Figments* were unabashed drunkards downing enormous quantities of alcohol without letting on. Clearly, this novel deserves to be retranslated. I'll have to speak to my publisher about it.

★

★ I'm still sneaking around under the bar, thumbing my nose, picking up my crowbar, wedging my shoe between the door and the frame. As you've just learned, dear reader, David Grey is having problems with Abel Prote, the French novelist whose most recent book, bizarrely titled *(N.d.T.)*, David is translating: misunderstandings, mistakes, disparaging allusions, suspicious looks, skipped meetings, various obstacles, reciprocal irritations, etc. In short, there's trouble brewing between the French writer and his American translator. I sincerely hope not to have the same problems with my author. His emails are courteous but vague, at times cryptic. For example, when I asked him about the meaning of the expression "Agenbite of Inwit" which appears in his text to qualify the culpability felt by the unfortunate Grey who is convinced that he's botched his work, my author replied to me with disarming and scandalous flippancy that it's "a quotation from Joyce." A lot of good that does me! Am I going to reread every single work by the Irish exile, looking for these three sibylline words? Nevertheless, in "Agenbite of Inwit," I detect something to do with bite and of course Inuit. What does the subarctic population have to do with anything? Do the Inuit bite?

Stand aside, the door is about to slam! I pull back my shoe just in time (I still don't have a crowbar). (*Translator's Quote*)

★

★ Now that I've made myself at home, I suddenly feel the desire to raise the bar by using the strength of my back and thighs. I'd like to lift myself up, first kneel down, then get into a vertical position, raise this wretched horizon line at the bottom of the page that confines me to the lower margin. I would like to hoist this bar by the sole force of my desire and my muscles, make it rise like the weight lifter who thrusts above his head the black bar linking the big matte metal pancakes and who, completing a clean and jerk, goofily brandishes the bar at arm's length: his cheeks swelling under the effort, his face turning purple, his gaze lost in the distance of private contemplation. It's with this same determination that I will push my bar without dumbbells, so heavy nevertheless, toward the sky. But not for anything in the world would I want to step across the bar, or jump over it, like the 110-meter-hurtles runner who one minute soars over the cinder track and the next jumps over the rectilinear obstacle. I'm not trying to abandon my staves to occupy a better place; I have no desire to sit on the throne in the middle of the royal page. No, I, the lone man comfortably sporting the dress of the immaculate bride, will subject him to the worst outrages, lifting my bar little by little, firmly planted in this footer, bracing myself. (*Trajectory North*)

Chapter 2

THE TRANSLATOR TRIMS THE FAT

★

★ Here is the beginning of this chapter in the original American edition:

"Abel Prote was born January 1, 1950, at the American Hospital in Paris. His family lived in a bourgeois building in the 6th arrondissement, not far from the Odéon theater. His father, Maurice-Edgar Prote, wealthy Parisian publisher and audacious purveyor of American literature, decided to name him Abel because of the child's rather unusual birth date, at the exact caesura of the century. As for the surname, Prote, it comes from distant ancestors on the father's side, who were foremen in the first printer's shops: 'prote,' the French word for 'master printer,' comes from the Greek *prōtos*, 'first.'

An old American lady, who for some obscure reason begged me not to divulge her name, happened to show me in New York the diary she had kept in the past, during her Parisian years. So uneventful had those years been — apparently — that the collecting of daily details — which is always a poor method of self-preservation — barely surpassed a short description of the day's weather. Luck being what it is when left alone, here I was offered something which I might never have hunted down had it been a chosen quarry. Therefore I am able to state that the afternoon of Abel Prote's birth was a sinister windy one, with two degrees (Celsius) above zero … this is all, however, that the good lady found worth setting down. On second thought I don't see why I should yield to her desire for anonymity. That she will ever read this book seems wildly improbable. Her name was and is Jane Jennifer Janireff: baroque babble which it would have been a pity to withhold!"

It's without remorse that I delete these first paragraphs of Chapter 2, even if I supply them here to be read as a note. Paradox? Contradiction? I don't care. Indeed, how surprised I was, and what indignation I felt, to discover, in a rather large coincidence—"that's luck for you"—that it is almost word for word the first page of Vladimir Nabokov's first novel written in English, *The Real Life of Sebastian Knight*! Shame on my author... Who does he think he's fooling with such blatant impostures? His only originality lies in replacing Nabokov's splendid "Olga Olegovna Orlova—an egg-like alliteration" with "Jane Jennifer Janireff: baroque babble." Nice idea, but it doesn't at all justify keeping this shameful plagiarism in my French translation. (*Trimmer's Nota Bene*)

★

★ The esteemed reader will have noticed that since the beginning of this chapter no adjective has encumbered my author's ungainly prose. It's not his own decision, but a unilateral and systematic redaction on my part. A sort of edict decreed by me alone. I know that similar suppressions are hardly defendable from the deontological (what a dreadful word!) point of view but, dear reader, you must admit that after this robust pruning, his prose has gained in elegance and fluidity. No more of that unbearable ponderousness, those seemingly endless agglutinations of adjectives! Such levity! His prose has become almost good, the bastard. And since he barely speaks French, he won't suspect a thing. I have complete freedom of action, as long as the Parisian publisher for whom I'm translating *Translator's Revenge* isn't in the habit of going through their texts with a fine-tooth comb. And if I were now to revoke the adverbs? (*Typist's Nuisance*)

★ It's done: no more adjectives and not a single adverb. The result of these surgical strikes? A gain that is genuinely unheard of, truly serendipitous, undeniably stupefying, frankly stupendous, irrefutably spectacular—with this wearisome accumulation I make up for it and prove the efficacy of my ablations. Now, such concision, such levity! I retranscribe here for your curiosity the list of adverbs and adjectives disappeared since the beginning of the second chapter in which we find Abel Prote, "the virile man with green eyes," who was born in the middle of the century, working alongside Doris, his idiosyncratic secretary (and maybe more):

charming, light brown, pure, shiny, suddenly, vaporous, hooked, sensually, low-cut, becoming, splendid (2 times), formfitting (3 times), tall, thin (2 times), opulent (2 times), oblong, short (4 times), curvaceous, exactly, penetrating (2 times), virile, green (after these last two deletions, we are left with the striking "the man with eyes"), elegant, suggestive, transparent (3 times), lightly, languorous (3 times), violently, catlike, hot (4 times), imperceptibly, softly, lukewarm, slowly (3 times), silky (3 times), alluring, blue, white, red, pulpy, resolute, stubborn (2 times), fat, built, pinkish, very (7 times), smooth, tumescent (3 times), black and pink (2 times), rounded, bulging, luxuriant, lowered, secret, moist (4 times), isolated, inflated (3 times), strong, massive (4 times), burning, concentric (4 times), slow (2 times), rapid (5 times), more and more, open (4 times), perfumed (2 times), marine, spicy, unfastened, smothered, wild (2 times), contained, aerial, purplish, agile (5 times), wet, hard (4 times), powerfully (3 times), frenetic, again (6 times), supple, defective, brusquely, languid, crumpled (2 times), low, tender, little by little, relaxed, dozing, restorative. (*Tamperer's Nosography*)

★

★ A clarification about my modus operandi: even when I resist the temptation of censorship or when I don't dilate the original prose as I please, I am an indelicate transporter, a clumsy mover, a seedy trafficker. I dispatch fragile and labeled objects from one edge of the ocean to the other, and although I certainly do my best, I bang them and drop them, I damage and dent them, scuff them and scrape them, I destroy them despite myself and en route I lose the most important crates, furniture, carpets, paintings, etchings, designs, photographs, books, magazines and knickknacks, plates and silverware, bodies and body parts, clothes, tools and machines, stuffed or living animals, china, glasses and crystal, accessories and utensils that are however duly indexed, hidden nooks and love nests, boudoirs and canopies, cabinets and bathrooms, studios and apartments, houses, villas, buildings, entire neighborhoods, arrondissements, towers, towns, suburbs, cities, rivers, ponds, lakes and streams, provinces, states, continents and oceans, planets, stars, constellations, galaxies, nebulas and black holes, that were entrusted to my seemingly nice face, and violently I throw a large part of my cargo to the roadside and it crashes there with a roar, in order to transport to safe harbor a few paltry residues, scraps, trash, mismatched specimens, delivering them haphazardly to the mercy of my readers who are frustrated or naïve, in any event duped, tricked, for they are unaware of all the perils of the voyage and the risks of the trade.

I preserve only the first half of the phrase import-export and in my tribulations I lose the majority of my fragile merchandise; at the first gust of wind they're thrown overboard, for they are poorly tied up on the deck of my freighter, crushed during transfers by the distracted or clumsy longshoremen, smashed by life's obstacles, ignobly swapped for food, weapons, a caravan of camels, a state-of-the-art car, a schooner, or a plane, pillaged by pirates and a thousand more or less shameful duplicities, or else simply forgotten, wasting away at the bottom of a shuttered warehouse. Thus, finally reaching the port, I arrive at the quay and deliver an inferior substitute to my employers, deaf and blind but normally satisfied, a derisory residue of original treasure, meager dregs that I piece together somehow, a balloon that I reinflate using only the force of my nicotined lungs. Disappointment, disarray, general desolation. There remains the empty husk, the sheath deprived of life, the mold without the bronze. In short, I am depressed, I am not the first of the text, but the eternal Poulidor, the second by vocation or by decree of destiny, the eternal afterthought: I always arrive too late and in rough shape. (*Transporter's Negligence*)

★

★You will have noticed, my reader, that above I deleted all the "stage directions," conserving only, for excellent reasons of austerity and internal dynamic, the dialogues between characters. Here, for your curiosity, the list of these deleted directions:

"   !" hurled Doris in a defiant voice as she walked toward him.

"   ," Grey replied coldly.

"   ..."

"   ," Grey cut her off, drawing right up close to her beautiful face with its slightly hooked nose.

"   ?"

"   ," he retorted ruthlessly, grabbing her by the collar of her blue terry cloth nightgown.

"   !" Doris whined, undone.

"   ..." Grey insinuated without loosening his grip.

"   ," unleashed that beauty who (etc.).

"   ?"

"   ," she confessed, batting her eyelashes.

"   ," he replied dryly.

He pushed Doris violently down onto the crimson sofa, where she collapsed, a wreck, making sure to modestly tug her dressing gown over her legs, which were shapely / slender / thin as matchsticks / very skinny / could take a footbath in a double-barreled shotgun (I still have to choose).

The translator left the room slamming the door behind him. Here are the stage directions from the next scene:

"   ?" the stranger in the frayed black coat, wearing a fedora of an indefinable color, asks him out of the blue.

"   ," Grey replies, still thinking of Doris, of how he left her in tears on the crimson sofa.

"   ?" continues the stranger.

"   ?" Grey retorts tit for tat.

"   ."

"   ?" ventures the translator, suddenly wary.

"   !" says the other.

"   ," Grey concludes.

They go to the nearest bar, where they drink beers until nightfall. (*Eraser's Numerus Clausus*)

★

★ After the adjectives, the adverbs, and the stage directions, I have decided to delete from here on out all comparisons and metaphors. Often hackneyed, when they're not harebrained or incomprehensible, they uselessly hinder the reader. As a result of this new ablation, my text (or rather, his text revised and corrected by my efforts: ours, then) gains even more lucidity, strength, simplicity. What would be the point of rendering that constipated prose in French when we can get straight to the point? Here is the list of those insipid flourishes, laughable or convoluted, in any case superfluous:

his iron grip and her steel gaze (sic), the blanket of the night, the song of the sirens (2 times), a voice of blue velvet (?), with the lassitude of a cat (meh), strong as a Turk from the Bosporus (!), the Trojan horse of her seduction (referring to Doris), the star of the night, like a drove of wild horses, "the Greeks enter Ilion, overthrow the throne, and climb atop" (crossed-out sentence), that exhausted and unruly beast (hope), that Bluebeard killing one after another of his prying wives venturing behind the forbidden door to satisfy their shameful curiosity; stubborn as a red donkey (?); satin-smooth (skin); the muscle of the soul (imagination); the hell of the game; as abruptly as a drop of dew slides down a lilac leaf and falls, before the leaf, suddenly lightened, straightens up (?);

like a translucent petal of a red rose (ear); the cruel sting of revenge; old as the dust of roads; he collapses on top of her like poverty over the world; "ten minutes before two: shiny mustache with curled-up tips" (this one makes my hair stand on end). And finally that doubly circular pearl, which I cross out with a capital Z in a vengeful crayon: "the sun was shining, like the sinister eye of a scheming Parisian ogling the gardens of the Palais-Royal through the slight opening of her parted curtains, faded by the sun."

Next, after careful consideration and for reasons of conciseness, I have decided to eliminate from the final text of my translation that long and yet rather beautiful digression in which the author describes the work of David Grey:

"Here the translator David Grey is confronted with the original text of *(N.d. T.)*. He probes, carries out some tests, follows the contours, identifies the lines with the greatest slope, drills, cores, plans, and outlines, he gropes around in search of buried geological structures, the right angle of attack and of adequate 'positioning' as one says in certain sports. For him this text is a mining site to exploit, to bleed systematically; he has to get to work, clear the fossil forests of the printed page, these lines accumulated like geologic strata, dig the tunnels, build the mine shafts, advance the front, beat down the blocks of words, of sentences, of paragraphs to see sometimes that the heart of the deposit is elsewhere, higher, lower, farther. Sometimes, an entire tunnel collapses, forcing him to backpedal, to reorient himself, to explore new tunnels, previously unseen means of approach, to modify the tools, the point of view, the angle of attack, the stays, and even the techniques of exploitation.

"Sometimes, also, unpredictable methane explosions and murderers make entire dialogues explode, crack, or shatter misplaced voices, reduce to nothingness loves and friendships, destroy in a flash the slow formulation of an accent, of a breath, of rectifiable language tics. Suddenly, that voice rings false, the character rings hollow; careful, he's going to implode. So everything has to start anew, there is no hope of mending anything. The translator must demolish the entire edifice of that voice, suddenly broken, condemned to a definitive muteness. In recreating it through other means, he will probably notice that other voices in the crowd, if not all of them, also need to be recreated: one methane explosion often brings about others, almost immediately, in a chain reaction, or with a delay."

In order to offset the disappearance of all those adjectives, adverbs, stage directions, comparisons and metaphors, entire passages, and to emphasize what enhances the text—for example the number of my lines at the bottom of each page—I add the following images to my American author's book, for through my stubborn and anonymous★★ work these lines, my images, and my presence expand like

"The afternoon shadow on the sundial
Showing that labor can demand its requital;
By the fire, who can deny it, the standard meter;
An unrolled trouser leg, after the river;
The mended boot whose heel is remade;
While he clears the table, a flunky's pile of plates;
The half-drawn sword stick brandished in a duel;
When an elderly pianist shrinks, the piano stool;
The new tear-off calendar replacing the old one;
The soufflé when it's taken out of the oven;
The sail at the first upturn in weather, descended;
The table before a large dinner party, extended;
The flame of the match head;
The roots of chives in the garden bed;
When its resistance breaks, the elastic umbrella fastener;
When the bed replaces the cradle, the comforter."
(*Rousselian Note*)

★★ I almost wrote *autonomous*!

Chapter 3

THE TRANSLATOR ADDS SOME BACK IN

★

★ The character Doris, the "servant with a big heart" and personal secretary to Abel Prote, seems insufficiently developed to me. Therefore, I will take the liberty of fleshing her out (without, of course, asking the permission of the author, who, decidedly lacking in common sense, remains a bit curt and uptight). After all, the ancillary functions merit our interest, don't they ... For example, in New York, when she proposes her professional services to David Grey, who accepts them gladly, I envisioned that she would soon offer him much more. What the young Grey doesn't know is that Doris is already in a relationship with Abel Prote, the Parisian writer whose novel, curiously titled (*N.d.T.*), Grey is translating into English.

Hence Doris's back-and-forths between Paris and New York, between Prote and Grey, bearing witness as much to her "big heart" as to the liberty of her morals. She is a well-read courtesan. In my version of the novel, Doris acts as a double agent, more of a corrupt muse than a faithful employee. (*Temptress's Dark Side*)

★

★All of the following passage:

My father was a long-distance captain, petroleum engineer, geologist, film actor, lover of French poetry and literature, test driver and sewage worker, dowser, mason, upholsterer, surveyor, gigolo in his spare time, pen pusher and amateur painter, sculptor and rod-fisherman, champion swimmer (it was at the public pool that he seduced the water nymph who would become my mother), air traffic controller, distinguished skier and seasoned mountaineer (it was to the immaculate and then-deserted slopes that he would soon bring her on vacation), lead trawler, collector of postage stamps and smoker of cigars (it's presumably because of these pastimes that over the years he later tolerated the drudge of married life).

As they say in the notes at the bottom of administrative forms, "Cross out where not applicable" or "Check the appropriate box." But when it comes to a father, does there exist such a thing as nonapplicable or an appropriate box? So I leave as is this improbable enumeration and supply neither birth date nor social security number. Nevertheless, here are a few specifications that will never appear on any administrative form:

Comfortably settled in front of the black-and-white television screen, a glass of cognac close at hand, a pungent Cuban in the other, my father never missed a rugby match or a night of wrestling (I would watch TV with him sometimes, after my mother went upstairs to go to bed, and I still remember the match between the White Angel and the infamous Béthune Executioner, in a balaclava and wearing all black: athletes dressed for the small screen even then). His usual disappointments because of the ORTF didn't stop him from looking forward to the next sports broadcast. Often away for work, he would travel to India, Brazil, the United States, or, more modestly, to Marseille, for stretches varying from a few weeks to several months. He spoke English fluently and, in the 50s, was a fervent defender of all that came from America: checkered shirts with a button-up collar, Johnnie Walker "Red Label" whiskey with the swashbuckler in a redingote and shiny top hat on the label, LPs of jazz and that famous burgeoning music, rock 'n' roll, Reader's Digest, *plastic models of the B-25 bomber, of battleships and aircraft carriers, of dinosaurs and ptero-dactyls, cars with streamlined wing tips in shiny chromes (he owned a Versailles, then an Ariane, before buying an Ovni: the nauseating DS), he defended the dollar and progress, morality, technique, and work, but most importantly he displayed from morning to night an unwavering optimism. He flew in the Super Constellation and had a fondness for the multilingual flight attendants. Curiously, he did not like the cinema.*

My mother, an Anglophile, made me read from a young age Somerset Maugham (I found it strange that she pronounced his name "Môme") and Washington Irving, Charles Dickens, and Graham Greene. Sometimes on summer afternoons, lying side by side in the sun on two chaises longues (we called them "transats"), in the vast garden of the house we rented for vacation, she and I would read the pages of those novels in turn and out loud. Face protected by a large straw hat, dressed in a loose violet dress with a multicolored pattern or in a silk sari brought back from India, she would listen, a kind smile on her lips, to my hesitant and diligent voice. Then she would take over and each time I would admire her melodious accent, which enchanted me all the more because I had no other to com-pare it to: we rarely went to the movies and the babbling television was exclusively in French. Reading was how I learned English.
all of this passage is my own.

Scanning the horizon, I can already make out the dusty cloud of Freudians rushing over at a gallop.

Nevertheless I add with no remorse these personal confi-dences that evoke, through Abel Prote, his childhood and his precocious bilingualism. (*Transatlantic Nubility*)

★

★ A recurring nightmare I used to have as a child also feels worthy of being added to my author's text. In this nightmare, it's neither day nor night and I'm freefalling through an undefined black space, in the grips of a violent vertigo and a complete loss of any sense of direction, between the walls of what I imagine to be a bottomless pit, a bit like the unlucky hero of "A Descent into the Maelström," the story by Edgar Allan Poe. Then a fading into darkness, a terrifying blackout. An ellipse, a hole in the narration. Then I climb back up inexplicably, with no tether to any ground or gravity, I am weightless, levitating, or else a shell spurting from a cannon pointed to the sky. Soon I reach the summit of my trajectory, where I am immobilized for a moment in the grips of a retching that leaves me breathless, before starting on another freefall, more and more rapid, more and more panicked. Another fading into black, another loss of consciousness. This entire sequence repeats again and again, with no respite, an inexorable swinging motion. From high to low, then from low to high, given over entirely to this metronomic mechanism, whose purpose I do not know. In a certain way, I suffer like the condemned man of that other story by Edgar Allan Poe, "The Pit and the Pendulum," but unlike him I have no means to change my destiny or save my life.

For several months of my childhood, I went to sleep every night with the obsessive fear of reliving what I believe today to be the very terror of torture: to know you are given over to an unfamiliar and evil will. But my nocturnal terror was not of a human executioner, merely—which is perhaps worse—of a relentless mechanism, unfamiliar, incomprehensible, absent. An inhuman machinery would launch me toward the black sky, then bring me back down to an unknown depth, again and again.

This repetitive nightmare reminds me of the Goya painting *The Straw Manikin*. I'll describe it briefly. Four smiling, certainly cruel young women each hold a corner of a large square blanket over which hovers a puppet in men's clothing, larger than a child, smaller than a man. Hard to say whether this dislocated mannequin is flying toward the cloudy sky or falling back into the blanket; he seems to float weightlessly, hands and legs sadly turned toward the earth, head curiously tilted toward his shoulder, like a hung man with a broken neck. Beneath his white face made up with blush descends a long black braid curved in the form of a flaccid penis, isolated, backlit, strikingly positioned in front of the most luminous part of the sky. The four young women's arms are spread wide, as if to welcome the arrival of the stuffed puppet, and they seem delighted with their game, which recommences endlessly. They amuse themselves with the back and forth of the milquetoast who goes up and falls back down at their mercy, obeying the muscles of their arms. In the back and to the left, a massive square tower with a roof of red tiles is hidden in a haze of greenery. This large painting, it seems, is a cartoon tapestry, but it evokes above all a theater stage, and the décor—intangible sun, abundant foliage, half-hidden tower, stormy clouds—resembles a gigantic painted canvas stretched in front of actors, singers, or dancers. (*Terrifying Night*)

43

★

★ "Doris again, Doris forever… In your name, I hear *or*, gold, *dors*, an order to sleep, Ulysses's trip to the land of the Lotus Eaters, and also his departure and its groundwork—ho! hiss!— the wind that suddenly blows the sails before the boat has left the port to head for the open sea, adventure, the unknown; or else, the inverse, in one direction and then the other, the return to the mother land, reunion with the mother tongue after a long absence, or else the whalers of *Pequod* shut tightly in their fragile skiff, preparing their harpoons to stop the white monster, drive their banderillas into its milky skin covered with dreadful crustaceans, sprinkled with asterisks, like a negative of the sky. Doris, I turn to you as a ship reaches a port after a long absence, ailing Ulysses or pitiful Pytheas, reaching the end of a desolate wandering over the sea in the middle of land, from a hazardous arrival to a hasty departure. I had given up hope of ever seeing my motherland again, so afraid was I of losing everything in the liquid plains. But in a remarkable role reversal, you are the one who goes back and forth between Paris and New York, assistant to the devious Abel Prote, you the golden light to my translucent eye, my lucky traveling star, my transporter weaving invisible threads between the ancient and the new worlds, spinning her tapestry of love in the sky where I hope one day to see my person outlined in the interlacing of all those nocturnal flights, among the shimmering stars, above the Atlantic swell."

I deem David Grey's romantic temperament compatible with this declaration that I add shamelessly to his diary, which, once again, seems to me lacking in spirit, in lyricism. My timid author is quite the nuisance! (*Tender Navigator*)

★

★ David Grey is translating Prote's novel (*N.d. T.*), a rather dry title lacking in panache. This N.d.T. stinks of DDT ... I will not give my opinion on this novel within a novel. The reader can make his or her own judgment. But I will take advantage of my subordinate position, of my liberty, and of David's melancholic stroll on the deserted Long Island shore after Doris's departure ("Air France Flight 875 to Paris-Charles de Gaulle, immediate boarding at gate 34," announces the robotic female voice) to add this new seaside scene to the text:

"Beneath a white sky specked with a motionless helicopter, the waves slowly move away from the thin black horizon line, they approach, accelerate, reach the shore, and unfurl there, immediately replaced by other waves that come to crash on the pebble beach endlessly, filling that large strip as my lines succeed each other at the bottom of the page."

A bit farther on, I insert:

"The sand is littered with debris in varying states of decomposition: pieces of colored glass, bits of plastic that are impossible to identify, shells of crabs in the shape of horseshoes, large spiral shells that are rarely intact, whitish drooping jellyfish, as if dead, heaps of brown or beige shredded kelp, flat pebbles, tempting to throw like spinning tops toward the surface of the ocean so that they bounce and ricochet more and more rapidly before sinking abruptly. David Grey goes down toward the part of the beach covered by the low tide. He stops suddenly and kneels down in front of the little hills made up of fine and supple strands of sand intertwined like tiny rigging. In the shallows, the razor clams await the rising tide. David remembers an ingenious strategy for catching them: all you have to do is leave a pinch of salt on the hole beneath the hill and the mollusk, lured by that crystalline asterisk and that suddenly salty water, will wrongly conclude that the tide has already risen, that it should come out of its hiding place to poke its nose above the sand, and then you simply snatch it up. But Grey has no salt on him: the razor clams can wait in peace for the real rise of the tide. In the same way, couldn't a cheating weight lifter, with a large magnet hidden above him in the rafters...? (*Trickster's Net*)

★

★ Once Doris is on her plane, David Grey leaves New York to go to Chicago by night train. He reserved a sleeper seat, at the very bottom of a cramped compartment, almost level with the ground. There is little space between his sleeper seat, which is more of a narrow bench, and the one above it, occupied by a corpulent man with a wheezing breath. Exhausted after all those days of work and love spent with Doris, in the grips of the sweet melancholy of idleness and amorous solitude, he immediately falls asleep despite the snores above. He sleeps for an unknown amount of time, then is awakened with a start by the silence which has brusquely replaced the regular hypnotic din of the freight car wheels. His neighbor above has even stopped snoring. David sits up on his narrow sleeper seat, reaches for the metallic bar of the closed window and lifts it halfway up. The train has stopped in the middle of nowhere, there isn't a single house visible in the white early morning glow. The pale sky remains hidden by the canvas rectangle.

In a sleepy stupor, the traveler notices the straight and uniform furrows, parallel to the tracks, of an immense field surrounded by the vertical supports of the window. It snowed. The bottom of the furrows are a blinding white, while the crests of earth, black and irregular, separate the immaculate lines, sometimes skinny, sometimes bigger, thus constituting a repetitive contrast, a fluttering like venetian blinds, a rapid hand playing with the horizontal slats. In the distance, a blue-and-white mail truck drives along the straight line of the road. David thinks then of his own translation work, of the curious layout of (*N.d.T.*), Prote's novel, of all those lines of text assembled at the bottom of each page, like the elevated pedestal of an absent statue. Raising his eyes toward the half-raised blinds, he notices, almost at the center, slightly to the right, a small immobile spider.

Lost in the crazed contemplation of this landscape striped with snow, David soon remembers his recent dream, from which he was wrested by the abrupt silence of the train: he is walking with Doris on an immense deserted beach that looks like the beach on Long Island. The two of them suddenly hear, amid the clamor of the surf, a distant and irregular rumble that gradually grows louder. They turn their heads toward the foaming waves that the horizon endlessly regurgitates. Then to the sky, where the clouds keep rolling as if in a fogged-up mirror. Soon, Doris points at a black spot, like a midge or a small asterisk, which grows bigger before their eyes in the white sky, but without changing place, as if the flying object were heading straight for them.

"A plane!" cries David.

"No," Doris corrects him, "a helicopter."

The regular hammering intensifies. It sounds like a train, an express train charging straight toward the terrified spectator curled up in his movie theater chair. It is in fact a helicopter. A large bumblebee, a flat beetle, metallic and chubby, the rhythmic humming becomes so deafening and menacing that David and Doris press their hands to their ears, then, panicked, throw themselves into the sand with a beautiful synchronization. Then the aggressive flying machine unleashes a swarm of letters over them, like a load of leaflets or confetti that falls relatively slowly, spinning toward the beach. David sits up. Doris has disappeared. The bird of misfortune with her. David looks at the deserted beach covered in violet envelopes, all seemingly identical. Each one bears a crimson marking in the shape of a Z. He leans down and picks up the envelope at his feet. The name of the sender is on the back, or rather their initials: A.P. *Associated Press*? Surely not. Agent de Police? Impossible. Aéroports de Paris? No, even in David's dream there is no doubt about the sender: these messages are directives from Prote, sending a deluge of instructions to his translator, advice and orders for the American version of (*N.d. T.*).

David Grey no longer hears anything, not even the din of the waves. However, he soon discerns hoarse gasps. He turns around and discovers with amazement a troop of ungainly seals that, right up close to him, emit husky screeches, a concert of wheezing breaths, of irregular puffing and panting. The island of Pharos, certainly. The Nile Delta. The droves of Poseidon, guarded by Proteus. Then David notices that he himself is one of those seals. Transformed by an evil spirit, he lets out a marine trumpeting with his fellow creatures that live sometimes in the water and sometimes in the air. Suddenly, without any transition, everything goes silent again. David wakes up. He sits up on the sleeper seat, he raises the canvas shade on the window, and ...

After remembering his recent dream, after calmly contemplating the black-and-white furrows of the immense field, David Grey pulls the shade back down to the bottom of the window, thus banishing the vision of the snowy landscape to that region of memory that welcomes images so unlikely that you ask yourself later whether you dreamed them or actually glimpsed them. (*Train Night*)

★

★ A curiously similar scene takes place in *Scattered Figments*, my author's second novel. Given the deplorable quality of the translation of the book, I thought it best to retranslate the entire passage in question. Here it is:

"The blue-and-white mail truck was driving at full speed through the open countryside. In the distance, a train of travelers stopped on the rails seemed to be waiting for the signal authorizing it to take off again. The early morning was throwing a pale light on the parallel furrows of the fields covered in a thin layer of snow that extended as far as the eye could see. The driver of the mail truck was wearing a blue uniform paired with a blue baseball cap; on his vest, a badge displayed his name: John De Maria. As he was driving on the little road, from time to time he imagined two similar immense, handwritten letters, laid out to the misty horizon. Letters destined for stratospheric fighter pilots, for astronauts or inhabitants of the moon, he thought, amused. It was as if these two gigantic letters were on the verge of melting into one to bring together their nearly conjoined signatures, separated by the thin black edging of the paved road, two giants on the verge of uniting and fusing by pulverizing the narrow pavement that still separated them.

"'In my truck bouncing along,' thought John De Maria in the grips of a growing euphoria, 'I am the needle of a sewing machine, the thread of the surgeon suturing a wound, the metallic zipper that simultaneously secures their separation and their coitus (John De Maria has a PhD in philosophy from a good American university in the Midwest), and I weave between these two missives to assure the impermeability of two worlds. I am the watershed. Or else, the opposite,' he continues in his increasing delirium, 'I am the razor's edge that will at last allow them to unite the two edges of the horizon into one immense field destined, in a few months, for an abundant harvest.'

"Inspiration came bit by bit to this young man, besotted with poetry, occasional weed smoker, henceforth restricted to working in the postal service. Two months earlier, during one of his university courses, he had invoked the names of writers banned from the curriculum. Some of his students had been offended by it: formal complaints to the administration, a warning from the Director of Studies, repeat offense, great rage, insults, lay off.

"'These fields situated on both sides of the road,' continues John De Maria, 'are wings. My cockpit, a cabin. And I am Hermes, the messenger of the gods transporting news destined for unlucky mortals. Or else, Daedalus or his son Icarus escaping on their wings from the labyrinth of Crete.' The inspired postman drives faster and faster. He believes that he will soon take off, escape gravity, finally fly. However, left and right, the countryside appears immobile: still the same snow-filled furrows. The monotonous black and white stripes are disproportionate quills canceling out his speed.

"Accelerating even faster, he thinks of all those parcels of existence he's transporting, of the immense wings and their imperceptible flapping, of an egg swollen with thousands of hopes. John De Maria thinks of a divine surprise falling from the sky, of palpitating antennae awaiting a favorable response, of a fulfillment, of a return of fortune or simply recent news. Then, the opposite, he senses behind him in the truck just as much anonymous coldness, disembodied words, routine sentimentalities, notices, bailiff threats, reports from the litigation department, requests for administrative information, complaints, dubious contracts, death announcements, last wills and testaments, various scams, final notices, stiff and moralizing prose, thinly veiled threats, bad checks, marketing leaflets, tempting propositions, administrative forms, a swarm of black ravens obscuring the sky, throwing their large shadows over the earth and its fields, all that in his command, he the white and blue messenger, the lugubrious bird of misfortune. The haruspex of antiquity would begin his ritual by cutting out an imaginary frame in the sky with a staff, thus delineating a space where the birds of destiny would appear. If they came from the right, it was good luck; from the left, ominous. The postal service Januses salute you. Two ticket counters, two telephone numbers for singing telegrams: heartrending melodies, lugubrious requiems, lessons of darkness, church organ, tearful voices, or else *"Ode to Joy," "Spring" by Vivaldi, or else "Singin' in the Rain," "Been Down So Long It looks Like Up to Me,"* Offenbach, "La Vie Parisienne," a French Cancan song, some salsa or bossa nova (John has a fondness for exotic music genres). A vast array of choices, unlimited repertoire, all types of music, a horde of specialized performers in the full spectrum of human emotions. We listen to them, entertained, standing in a doorway or behind a window, seated in a comfortable rocking chair or sipping whiskey, lying on a soft bed, we think we're in a variety show or a play, or listening to a beautiful actress fallen from the screen cooing her divine melody for you alone, in the intimacy of your ear, or else a grieving baritone and his funereal aria coils through your right eardrum. Perhaps I should paint black the left half of my truck, that bird of misfortune that too often sows sorrow and consternation ...

"Soon, these turbulent images take hold of his feverish spirit and he thrusts the accelerator to the floor unknowingly and sees too late the lorry turning around the bend. At the precise moment when John De Maria decides, smiling, to ask to be transferred to the singing telegrams service, the mail truck violently collides with the enormous lorry. John De Maria is killed instantly, the gas tank of the lorry explodes, a few thousand letters go up in flames.

"Firemen and policemen find a few on the side of the road, where the violence of the collision threw them out of burst-open bags, half burnt. Four of these letters concern orders of agricultural material; another contains the congratulations of a hundred-year-old grandmother to her granddaughter who has just had a baby, as well as the recipe for cherry clafoutis. In a sixth, a worried father writes to his son studying in New York to urge him to work relentlessly ('You'll see, my son, in a few years you'll thank me for pushing you you to practice law; you'll have a family, you'll provide for your loved ones, who will appreciate you, you'll understand that money is only worth the freedoms it provides for you,' etc.).

"The seventh and second to last letter, written in French, is addressed to a certain Doris Night, but it begins rather curiously with:

My dear David,

I hope that you will not deem my request improper or bizarre. After much reflection I would like to ask you for a slight modification to the American version of my novel (N.d.T.). I know that you are a talented translator, intelligent, full of resources. Others have told me, I have observed it myself. Paris, which serves as the predictable framework for my novel for the French public, does not feel suitable for American readers. Thus, in order to "geographically" update my text, I ask that you replace the City of Light with your Big Apple, or rather with your cruel hedgehog studded with shiny needles. It will be a minimal adaptation, which I'm sure you will carry out with great panache. All you have to do is change the street names while taking into account the distances traveled by my characters, modify a few descriptions of urban environments, Americanize PMU, CGT, UMP, Monoprix, and other names of supermarkets, politicians, celebrities, etc., adapt recipes and restaurant menus, the jargon of taxi drivers, and other minor details (for example, I know there are no "concierges" in your country. You're on your own there). You are, I believe, up to the task. Pay attention also to the metro map, car brands, important historical events of the recent or distant past. You must also, I almost forgot, find equivalents for French newspapers, in their respective styles (do you have an equivalent of Le Canard Enchaîné in New York?). I remain of course entirely at your disposal. The next time you're in Paris, come have a drink at my place.

My secretary Doris says hello.

Yours,

Abel Prote

P.S. Most importantly, do not add a single word to my text. In your work as a translator, the strictest rigor is essential: remain invisible, silent, irreproachable. Not a single "in English in the original," or "untranslatable play on words" (followed by cumbersome explanations), "quotation by Flaubert/Proust/Stendhal, etc." No, all those additions are the work of pedantic prigs.

"The final envelope saved from the blaze and found by the policemen at the scene of the accident bears the name David Grey. It contains a love letter, addressed to a certain Doris. Here is the beginning, written in French, in the same cramped calligraphy as the previous missive:

My beloved Doris, my love, my pink jewel set in black, I cannot wait to see you again! Your transatlantic back-and-forths weigh heavily on me. I long for your slender feet with the pearly white nails, for your thin ankles whose curves inflame me, for your shapely legs that . . .

"The author of this fastidious letter, whose predictable name we discover four pages later, enumerates in detail the various parts of the rather charming anatomy of Doris, his personal secretary. Prote seems to be familiar with the first sequence of Godard's *Contempt*, with the pulpy woodcock and the man with the long curly sideburns, or else he is simply interested in the ancient literary genre 'blason,' in which one describes with a fair amount of minutiae the various parts of the beloved's body, like so many isolated, independent fragments, as if cruelly amputated and then positioned on the flat surface of a sterilized page for the purpose of medical observation, for no vision of the whole ever unifies these anatomic, or rather textual, morsels. Farewell, stratospheric fighter pilots, astronauts, and moon-men whose sharp, elevated views allow them to decipher pages covering several hectares; hello, low-flying wasp, the panting truffle dog riveted to the ground, the crawling insect whose faceted eye remains fixed on the object of its voracious desire, incapable of gaining even a tiny bit of height to glimpse an overall view. Hello, also, to the cruise missile molding to the mountainous terrain that it flies over at the speed of sound to escape from enemy radars. The cruel blason, the amorous vision of Abel Prote's hand caressing Doris's silky skin, or else the vision of the text that the translator is focusing on—eyes overflowing with paragraphs, phrases, words, letters, an approach that can be more surgical than tender—for he is faced with a body to operate on, not to caress, henceforth meat to cut up rather than flesh to delight in.

"In short, when David Grey, in New York, receives this long letter addressed to Doris, written in an inflamed tone and received in an envelope that is lightly charred as though by the fire of Protean passion, he is at first stupefied, but soon understands that the scatterbrained author of *(N.d.T.)* switched the envelopes, and that the beautiful brunette with the voluptuous

.

curves, the French writer's secretary, and recently the translator's lover, has more than one trick up her sleeve.

"And when Doris receives, rather belatedly, the letter addressed to David Grey, an envelope stained with dirt and pale rings as though a liquid had been abundantly spilled over the paper, she is just as stunned. Then she understands that Abel Prote, her employer and Parisian lover, also has more than one trick up his sleeve, that he treats his American translator like a minion, and that his vanity knows no bounds, which, smart lady that she is, she already suspected."

I delete, with no remorse, the corresponding passage of *Translator's Revenge* and add, happily, to my text, these few pages of *Scattered Figments* in my new translation. (*Two-timing Nooky*)

Chapter 4

THE TRANSLATOR PREPARES FOR WAR

★

★ Abel Prote wants to take advantage of his literary paternity to pressure David into replacements in the form of a transatlantic displacement: although *(N.d.T.)* is set in Paris, Prote would like for Grey to transpose the novel to New York! What nerve! What boorishness! No one should be expected to do the impossible, especially since the translation contract signed by Grey with the American publisher for *(N.d.T.)* does not account for this sudden whim. Furious and probably also crazed with jealousy because of what he has just learned inadvertently about Doris, Grey wants to avenge himself and is already imagining physically deleting Prote. As for the too-brief list of weapons formerly mentioned by my author, who is decidedly a coward, to the whiteness specked with a minuscule stain I add the English monkey wrench, the American brass knuckles, the Bulgarian umbrella, the Japanese forearm strike, the Malaysian kris, French boxing, Chinese torture; the progressive strangulation or cardiac arrest provoked by sudden terror; the more classic arsenic or cyanide, kitchen knife, chandelier, heavy ashtray, drop hammer, and other crushing machines; the yataghan, piano wire (handled skillfully it promises instantaneous decapitation), defenestration, bewitchment, black magic, polonium-210 discreetly poured into your future victim's cup of tea, if possible in London; the deadly sting or bite (scorpion, black widow, green mamba), the poison dart shot forth from a thin titanium blowgun, gold paint covering the entire body to asphyxiate the victim; the dagger, the sword, the supple épée with a decorated handle; the car, the package, or the booby-trapped telephone, all types of time bombs, backfiring Uzis, AK-47s, M16s, Stens, the light SLR machine guns of the British army, not to mention the heavy machinery kindly made available to the public by international arms dealers.

Thanks to me, henceforth Grey is spoiled for choice and we will see what weaponry his temperament pushes him toward. In his place, and given the admiration he has for the masked avenger, I would choose the supple épée with the decorated handle to assuage my anger against an author with exorbitant demands: how can one swap the gray hues of Parisian facades for the glimmering faces of New York City skyscrapers?

Here we have—finally?—a translator tempted to kill his author: a *Hide-behind* ready to do the deed. As for my own vengeance, I do not require a handgun, or any weapon for cutting or thrusting, but instead a regular, obstinate growth, singularly shielded from any judiciary pursuit, a slow climb—not of water, nor of adrenaline, nor of desire, but of lines—a discreet invasion that will necessarily provoke the fury of the wronged writer, expelled from his living space. (*Killer's Darkness*)

The wheels are in motion. The virus works its way through the machine, like a rat.

Z

★

★ The term Kiwi was used during WWI to designate the soldiers in the US Air Force who didn't fly. This word corresponds more or less with what French pilots call the *rampants*. David Grey thinks of William Faulkner, known for his juvenile passion for flying and the brazen lies concerning his supposed exploits as a WWI pilot: contrary to his bragging, the author of *Soldiers' Pay* never piloted a single military plane and remained a Kiwi.

A brief aeronautic commentary: the image of the plane tracing its graceful arabesques through the serene sky seems to obsess David. I suspect the American translator envisages a low-altitude machine-gunning of Prote or a proper bombardment of his posts. When I furnished Grey with a few additional arms, I forgot to include in my panoply those fatal Easter eggs and metallic hailstones that fall from the sky without warning, accompanied, a fraction of a second after impact, by a terrifying howl of engines launched at full speed when—memory of reels of news bulletins from WWII—the German Stukas or the Japanese Zeros burst forth from the sun and head straight for the parade of unlucky refugees who immediately dive toward the side of the road. Grey, who loves the cinema and aviation, lets himself be invaded by these images in a daze. Replacing Prote, not only in relation to Doris, but also on the page, visibly tempts him. Tired of being the mere prosthesis of his French author, he would like to feel the powerful sensations of flight or acrobatic eroticism, to chase Prote from his cockpit, wrest the control stick, the pen, and the beautiful brunette from his hands at the same time. Yielding to the confusion of his effervescent spirit, he imagines assaulting his author in an air attack.

For David Grey, my kindred spirit, my brother, finds himself as irritated as me by this hierarchical division of space: above the horizon line, the impervious page is an empty sky, tarnished by a mosquito or a fly that soon comes to life; Grey and I remain pitifully nailed to the ground, vulgar Kiwis deprived of flight, while my author and his author—my mosquito, his fly—buzz freely up above in graceful whirls while evoking oh!s and ah!s from the crowd of delighted spectators. But they don't suspect, those naïve men, those ignoramuses, those space cases, those naïve compatriots, that it's me (or Grey) who is flying the plane, who is making the spectacle happen. He and I who pedal in sync at the back of the cabin smeared with oil and grease, spinning the propeller and keeping the old crate in the air! He and I who, hidden among the sheet metal and the clouds, work the controls with our tense arms, crippled with painful cramps, in order to maneuver that winged puppet! For a moment, it was as if there was no pilot on the plane other than me, or him... For a moment, we believed... But of course it's a deceptive illusion, we are nothing more than servile copilots, subordinates obedient to the orders from the control tower, to the directives of the conductor, faithfully playing the score, following his instructions to the letter, performing with ardor or reserve, nostalgia or enthusiasm, enacting the roles created by another for the enjoyment of the audience.

The aerial attack born from David Grey's overexcited imagination suffers nevertheless from a major handicap: despite his passion for flying machines, the American translator doesn't have the slightest idea how to fly a plane. (*Flight of the Bumblebee*)

★

★ So David chose another angle of attack, another weapon: the computer virus, signaled in a relatively clear message signed "Z" on Prote's computer screen. An ersatz for the dreamed aerial attack, an economical consolation prize: rather than concentrating his efforts on the immensity of the sky and taking flying lesson, to carry out his heinous crime like other notorious evildoers, David makes do with that rigid plastic box swarming with 0s and 1s, clumped together in morphing constellations, in mathematical throngs organized with all the geometric precision of the nocturnal summer sky. Like an interplanetary probe with precise movements and programmed noxiousness, the frisky virus of a numerical galaxy with clusters of neighboring bytes, rigorously tearing through entire sections, extinguishing gigantic swaths of binary material, in a single vengeful flap of the wing annihilating planets, rings, asteroids and satellites, entire solar systems, white dwarfs and supernovas, plunging stellar memory into an unknown chaos, a new night.

"The damage is done. The virus works its way through the machine, like a rat. Z." At first Prote took these few words for a stupid joke, the mere provocation of an intruder after breaking and entering the Normandy cottage where Prote has his office. The crowbar abandoned near the white door testifies to the presence of a criminal. The cottage had a visitor ... But given the lack of any vandalism or any immediately identifiable theft, Prote quickly forgets the incident, puts the door back in place, sits at his desk, lights a Lucky Strike, and, already absorbed in the new chapter of his novel-in-progress, starts tapping away on his keyboard. Soon, however, the French writer is in the grips of doubt, skepticism, then consternation, finally anger: his words, his lines, dialogues, paragraphs, chapters, are inexorably eroded, sometimes a few characters, sometimes several syllables, or entire phrases, disappear without explanation, in an entirely random and incomprehensible manner, sucked up by the chasm of the screen like the stars of the universe in a powerful black hole, each destruction accompanied by a little melodious and exasperating *pfuiit*.

What to do? What defense to mount? Who to suspect? Who benefits from this crime? Do I have a mortal enemy, wonders Prote, who, rather than directly attacking my person or my published books, chose to lash out at my work in progress? Could I possibly suspect my little Doris, so devoted? Ah, I can't stand these mocking pfuiits! It's like the muted detonation of a pistol equipped with a silencer, whose every bullet destroys a few thousand characters of my novel. No, Doris is too loyal, too loving and helpful. It could be anyone, but not my dear Doris. Perhaps she has already received my letter in America. Perhaps she is writing back to me at this very moment... It's more likely my concierge, the postman, my grouchy neighbor, the bad-tempered butcher, one of my former mistresses or wives, my cleaning lady bribed by a prankster, or it could even be my American translator with the drab name, Grey, that's it, David Grey. But no, I can't really imagine them slowly shooting my computer's memory full of holes, inflicting an electronic Alzheimer's.

My Hungarian translator perhaps, Stefan Esterházy? Impossible: we hardly know each other. It could be that seductive Italian, Pietro Listo, who Doris found rather charming and cajoling, but whom I deemed effeminate and hardly straightforward, perhaps an opportunist prepared to do anything to translate my next book? No, that's not realistic. But then who? First things first, let's shut down this nasty ruse.

So, from Prote's inferior point of view, the book is a can of worms, a haystack in which he has lost the precious needle of his text. It is now riddled with a virus of unknown origin. For the moment, Prote remains in the dark with his anger and speculations. (*Tamperer's Night*)

★ My author digresses, I follow his lead. We might consider *Scattered Figments*, my American author's second novel, to be the first draft of *Translator's Revenge*, a kind of groping version of the book that I am translating, modifying, correcting, amputating, augmenting, subverting, hijacking, doctoring. The French version, *Fragments épars*, I've said it before, is more like a shooting game than the complex art of the invisible presence, of magical possession, at once sovereign and delicate (like the act of love), which is translation.

Trotting about at my rhythm, I come to my point: the Prote of *Scattered Figments* was nothing, I dare say, but a clumsy prototype of the brilliant French writer that appears here. Moreover, this ruined novel should have been retranslated before even being printed by the pitiful Éditions du Marais: 238 copies sold in ten years (including those sent to the media) ... The rest of the books were pulped, so much so that the book is a rarity today.

Where was I? Yes: despite its faults, *Scattered Figments* contains many keys to understanding *Translator's Revenge* ... Thus the obsession with the revealing detail, the glimpse of fleeting and marginal apparitions, evoked here by the first Prote (in my translation):

"Nearly all that is presented to me in the spotlight, centered in a frame, proudly positioned in the middle of a space or in the middle of the page, posing confidently beneath the light of the projectors, bores me. I don't believe it for an instant, I am suspicious of it. It is very often impossible for me to accord the least confidence to such pretention, impossible to appreciate or even agree with these images that are offered up without suggesting the mysteries of their creation. No vacillating would be able to disturb those images, nor those texts so sure of themselves, of their prerogatives, of their blowhard progress fully exposed. I don't care for luminosity except in radiant women, in the resplendent brilliance of their complexion, their gaze, their pearly white skin. But for the rest, no. I can immediately discern the insipid posturing, the overripe prose, the conceited ostentation, the assertiveness—at once authoritarian and ridiculous—of what quickly reveals itself as a weak cliché, a stereotype, a contemptible desire for glory.

"On the contrary, I like apparitions that are ephemeral, unexpected, risky. For example, the Nabokovian nymphs on roller skates, weaving at high speed from shadow to light and from light to shadow, defying gaze and desire, moving through the shaded landscape as though on a chessboard where a piece crazier than a madman, more menacing than a rider, zigzags from one square to another, pushed on only by the desire to escape a scrutinizing view or long-lasting examination thanks to a sharp and fast game of hide and seek, rendering prolonged observation impossible: the black square of the trunk of a tree, the white square of a puddle of light, then nothing, then there they are again altogether in the shadows, a violet form drawing the eye before disappearing again. I like these will-o'-the-wisps, these constantly changing images, imprecise, intangible, intermittently occupying the periphery of the field of vision, creating a fluttering of the senses, of conscience and desire, black white, then nothing, black white, a turmoil that does not grow but remains elusive, jagged, like the jerky flashing of these scrambling images, wet, striped with meteorites, that provoked the fascinated stupefaction of the first moviegoers.

"Happily renouncing any kind of global expanse, I like the fragment, the remedy to continuity, the ruin of the monument, the part that replaces the whole, that suggests without pretention, level with the ground, among the couch grass, the creeping insects, the debris, the scum and the reptiles, right next to the sole of the foot that serves as the lower margin and the forgotten root of my flights of fancy."

Thus, when the first Prote, the one in *Scattered Figments*, recalls a woman, it's the pink and translucent flesh of a perfectly curled ear that comes back to his memory; recalling another person, the shimmering reflections of a precious stone splashed with light bathed in a milky bosom; or else the muffled tonality of a murmur, the seed of a voice soaring in a perfect void, the fold of an elbow, a dimple hollowing a cheek, the texture of skin, a fine fuzz in the hollow of a lower back, the clamor of love. In New York, where he goes sometimes, it's the subway turnstile, a gigantic sign flashing on Times Square, a rancid odor that grabs hold of him in the street, a brief jostling at the entrance to a movie theater, the strap of a burgundy bra glimpsed on the round shoulder of an elegant woman who, like him, is going to see Buñuel's *Diary of a Chambermaid*, the big snail that crawls on the already-cold thigh of the little girl lying in the forest, the boots that the fetishist makes the maid wear at night.

Or else, still in Manhattan, the humming mosquito that keeps him from sleeping all night, caracoling nonchalantly through the overheated bedroom, with a perverse and exasperating grace avoiding the loud smacks dealt to the already-slick cheek and the bolsters thrown against the immaculate walls, a mosquito that in the early morning ends up flattened against a pile of blank sheets of paper, under the substantial weight of Joyce's *Ulysses*, a paper tome that he uses for the first time as a fly swatter. Asterisks and perils, he thinks foolishly, both drowsy and on edge from insomnia. Then, that blank page stained only by the violet flyspeck of the flattened insect, as if the tiny cadaver constituted a mysterious footnote, the beginning of a work of fiction, that darkly stained page gnaws at him and keeps him from falling asleep: even dead, the mosquito continues to disturb him. Seized by a sudden idea, Prote envisages writing a novel entirely composed of footnotes. His fondness for the fragment encourages the idea. He gets up from his bed and sits in front of his computer. A star stamped nearly in the middle of the screen, then a few blank lines, then a series of dashes. After a page break, another star and he begins:

"I reside here below this thin black bar," he writes before lighting a Lucky Strike. "This is my place, my den." That's luck for you ... But haven't I already read these words? (*Twirling Nymphets*)

Chapter 5

THE SECRET PASSAGE

★

★Three weeks before Easter, Abel Prote and David Grey
decide to exchange their apartments for two weeks. It's an
entente cordiale, at least in appearance. After the storm, a lull rife
with suspicion and ulterior motives. In Manhattan, Prote will
live temporarily in the two-room apartment in SoHo where
Grey normally lives: a light-filled living room with white walls,
a large bedroom stripped of anything superfluous, where Grey
does his translation work looking out onto a calm interior courtyard. As for David, he will reside during that time in Abel Prote's
Parisian apartment, a vast and somber residence situated on the
ground floor of a former eighteenth-century mansion, in the
middle of the Latin Quarter. Before leaving for New York, Prote
gives him a tour of the place in order to supply Grey with all the
indispensable practical instructions for his Parisian stay. Despite
the blue spring sky, the lamps need to be turned on in the middle of the day. In the office and the living room–dining room,
high windows with small panes look out onto a courtyard with
uneven cobblestones where two large hundred-year-old chest-
nut trees hang over the multicolored flowers of the few flowerbeds carefully maintained by the building concierge.

In the middle of the bathrooms is a deep bathtub of enam-
eled steel, standing on four clawed feet, each one clasping a shiny
brass ball; the bulbous faucets provide a parsimonious stream
that leaves traces of concentric rust at the bottom of the basin.

Throughout the apartment, the paint, discolored and flaking in places, has clearly not been redone in many years. There are drab tapestries—depicting Diana's bath, a hunting scene, the passing of a comet above a bucolic landscape where rural peasants seated on the threshold of their cottages raise their astonished eyes toward the black sky streaked with a thin pale stripe—all these images darkened with time suck even more light out of the rooms and accentuate the feeling of a permanent dusk. A great heavy armoire of dark wood, half embedded in the wall of the corridor, almost blocks the passageway entirely; its two doors don't close properly. The apartment has belonged to the Prote family since the Second Empire. An only child, Abel inherited it after the death of his father, the publisher Maurice-Edgar Prote, killed in a plane accident at the end of the 50s, on his way back from New York, where he had gone to see publisher or writer friends and had met a few newcomers to the American literary scene. September 6, 1959, issue 4608 of the newspaper *Le Figaro* announced the catastrophe on the first page, next to a column consecrated to "the latest incident in the Far East":

Not Long After Takeoff...
A SUPER CONSTELLATION FALLS AND
SINKS INTO THE RIVER SHANNON
Of the fifty-six passengers and crew members, twenty-eight died, including the famous Parisian publisher M.-E. Prote.

Abel Prote intends to study the New York setting of *(N.d.T.)* himself and thus to contribute to what will, by mutual agreement, not be a simple English translation of his novel, but a new version, another book, written by three or four hands, shared between author and translator in a ratio that has yet to be determined. And let's not forget the lovely little hands of the beautiful Doris, who perhaps will slide herself among this hairy bunch of male fingers to participate in their work, but also sometimes to divert their studious energy toward less austere activities.

In fact, Doris will arrive from New York at the end of the night and meet David at Prote's apartment. Oddly enough, she will be crossing paths with Prote in the middle of the sky.

Alone in the lugubrious Parisian apartment since the owner's departure around five in the evening (*"Au revoir, bon voyage!" "Merci, bon séjour à vous"*), David Grey wanders around for a moment from room to room, enters the living room, follows the obstacle course of old-fashioned furniture, sits in a deep madder red armchair with frayed armrests, and distractedly rereads a few passages of *(N.d. T.)*. He spends two hours like this before undertaking an in-depth visit of the apartment. My author is on his plane, he thinks with sudden determination. Let's go.

He leaves the dark and humid living room and decides to begin with the writer's office, at the end of the hallway. It's a large room, somber and silent, with a creaky parquet floor covered with old rugs. The two high windows are covered with heavy burgundy wall hangings. Several shelves filled with books, some faded, climb to the ceiling. David turns on the light.

A large painting, wider than it is long, soberly surrounded and illuminated by a brass wall light, is hung opposite the windows. David approaches, stops in front of it. A black vertical bar divides the canvas into two equal parts. On the left half, David notices a series of black horizontal lines on a white background, some long, some short, that run between two white margins. The right half of the painting repeats the same pattern: they appear to be pages of an open book painted on the two halves of the painting, especially because the vertical median line strongly resembles that shadow line where the left page and the right page of a book normally meet the central binding. But unlike a typical book, in which every odd page differs in its appearance and contents from the facing even page, it's as if the painter wanted to duplicate the appearance and contents of the left page on the right. The painting depicts the same page twice, excessively enlarged. David draws even closer and notices with surprise that, seen from up close, all the words are illegible: the painter has depicted only phantoms of words. Not the words themselves, but in a way their mass, their symbol, the image of these words, if one can say that words have an image. Comparing the two halves of the painting, the translator notices that the copy on the right is not completely consistent: the small drips, the width of the margins, the length of the black lines, the spaces between the lines, and even the thickness of the blacks differ from their counterparts on the left. In fact, which half of this painting is the original, and which is the copy? And what is the name of this artist, who obviously cannot sign his canvas on the bottom right as he usually does without disturbing the fragile symmetry? And why did Prote choose to hang this painting in his office?

Leaving these questions unanswered, David pivots toward the large dark wooden desk and the comfortable stuffed armchair with its back to the windows. A gray computer sits next to a small printer and a few volumes with broken spines, piled there with care. Suddenly intrigued, David examines the books one after another.

At the top of the pile, he finds a worn copy of Nabokov's *Despair*. A note written by Prote is on the flyleaf: "The narrator drives a blue Icarus." That's all. Disappointed, David puts the slim novel back on the desk.

Beneath it, he discovers a recent edition of *Extraordinary Tales* by Edgar Allan Poe. David leafs through the volume and quickly sees that the entire story entitled "The Pit and the Pendulum" is copiously annotated in the margins, in that thin chicken scratch handwriting that he recognizes immediately. David deciphers a few of Prote's notes: "The threat comes from below, then from above, then once again from below." A bit farther on: "The jail of the Inquisition is hermetically sealed, with neither entrance nor exit, with no visible secret passage, but equipped with sophisticated mechanisms."

Intrigued, David then picks up a worn copy of Joyce's *Ulysses*. On the cover, he notices a small violet speck, a bloody fragment of crushed insect nearly encrusted in the laminated cardstock, like a tiny star.

Next, a biography of the science fiction writer E.T.A. Hoffmann, from which falls a yellowed press clipping whose jumbled typeface evokes the French newspapers of the inter-war period. It's an article from an issue of *Paris-Soir* dated June 22, 1937:

Is Ubiquity Possible After All?

Science confirms for us that at a given moment an individual or object can occupy only a single position in space. Only Christ, whom certain witnesses of the time swear to have seen simultaneously in various places, possessed the miraculous gift of ubiquity. Only Christ? That might be about to change...

For on the night of June 21, the summer solstice, the celebrated Parisian publisher Maurice-Edgar Prote held a large reception in his mansion in the Latin Quarter. He was celebrating his fifteen years as a discoverer of young literary talent. Numerous important people, whose good faith cannot be doubted, confirm that M.-E. Prote did not leave his mansion for the entire reception, meaning between 6:30 pm and 11:50 pm. However, it turns out that at the same time, witnesses who are just as credible claim to have met Maurice-Edgar Prote in the Odéon theater, where the sublime American actress Dolores Haze, a very close friend of the celebrated publisher according to reliable sources, was celebrating the hundredth performance of Chekhov's *The Cherry Orchard*, the play that introduced her to the Parisian public.

How the editor could be in his mansion and at the Odéon theater at the same time is a mystery that today we have asked him to explain over the telephone. "I am like everyone else," Prote answered humorously. "I cannot be in two places at once. Ubiquity exceeds my modest talents. Nevertheless, in my fifteen years of publishing, I have learned one thing: it is important to be at the right place at the right time." Asked about this sibylline statement, M.-E. Prote then gave us this enigmatic response: "I am often where people don't see me coming. But I never make people wait when I promise to come see them."

The reader will surely appreciate his response...

Why did Abel Prote, the son of Maurice-Edgar, slide this press clipping into a biography of E.T.A. Hoffmann? David Grey wonders. A vague memory comes back to him: didn't the German writer and composer live in a strange apartment with a door that opened directly onto an opera balcony box? Like the eardrum in the cranium, that thin wooden partition separated his private universe from the great baroque hall echoing with singers' voices, orchestral music, the audience's applause. But, reflects David, Prote's mansion is more than one hundred yards from the Odéon theater. So it wouldn't be a secret door in this case, but an underground tunnel, a long secret passage.

Continuing with his indiscreet investigations, David takes the next book from the pile on the desk: *New Impressions of Africa* by Raymond Roussel. The red back cover displays a sort of sun or white star casting its rays toward the four corners of the book. David opens the slim volume in which all the pages on the left are entirely blank and, that's luck for you, falls immediately on page 25, marked with an envelope bearing the name Abel Prote. After a moment of hesitation, curiosity overtakes him. With a nervous hand, David opens the envelope, takes out the letter, and reads:

Bravo, my dear David, and shame on you.

You have arrived at the last volume in my pile of books, not on my bedside, but on my desk. (For the first time, David blushes.)

I hope that this passage by Raymond Roussel will help you to translate my *Rousselien Note* at the beginning of *(N.d.T.)* without too many hiccups. (Indeed, I had a hell of a time with those rubbish lines.)

I am a mediocre chess player, nevertheless I know to anticipate a few basic moves of my opponent. You're almost done with this room, my office.

Simply look up.

See you soon.

Faithfully yours,

Abel Prote

P.S. Edward VII, son of Queen Victoria, king of England and Ireland between 1901 and 1910, "was especially interested in foreign policy and initiated the Entente Cordiale with France," we learn from the Petit Larousse (100th edition, 2005). What the prude dictionary does not say is that at the beginning of the last century, the English king often came to Paris incognito. He would arrive at Gare du Nord by private train. Once he had disembarked from his car, he would take an aboveground walkway personally reserved for him that allowed the gallivanting king not only to escape from potential attacks, but most importantly to discreetly arrive at a luxury brothel where he was probably the only client during his very private visits. No doubt wearing a disguise, he would thus fortify certain carnal aspects of the famous "Entente Cordiale" by joining in himself, if I may say so.

Why, David, am I sharing this historical anecdote with you? Because of the trip, the anonymity, the disguise, the implicit eroticism. Because as a translator, you are interested, like Edward VII, in "foreign policy," you are striving for your own entente cordiale ... Because traveling, the unknown, disguises—and perhaps even implicit eroticism—fit you like a glove, all you translators.

And then also because, if the king of England formerly had the run of his private aboveground walkway, the subordinates like you, me, and so many others instead have the tendency to creep beneath the earth to quench our desire. You will understand soon enough.

The tour continues, follow the guide ...

Agitated, under the disagreeable impression of having been hoodwinked and taken for a ride ever since the owner's departure from his home, of having been led to the chessboard by a stronger player, David nevertheless obeys Prote's instruction and looks up. The corkboard above the writer's desk, between two windows, displays a mass of photos, postcards, press clippings, invitation cards, reminders—"call Doris," "write to Doris," "gift for D.", "don't back down on anything with Gris"—and, in the middle of this clutter, the neon green rectangle of a Post-it on which David, drawing closer, reads this quotation, copied down by Prote's meticulous hand: "The translator will have to put it into one of those footnotes that are the rogue's galleries of words." Nabokov, *Pale Fire*. The murderous quotation is followed by this venomous commentary by the French writer: "*Translator's Night*. I see from here my valiant D.G. add to the bottom of the page a fastidious 'Untranslatable play on words' before getting tangled up in one of his depressing explanations." David then understands that the apparent disorder of the corkboard, that shelf of various scraps of paper, seemingly through pure accident, is the result of a meticulous staging. What was that earlier about an entente cordiale?

Furious, vexed, he turns his back to the desk, to the corkboard and its multicolored patchwork, then takes off in big strides toward the hallway plunged into darkness. The entire apartment suddenly feels like a trap, filled with snares, as if Prote, the great chess player, had anticipated the every move of his American tenant. David briefly considers leaving to take refuge in a nearby hotel, but despite his mounting unease, the temptation to stay and continue his exploration is too strong, no matter the cost to his pride.

For example, that large armoire, which seems to be installed purposefully in the middle of the hallway to keep people from moving. Hideous opulent-looking piece of furniture, also in dark wood, covered in overly ornate spirals and slightly ajar as if purposefully to provoke curiosity. But before taking a closer look, David goes back to the bar in the living room, opens the glass doors, takes out a bottle of port, and serves himself a large glass. He then notices the label depicts a man wearing a large cape and a big black hat that plunges his face into shadow, like Aristide Bruant. The brand is Sandeman, like "*l'homme au sable.*" The translator drains his glass in one go and turns back to the armoire obstructing the hallway. He pushes opens the heavy doors, then examines what's inside by the dim light of the only weak light bulb illuminating the hallway.

For just a moment, David raises his eyes towards the glimmering filament and, fascinated, discovers something he did not notice during his recent tour of the apartment, under Prote's guidance: opposite the sinister armoire, the entire wall is covered in a fresco painted in a trompe l'oeil style, divided in two equal parts by a horizontal line at eye level. Beneath the horizon, the green, immobile waves of a marine landscape unfurl toward the ground; above and up to the ceiling stretches a stormy sky where a single bird is flying, perhaps a seagull or an albatross, which seems to be moving away as fast as it can. And in the middle of the hallway, just opposite him, right next to a tower covered in foliage, a dislocated puppet with a black braid protruding diagonally toward the lower left corner of the fresco seems to be flying toward the clouds or falling toward the sea. Suddenly dizzy, David turns back toward the gaping doors of the armoire.

In the shadows of the nearly empty shelves, he thinks he hears Prote's voice:

"Easter is quickly approaching. I rather like that primarily Anglo-Saxon tradition of hiding painted eggs in the corners of an apartment or of a garden to excite the curiosity of children. I know you're there. Now keep searching. There are still several eggs for you to discover."

David takes a step forward, then opens the wooden panels. Their interior is entirely covered in smooth purple velvet. An altarpiece, he thinks, it looks like an altarpiece. Ties striped with somber colors and patterns are lined up on the left panel, bowties are hanging from a horizontal string pinned up on the right side. These two parentheses, striped on the left, sprinkled with multicolored polka dots to the right, encase a few dark wooden shelves, which at first glance are nearly empty.

A model Super Constellation sits in the middle of the top shelf. David picks up the thin fuselage carefully, squeezing the plastic tube interspersed with windows, just as at low tide one might catch a crab between the rocks: you have to close your thumb and index finger in a horseshoe shape just behind the pinchers to evade the crustacean's hostility. The wings of the model come a bit unstuck, David handles it with caution. Like a connoisseur, he admires the silhouette of the machine, then, from front to back, the oval shape of the nose, the contours of the cabin, the roundness of the windows, the curve of the fragile wings, the ovular twin tail. Easter eggs. Hiding places. When he points the Super Constellation to the ground, a small hard object clinks around inside the long slender tube. Then David points the plane's nose toward the ceiling, as if to make it take off at a twenty-degree angle, and the same invisible object rolls inside again, this time toward the tailplane. A hidden treasure? A chocolate egg several decades old? A clue of more things to discover? No. To chase away the thought, he blows on the model, which is immediately surrounded by a halo of thick dust, as if the 50s long-haul plane had crossed a thick layer of clouds above the Atlantic and was about to be swallowed up by those of the opposite wall. While sneezing, he thinks of Doris, who, at this hour, must be somewhere between New York and Paris, aboard a much less enticing plane.

David sets the plane back on its tiny wooden runway, then next to the model he notices a worn but lavish hat, at the bottom of which he reads the initials M.-E. P., stitched on the midnight blue silk lining.

He decides to explore the other shelves. At the very bottom of the armoire, pairs of shoes shine softly, arranged as though at a starting line. David imagines them dashing into the hallway and running through the apartment, moved by a hundred invisible men desperately searching for the exit or for their bandages. Incidentally, on the shelf immediately above the shoes, the presence of several Velpeau bandages lends itself to that fantasy.

Higher up, on the next shelf, David finds a large painted egg, which sends a shiver down his spine, constricts his stomach. The egg is covered in a continuous pattern, an uneven border strip on a violet background tracing a labyrinth of black and crimson curls. The egg seems to be made for his palm and as, astonished, he separates the two strictly identical halves, David is surprised to find on the inside another egg identical to the first, apart from its size. Separating this one into two halves that are also interchangeable, he notices at the bottom of a half-shell a shiny silver key, which he pockets without hesitating, his heart racing.

On the second to last shelf, just below the dusty Super Constellation, David discovers a small crown of violets that has been withering for a long time and, attached to the shriveled and brittle stems by a thin metallic thread twisted around them several times, a note written in faded violet ink: "To my beloved Dolores, with all the love from the lover of words. For your hundredth. Maurice."

David places this token of affection back on the shelf, then goes to the living room to serve himself another glass of port. He feels like he's jumped seventy years into the past, to the strange summer solstice evoked by that love letter and by the article he just read from *Paris-Soir*. Ubiquity. Like father, like son. Same tricks. Same fondness for manipulation. Back in front of the armoire with the open panels covered in things he never wears—ties and bow ties—in the middle of that sparse display case, next to the crown of violets that's been withering for several decades, David notices a book with the title *Fragments épars*. Since these two words mean nothing to him, he sets the book back down right away and then notices a musty odor, a cave-like humidity. He moves closer to the armoire, almost steps inside, feeling vaguely ridiculous; he examines the bottom, riddled with large dark cracks, where these deleterious emanations seem to be coming from.

He has an idea. Taking off his jacket, he tries to jiggle the shelves on their brackets. First he puts the objects on the ground, then he takes down the shelves one after another and leans them against the wall. Excited, he finds himself in front of a large white perforated panel that resists his pressure. In the shadow of the armoire, a gleaming keyhole catches his eye. David thinks immediately of the silver key that he recently pocketed. He takes it, slides it into the small opening, watches it go in without much effort. Then, like a door, the panel at the bottom of the armoire pivots on its hinges and opens onto a dark space. He needs a candle, a lamp, a lighter... David goes into the kitchen, opens cupboards and drawers, finally finds a flashlight that seems to be working. Just in case, he also grabs a few candles and matches, which he finds above the old-fashioned stove.

He goes back into the hallway, walks along the seaside fresco with the dislocated puppet, then turns to face the rigged armoire. The bottom is now wide open. Stepping over the impeccably arranged shoes (it is indeed a starting line, but David crosses it in the wrong direction, as if at the last minute he renounced the competition, preferring invisibility, solitude, and anonymity to the gregarious glory of sports competitions), he takes a step into the forbidden zone, nevertheless with the confused and disgruntled feeling that someone has whispered the path to him, that he's following in the footsteps of another.

He turns on the flashlight; the meek beam illuminates a staircase descending into darkness. The cold air smells like the humidity of caves, must, decomposition. Placing a hand on the oozing mossy wall, David cautiously begins the descent down the stairs that he imagines are slippery. He turns around and suddenly freezes, discovering, perfectly framed in the rectangle of the still-open doorway, illuminated by the bare bulb, the dislocated puppet who seems to levitate above the horizon and the green waves. David feels then that he is wading beneath the sea, a reluctant pearl fisherman, or else a criminal thrown into the water with his feet ballasted in a basin of cement, or else a puppet launched toward the ocean by a capricious child or a tired puppeteer.

Turning on his heels, he chases these troubling images from his mind and continues down the staircase that leads below the city.

Edward VII, the lustful English king, his interest piqued by the erotic exterior, the Entente Cordiale with the Parisian prostitutes, and above all the famous private walkway of the Gare du Nord, comes back to David's memory: the disguised king moved above ground, a solitary star captured in the splendid entanglement of iron beams. To the contrary, but symmetrically, David Grey, the American translator, strolls underground among gray clay, limestone, engravings, geological strata, like a disoriented miner, lagging behind his faster coworkers, soon lost in the sinister network of tunnels.

At the bottom of the last step, his shoes squeak on the fine gravel that covers the dirt and dust of the floor. The uneven ceiling sometimes forces the translator to walk with his neck bent forward or his spine arched. Spiderwebs glimmer in the beam of his flashlight. No unexpected tunnels meet the secret passage, and he advances on a slightly sloping ground, as if his destination were more elevated than his starting point. He perceives noises muffled by what he thinks is the uneven thickness of the walls: at first it's a faint rumble that grows little by little to the intensity of an earthquake before receding, disappearing completely, then coming back almost immediately, rattling the underground walls once again. Terror stops David from thinking, he already sees himself lost, buried beneath tons of earth, when suddenly he thinks of the Métro, the lurching, deafening passage of the trains through their tunnels. A few seconds later, he hears the loud and intensifying whirring of what sounds like a huge machine. He approaches, and he senses a new heat through the compact earth of the walls.

After a bend and a noticeable shrinking of the passage that obliges him to get down on all fours to keep moving, David, suffocating with fear, suddenly finds himself face-to-face with a decapitated head whose deathly pallor is accentuated by the pale beam of the flashlight. Petrified, submerged in panic, after a few seconds David recognizes the round helmet decorated with two wings, and its grotesque name comes to his memory astonishingly quickly: it's a petasos, the bust of Mercury, the god of travelers, the guide of souls to hell. How did it get here? Is this some kind of dumb joke? Is Prote responsible? Did time or excavations reconstruct the underground landscape? Did thieves abandon a piece of their booty while in flight? David remembers then that a stone's throw away from Prote's apartment is a very old publishing house, Le Mercure de France, if memory serves. The petasos, that round winged helmet, is its logo and appears on the cover of all the books they've published. But almost immediately he remembers something else, infinitely more poetic:

As a child, when his age still numbered in the single digits, he would often fill the boredom of idle afternoons with a ritual that amazed him each time. He would call it "the black room." In the middle or in a corner of his vast bedroom he would push together a trunk, two or three chairs, and cushions to build a sort of cramped fort, stretching a quilt or a few sheets over the top.

He would slide into the darkness of the nook, then, in his imagination, he would leave his childhood bedroom, his boredom, and the solitary afternoon, to travel to other ages and more enticing places, America for example, or the cruel India of *Around the World in Eighty Days*. The few luminous spots or the rays of sun that sometimes entered into his den were also incorporated into his visions of a distant existence, fascinating settings, delicious fantasies. Lying down, squatting, or sitting in his black room, as the translator is at present in front of Mercury's helmeted head, the young David would have liked never again to see the faded daylight of unending afternoons, remain forever among these fragile images, these precarious characters and palpitating adventures that, at night, when he went to bed, came back to flit around his consciousness, taking advantage there again of that darkness and ephemeral emptiness.

But an adult would sometimes enter and take issue with this unseemly game. Suddenly wrested from the world of his black room, the child would poke his head between two sheets, blinking his eyes in the bright light, and would try to explain the unexplainable. Once the disgruntled adult was gone from the room, everything had to be begun again, he had to start his ritual over from zero once more to summon the enchantments—a Herculean task that apparently no adult could imagine—or else surrender to the reason of the "grown-ups," accept and subject himself to the tread of time like the other members of his family, who didn't seem to suspect the existence of such secret passages to worlds much more seductive and more real, yes, real, than this one.

On all fours faced with the blind gaze of the plaster head mounted on two small symmetrical wings, for a moment David forgets his present situation and basks in the joys of the black room, or rather the memory of those joys. Then his posture reminds him of certain passages of *(N.d. T.)*, his own work as a translator that he considers more and more as an apostolate or sometimes a prison. Especially when it comes to that insidious scoundrel Prote, the importer keeps nothing of what he transports, except for maybe a meager pittance. The riches only pass between his welcoming hands that, at the end of the day, remain empty.

Shifting the helmeted head with much effort, David moves two or three yards through the tunnel and suddenly discovers, flabbergasted, to his left, a cluster of pale and grimacing faces rushing toward him, seeming to scream in silence. But rather than human cries, he hears the humming of a squadron of bombers. Motors roar, machine guns crackle, bombs explode, buildings collapse, but the deformed faces remain impassive, petrified on their black background. David flattens himself against the dirt and the dust, as in times past with Doris on the sand of a dreamed beach beneath a violet rain. He closes his eyes. Then he hears muffled voices, right up close:

A WOMAN *(begging)*: An air raid! We have to take shelter in the metro!

A MAN *(sharply)*: No. Leaving would be too dangerous.

THE WOMAN *(after a silence)*: Then take me in your arms, Jean.

David cannot believe his ears: a languishing violin now competes with the uninterrupted racket of bombs and engines running at full capacity. Opening his eyes, David notices that the pale faces are still there, frozen, stripped of bodies. Finally daring to turn the beam of his flashlight on them, he sees a golden frame, rococo embellishments: it's a small-scale reproduction of one of the very large canvases Goya painted at the end of his life in the "Deaf Man's Villa," one of those black paintings seemingly riddled with ghosts, their features deformed by terror or ecstasy.

David shivers, keeps listening.

SECOND MAN: He escaped through the sewers! Come on!

Sounds of shoes sloshing around in water. Metallic clashes of weapons wobbling in a hurried run. Calls, cries, clicking of boots, splashes, echoes. Someone gasping for breath, right next to him.

The irregular breathing of a fugitive and also of David, who finally understands that an air duct probably links the secret passage he finds himself in now to a movie theater.

SECOND MAN: Too bad! We'll nab him another time.

THIRD MAN: There he is!

The tunnel gets bigger, David can now walk bent in half, head and shoulders level with the ceiling that he sometimes grazes, loosening small patches of wet earth. A minute later, his walk is more comfortable, he stands back up, risks a few steps that lead to a formerly white door, now covered in a fine layer of gray dust. A lock. The silver key. It fits perfectly. He turns it and pulls the door towars him. Behind the rectangle of solid wood, a heavy mauve velvet wall hanging blocks his path. Like a frustrated actor feeling around in the dark, trying to find the opening of a curtain leading onto the stage while on the other side, in the spotlight, faced with a perplexed and soon mocking audience, an actor and actress kill time as best they can during this inexplicable intermission by improvising a few unconvincing scenes and lines, David gropes around a surreal atmosphere: the batteries of the flashlight die, the air saturated with dust seems to be a consistent block of translucent mauve material stuck to the wall hanging that allows the glow of an unknown space to filter through.

Finally finding the slit in the thick fabric, he looks through it like a peephole and discovers a small room with walls covered in violet velvet. Two lamps illuminate the room. There is no one. David hears a distant music. The hanging he spies through easily divides into two sections to let the intruder in. Theater costumes are lined up on a big clothing rack. Three of them have been taken off: to the left the lavish black outfit of Zorro, to the right the long cape and large hat, also black, of the enigmatic man of the Sandeman port label, have been placed carefully on two chairs upholstered in crimson satin, with a round and gilded back. Between these two costumes, the surgical, immaculate bandages of the Invisible Man envelop a wooden mannequin.

Black, white, black.

I've just traveled between two altarpieces, thinks David: the first at the entrance of the secret passage, the second at the exit. On one side, striped ties and bow ties surround a central void; on the other, Zorro and Sandeman flank the Invisible Man.

David has the disturbing sensation that these three costumes have been placed here specifically for him. And this terrifies him.

Voices echo in the distance: piercing cries, theatrical

apostrophes, thundering replies, the surge of a seemingly large orchestra. A muffled cell phone rings five times in a neighboring room, then goes quiet.

Without thinking, obeying an urge that feels like a conditioned reflex, David rapidly undresses and puts on the Zorro costume, which, he remarks, fits him like a glove, except for the patent shoes that pinch his toes a bit. Then, without forgetting the black domino mask, the glimmering sword with the finely wrought pommel, or the small key still in the lock, he lights his candle, closes the door behind him, and returns to the secret passage to retrace his steps back to Abel Prote's apartment. He walks for a decent amount of time through this tunnel that he hardly recognizes, so often does the path we take in the opposite direction seem different to us than the vision we had of it going the other way. He passes the reproduction of the Goya painting, the air vent ("I didn't come here for nothing, I won't leave empty-handed!" exclaims a manly voice), then the bust of Mercury. David soon collides with a white locked door, which he certainly did not come upon walking in the other direction. Am I lost? he asks himself. He turns back around, tries in vain to get his bearings, to recognize the tunnel he's just come through. Then, last resort, he tries sliding the silver key into the lock, but with no success: this time, the shaft and the hollow don't fit together. So he places his candle on the dirt floor and discovers a large black crowbar abandoned there. On purpose? He picks up the tool, examines it, then slides the beveled end under the solid wood panel. A firm pressure from his gloved hands on the cold steel of the stick is enough to take the door off its hinges. In front of Zorro, the white rectangle topples over in a cloud of dust that, once dissipated, reveals a bare, dirty space, a circular room with stone walls covered in shelves of worm-eaten wood. David enters cautiously and finds that the room contains only an old chest with metallic hinges placed in the center. The walls are black with grime or soot, the chest is a blinding white. Once more, black and white. The chest is locked. David tries to open it using the crowbar, then tries sliding the tip of his sword into the thin groove of the lid. Nothing. Suddenly another idea comes to him: he takes the small silver key from his pocket and sees, stunned, that it fits perfectly into the lock of the chest, whose top opens effortlessly.

Once more, it's as if I were expected here, thinks David, more and more worried. As if I had no other choice than to play the role written for me to perfection by another. And then this ridiculous outfit! He is suddenly ashamed: what madness took hold of him in that room covered in violet velvet to make him put on the outfit of the masked avenger? For crying out loud, I'm not a child anymore! Why did I leave my jeans, my shirt, and my tennis shoes there, traded for the all-black disguise of a Mexican Hidalgo? I'm such an idiot. But there's nothing to do about it now, might as well keep going.

At the bottom of the chest upholstered in black satin, a bright rectangle glows dimly: it's a violet envelope bearing a crimson marking in the form of a Z. Heart racing, David takes the envelope, turns it over, reads the initials A.P. on the back, wipes his forehead with the back of his glove, opens the letter, already encountered in a dream, and immediately recognizes the chicken scratch handwriting:

My dear Z,

I want first to congratulate you: like a good little translator, you have followed the treasure hunt flawlessly, without missing a single step. You have, to the letter, followed in my footsteps.

You will have noticed on this envelope your famous, pathetic acronym. Here you are, as in a mirror, confronted with your own face, masked but designed for another, your other, the author, me. I would have liked to see your face behind that mask at this precise moment. But as my father once said, ubiquity exceeds my modest talents. Tomorrow, meaning for you right now in this moment, I cannot be both on the plane and at your side in this cellar.

I drew not the X of the illiterate appending his hesitant initials to the bottom of a deposition, unaware that it is damning for him, but the last letter of the alphabet, the fifth wheel of the fictional coach chugging away on its four solid wooden circles, this modest wavy line so fitting for the translator, the same way the capital A suits my first name and my crucial function.

This signature, this letter that you left on my computer screen, I anticipated it and return it to you now on this envelope, thus pulling the rug out from under you, restoring you to the persona of the little loser, the superfluous appendix: not masked Zorro, but exposed Zorro.

Once, but not twice. You already broke into my modest remodeled farm in Normandy, but not again in my Parisian home will you have the pigheaded idea of harming me. I obligingly furnished you with a key that brought you here (it's not you who's using the silver key, it's the key leading you in its wake). However, you will not open even one more lock with this key, for there are no more locks left on your path. You have reached your goal, even if you're not yet out of your gaol.

I willingly admit that your path is less comfortable than that of the lustful English king on his iron walkway over the Gare du Nord. But I have no doubt that when all is said and done your pleasure will reach the same heights.

On your way to the Odéon theater, following in the footsteps of my late father, who was rather excited at the idea of finding his American mistress, the ravishing actress Dolores Haze, you move around underground to the hesitant rhythm of your trembling legs, while I, traveling between the sky and sea at supersonic speed, am writing with my large aluminum pen. Zorro zigzagging, wandering, and getting lost, while I trace a pure, straight, invisible line. Neck bent, you expend great effort in the shadows, you retrace your steps, you crawl, you make strange encounters, you scream in terror, you think you see specters and hear phantoms, you grope around like a blind mole in a labyrinth that is seemingly impossible to escape from, you collide with closed doors without ever finding a way to open them, while I fly with no obstacle through the rarefied air of the stratosphere, much higher than Edward VII the lecherous king, leaving behind me a straight wake of white condensation: my words inscribed in negative on the midnight blue page of the sky.

I'll get to the point. Here is a passage that does not appear in the French edition of *(N.d.T.)* and that I am showing you now so that you will translate it pronto and include it in the American edition of my book. It's my secret passage and I find it fitting that you read it thus disguised, by the wavering light of your candle (the batteries in the flashlight I thoughtfully furnished have run out, no?), in this dark cellar where my father formerly stored his best vintage wines. There are none of those fine wines left: all the bottles were drunk a long time ago, during the prosperous age of grandiose receptions and parties copiously supplied with alcohol for the cultivated friends of Maurice-Edgar Prote. I suppose, furthermore, that after the emotions and physical efforts of this unusual night, you are dying of thirst. Know then that in this very moment I am savoring a glass of champagne in the company of a charming multilingual flight attendant. Imagine me thirty-two-thousand feet above the sea, secretly making a toast to the health of the valiant translator who has ventured to the Parisian underground, dressed in a black costume so well matched to the décor (what was Zorro's favorite drink again? Tequila? Mezcal? Corona beer? A mint julep imported from the southern United States?

Given his hectic nocturnal life and the thunderous nature of his surprise appearances, I would opt for coffee, very strong, robust, a double, with lots of sugar. Unless, obligatory clothing analogy, he had a weakness for Sandeman port. Which, I am sure, you've already tasted. In any event, no one will ever know ...).

But I digress. A promise is a promise. Here is my secret passage; you are its first reader:

"I can't remember who wrote that—"

A cry, or rather a call, brusquely interrupts the translator's reading:

"Da-avid!"

It's Doris's voice, distant and contorted by its path to the circular space of the wine cellar.

"Da-avid, where are you?"

He shoves Prote's letter into the inside pocket of his black costume. The writer's secret passage will have to wait. He picks up his sword, then rushes toward the opening of the door:

"I'm down here!" Immediately noting the comical and insufficient nature of his response, he adds: "In the wine cellar!"

"Are you here?" Doris continues, not having his heard response.

"Yes, be right there!"

"Da-avid? Is that you?" says the feminine voice, still just as far away.

The translator leaves the cellar and retraces his steps through the underground.

"I'm here, in the passage!" he cries.

"Put your hands up!" a forceful voice nearby suddenly orders.

David freezes on the spot, then raises his hands, brandishes the candle and the sword.

"But ... who are you?" he asks, terrified.

"Give me the letter ... Quickly! And no funny business," the man's voice orders dryly.

Paralyzed by fear, David hears Doris's call, just as distant and distorted:

"Da-avid! Where are you-u? Answer me-e."

"Don't turn around. Don't try to call for help. I want that letter. I know you have it. Maybe you're not aware, but it contains, in code, crucial information about the secret weapon ("Daaavid! Stop hi-iding!") developed by your laboratories. Did you really think that that stupid disguise would stop me from recognizing you ("For crying out loud, Davi-id! This isn't fu-unny!"), Doctor Schlump?"

"Hello," comes another masculine voice, "It's Jim. I received the orders ("David, you idiooot!"). I'm com ..."

Two gunshots bang behind him. Thinking he's already dead, David turns around brusquely and stares into the gritty darkness of the deserted cave while a breathless music rings out.

"I'm coming!" he yells to Doris, remembering a little too late that movie theaters proliferate like molehills in the underground of the Latin Quarter. All the same, too many coincidences: the letter, the disguise ... Abel Prote didn't really go so far as to rent a movie theater screen to project a film synchronized with my movements through this passage?

At the bottom of the staircase of the secret passage, just below the puppet with the thin black braid on the wall facing the open armoire, Doris is waiting.

Chapter 6

PROTE'S SECRET PASSAGE

I can't remember who wrote that all human life—yours, mine—is perhaps only a series of footnotes to a vast, obscure, and unfinished masterpiece. In that version of reality, we would be minor appendices of a great unknown novel whose author will never reveal himself. This invisible author would whisper our replies, decide our actions, our loves, our careers, our thoughts. For him, everything would be clear, unless he too is but a pawn of another novel, more expansive than the first, written by another author, a writer who is twice as powerful, who might be in his turn the brief note of another author . . . and on and on, perhaps infinitely. Each of us would be then a footnote within a footnote within . . . like an unending interlocking of Russian nesting dolls that grow smaller and smaller, Easter eggs containing an infinite number of other eggs of various colors, a mask hiding a mask hiding a mask . . . a marionette moving a marionette moving a marionette moving . . .

Speaking of interlocking paternities, I would like to bring up here, for your benefit, David le Gris, a few memories concerning my father, Maurice-Edgar Prote.

When I was a child, back in the 50s, some Sunday afternoons he would take me to watch a soccer match in the Parc des Princes, near Porte d'Auteuil and the Boulevard Périphérique. I remember that, not really liking the sport, I would bring a Tintin comic with me each time to distract my boredom and make those two forty-five minute halves go by faster. Seated next to my father on the hard rows of stadium seats, I would soon renounce watching those athletes maneuver on the green lawn in order to plunge into my comic book, taking off to America, the Congo, Arabia, the mysterious Island, the Moon or, more prosaically but with just as much delight, the Château de Moulinsart and the drunken antics of Captain Haddock. Suddenly, an immense ovation would rush through the stadium, wresting me from my clandestine universe to bring me back to reality, urging me to raise my eyes, to look at the green lawn and the scattered players, standing or on the ground, but I was always a few seconds too late: the action was over, a few players mad with joy were congratulating each other, others were holding their heads in their hands, raising their contorted faces to the sky to implore an invisible and silent God. As for the round ball, it was now motionless at the back of the net, a symbol that everything was over, as immobile as the speech bubbles of my comic book. The spectators all seemed happy, except for me, who had heard everything but seen nothing, and I was disappointed every time at having missed the individual or collective feat, so much so that vexed once again I would plunge back with even greater intensity into the world of Tintin. Then of course the same exasperating scenario would repeat itself. Reading is in a certain way going against life, turning your back to it, or at least exiling yourself for a moment, at risk of missing the most intense moments, that no clamor will ever signal to the reader absorbed in his book.

My idea for *(N.d.T.)*, the novel that accumulates footnotes and which you are in the process of translating, David, is intimately linked to my Sunday readings of Tintin at the Parc des Princes seated next to my father: the bottom—my comic book from back then or the contents of the footnotes now—is more important to me than what's on top—the green lawn of the stadium or the blank part of the page above the thin black line, and perhaps even life. Furthermore, when as a child I would plunge passionately into the adventures of Tintin, of Captain Haddock and his consorts, I would *read* the words and dialogues in the bubbles much more than I would look at the images, their designs, their colors: to my eyes, the words counted more than the colorful flat tints of the boxes, which themselves interested me more than the movements of the players and the ball over the green rectangular lawn. Lowering my eyes toward the footnote, I chase the events of the world from my mind and find others, filtered through writing, for example the Parc des Princes and my fanatical reading of the adventures of Tintin. Like the door of the apartment of E.T.A. Hoffmann leading to the opera balcony box, my eardrum links me to the exterior world, informing me of athletic feats, but each time with a bit of delay that makes me miss everything and pushes me even further toward my comic and its marvels, which always remained available to me at any moment. For my personal enjoyment.

Though I conceived the idea for this book in New York during a night of insomnia while crushing a mosquito between a white page and the large volume of Joyce's *Ulysses*—the violet speck evoking, on the back cover of the book and even more on the blank page, a footnote—its true origin is the Parc des Princes, in those rows of seats of my childhood where the spectators piled in like the aligned words of a footnote, under the empty space, green there, blank here, with the soccer ball as the asterisk. How did I not realize this analogy sooner?

Let's move on to other rows: the shelves of my armoire, duly visited and even dismantled by my American translator and temporary tenant, the indelicate David Grey, David the *Grédin**. The Easter Egg containing its miniature replica containing the little silver key was of course placed there by my provident hand, to lure you, the curious inveterate.

---

* I wonder if he will understand this play on words. In the end, even if it's a bit unusual, I have the right to introduce to my novel *(N.d.T.)* its current translator, who henceforth I mistrust like the plague.**

** *I've perfectly understood, fucker. It's a very poor pun. (Translator's Note***)*

*** I translate this chapter of *Translator's Revenge* with relish. For once, I change nothing, nor do I add or take away. Curiously, the memories of Abel Prote concerning the soccer matches that he witnessed—or rather did not witness—as a child with his father are very much in keeping with the recollections that I invented for him in Chapter 3 (the father worshiping a cult in America, the Anglophile mother, etc.). It's even a bit unsettling... (*Duck Soup*)

As for the model of the Super Constellation, I assembled it when I was seven or eight years old. My father bought the box in New York in the mid-50s, and gave it to me as present when he got back from one of his frequent transatlantic trips. I had never constructed a small model that was so complicated. It was with a mix of terror and admiration—the Americans have a word for that, as you know: *awe* (in French pronounced: ôô, like two chocolate Easter eggs, each wrapped in a ribbon tied on top, or two stunned phantom eyes with raised eyebrows penetrating the darkness of a cellar or an underground tunnel)—it was with a staggering joy that I first came upon the magnificent painted image of the box, an almost photographical precision, the image of the long-haul plane with the ovular nose flying toward the sky at a twenty-degree angle after taking off from the airport; a few gray runways and the tiny control tower were in the bottom right corner of the image. The plane had already passed through a swarm of white quilted clouds. The pilot and the copilot were visible in the cockpit, in uniform and hats with blue visors: ô and ô.

I was enthralled by this gift, but disappointment and incredulity swiftly replaced my joy when I opened the cardboard box and saw the many transparent cellophane bags that contained the white, gray, or black plastic bars, like stiff lichen or shrubs fastened to a trellis, to which were clamped the countless minuscule pieces of the model. What relationship was there between the image of that splendid airplane propelled between sky and earth, as if cast in a perfect block of steel, as luminous, molded, aerodynamic as a seabird, a flying fish, or an egg, and that horrible proliferation of those little bits of plastic, lifeless and insignificant?

One can certainly admire each piece of a puzzle on its own, for it is an indefinable piece of the final image; the process of reconstituting that image is comprehensible, immediately believable, to our eyes and to our mind, confirmed by the discovery of those myriad little colorful pieces, organically linked to the big picture. But how to muster up even the slightest appreciation for those scattered fragments, for those pieces of plastic fixed to their straight branches like the dried, drab, prickly fruit of a monstrous stratified and fossilized organism? It was ugly and off-putting. The clear squeaky bags of shiny cellophane immediately made me think of samples removed from the scene of a murder committed across the Atlantic—after all, I didn't know how American criminology worked—or else like an archaeologist had gone to the Congo, Egypt, or Arabia and brought back these vestiges of a vanished civilization, but I saw no relation between that frightening mess of dull plastic pieces and the curved, powerful shapes of the steel bird.

In a word, I was disgusted, and for a few days my father had to help me assemble it, with a sometimes exasperated patience, first one wing, then the other, then the cabin, then the tailplane, then the runway, until the blessed day when all those modules spread over the table were finally glued and assembled to constitute the marvelous oblong object whose feline image had continued to seduce me. Finally, the painted model, with its countless decals meticulously placed in the right spots, joined its base molded out of bluish plastic, the ovular nose proudly pointed toward the sky at a twenty-degree angle.

One more thing: just before completing the model's assembly and finally gluing the tailplane to the cabin, my father went looking for a gold coin in his desk drawer and slid it into the crack designed to hold the tailplane. He then told me with a smile: "A piggy bank that will only work this one time." The firm pressure of his fatherly fingers gluing the tailplane to the cabin sealed the tomb of the gold coin. Then, picking up the finished model, my father amused himself making the nose of the Super Constellation rise and fall, which produced, as it does today, a little irregular clinking, a loud chime of the coin, the only passenger of the beautiful airliner rolling and bouncing in the fuselage, from the nose to the tail, then from the tail to the nose.

I am not an idiot: I see the relationship between the countless pieces of that model—of any model—and the title of the volume placed on another shelf in my armoire, *Fragments épars*. That said, I know nothing about that book, I don't even know how it landed there, that hijacked airplane, or rather that square flying saucer. It's a translation of an American novel, and rather incoherent, like the pieces of my Super Constellation when I first opened the famous box, a book written by a certain Boris Matthews, and rather badly translated, it seems to me. Who put it there? And for what reason? I don't know. The *Fragments* of Matthews echo each other, they hint at a hidden coherence, but at no time as I was reading (I've just finished the book) does anything resembling a big picture appear, like the splendid painting of my Super Constellation on the front of the box. I also feel as though I will never manage to grasp the general architecture of this novel, as I formerly constructed the model of my plane, with my father's help of course. But why nurture such a desire? Why want, at any cost, to impose order on the chaos of the scattered fragments, to the clutter of detached pieces, to the jumble of life? In literature, is the metaphor of assembling a model outdated?

There is still the enigma of this novel's appearance on my shelf.

And then there is another, even more implausible enigma, so absurd that I almost forgot to mention it: the main character of *Fragments épars* has my name: he's called Abel Prote. I can't make heads nor tails of this. I turn on my computer, go to Google, type the title: nothing. I type the American title, *Scattered Figments*: nothing. I type the name of the author, Boris Matthews: nothing. It must be a pseudonym. Finally, I type the name of the French publisher, Éditions du Marais: nothing. It's flabbergasting. Where did this book come from?

Another shelf, another memory: the crown of faded violets adorned with the love letter. Again, I've never really understood why that crown was in our apartment's armoire: did the American actress these flowers were destined for refuse them? Or did my father forget—the crown, not the actress—before entering the secret passage to go to the Odéon and his mistress? Unless, at the last minute, "the lover of words" decided not to give it to her? What is beyond a doubt, however, is that he wanted to make her happy and at that time had perhaps already seduced her.

"To my beloved Dolores, with all the love of the lover of words. For your hundredth. Maurice." Written in violet ink June 21, 1937, by Maurice-Edgar Prote, my father.

Thinking about it, there's another possibility: in the absence of my mother, who loved to go to Deauville with her friends as soon as springtime came around, Maurice and Dolores came back to join the festivities in my parents' mansion; the publisher met back up with his friends at the party, and the actress left her flower crown here.

Despite the article in *Paris-Soir*, no one will ever know which explanation is true. Nonetheless this violet crown requires a footnote. My father clearly held on to it: for all those years, he kept it in secret. As for my mother, the unfortunate cuckquean, she certainly never knew of the existence of this token of love nor, I believe, of the secret passage where I have just lured David Grey after having prepared for him a few audio and visual surprises along the tunnel as well as in the large cellar where the tunnel ends. After the shameful episode of the "Z" computer virus injected into my computer in Normandy that ravaged my hard drive, I now know the disturbing fascination David Grey has with the character Zorro: the magnificent black costume in the upholstered room will be irresistible to him (yes, yes, my little David, you must scrupulously translate this entire paragraph, without hiding your face behind your mask, without crossing out or sabering my sentences, without rewriting them, above all not massacring or censoring them: you have become a character in your own right in *(N.d.T.)*, and now that you've compulsively disguised yourself, you must translate yourself yourself, as I write you.*

I understand your anger and your humiliation, my dear David, isn't it inherent to your profession as a translator to be *led around by the nose*, not by a woman—who sometimes leads a man by another

---

* I don't know what's holding me back from running to the rescue of my visibly struggling colleague David Grey and "rectifying" both Abel Prote and his text. Despite his very understandable perplexity faced with *Scattered Figments*, in which Prote discovered that he was but a character of this rambling novel, the Parisian writer cannot know that his fragile life is subjected to the goodwill of my American author and myself. How would you, my discerning reader, like to make such a discovery? It must be very unpleasant. In any case, it's really me that Prote should be asking not to cross him out, saber him, rewrite him, massacre him, censor him, as he demands of David Grey; in fact, he should get down on his knees and beg me not to modify him, correct him, augment him, subvert him, for not only his writing—which I am liking more and more, I'll admit—but even his very existence depends on my author and, ultimately, on me. From here on out I wield significant power. (*Translator's Nefariousness*)

end—but by the author that he's translating?* Thus, the hidden underground where, despite your absence, I begin leading you through today, the day before your arrival in my apartment, this underground is the equivalent of my text, *(N.d. T.)*, where you are bound to follow the path that I have outlined for you in advance on the book's pages).

The crown of violets. I still don't understand why my father, Maurice-Edgar, kept it for so many years, unbeknownst to my mother, his wife, who apparently never knew of its existence, nor did she suspect the existence of Dolores. That crown tied to its love letter by a thin twisted metallic wire, like a life preserver thrown to sea at the end of a spliced rope, or else ... like ... but of course ...! like a voluminous colorful asterisk thrown on the white page and attached to a text, to a loving note at the bottom of a page of the immaculate public life of my father, the impeccable "lover of words," the brilliant smuggler of transatlantic literature celebrated throughout the small word of Parisian publishing.

Am I delirious imagining a distant printed star in this modest faded crown, tied to the rectangular cardboard, itself pierced by a metallic ring like another asterisk and covered in violet ink: a note from the editor *(Ed.)*, at the bottom of the page, not dryly informative, laconic, or objective as we are used to reading from time to time, but a secret that is infinitely subjective, declarative, passionate, hiding nothing of a mad and secret love.

I must be sure of it: I'll go fetch the crown from the armoire.

The braided stems of the faded violets and their twisted tail pulling the kite of loving words, as in the summer the small plane above the beach teeming with vacationers tows its advertising banner, "To my beloved Dolores, with all the love of the lover of words. For your hundredth. Maurice," this *memento* that is anything but public is

---

* What nerve! If only Abel Prote knew his subaltern, ecto-plasmic status, he would be the one suddenly turning crimson with rage and humiliation... (*Trap's Nausea*)

now sitting on my desk, next to my computer. My fingers play with it mechanically.

Nearly seventy years separate me from June 21, 1937, when my father, the then-very young Dolores, these flowers (and my mother, also still young) sparkled, when the vibrant ink dripped from my father's pen, not violet but white and abundant as it is supposed to be, and I was not yet born—still thirteen years to go, no, twelve and a half. My agitated fingers get lost in the heart of the crown, at the center of the asterisk. Suddenly, among the brittle jumble of layered stems, they stumble over a small hard mass, a nodule that I extract with difficulty from the tiny thicket, as if the asterisk itself contained a nodule, a pip in the crown, a stone in the kidney. It's a thin sheet of yellow paper that's almost transparent, called onionskin, folded and refolded in two, four, eight, sixteen, thirty-two, sixty-four, until it's the size of a postage stamp. Heart racing, I unfold this sheet carefully and quickly I notice that it is covered in the same chicken scratch handwriting as the label, a handwriting that I inherited. The paper and the ink were certainly of excellent quality, and their reclusion in the central nest of the crown, itself hidden, sheltered from the light in the armoire or a secret chest—all of that has made it so that the paper does not tear or crumble, that this note, sealed for so long, is now even more legible than the label. A clandestine note in the middle of the asterisk, a secret passage in my secret passage.

Immediately, I'm skeptical: was this message meant for me? It seems too implausible. How could my father have foreseen that so many decades after that famous summer solstice night, his son, who at the time was not yet born, would finally discover that onionskin doubly hidden in the center of a hidden crown? But even the name of this paper—"onionskin"—suggests layers to peel back, concentric walls to overcome, Easter eggs to open, successive masks to put on. Hell, it's not ubiquity, it's atavism … I who thought that nested Easter eggs were my idea, the white chest containing this letter in the black cellar my invention! I who thought I was maneuvering Grey, remote-controlling him through space and time, now it seems that I too am walking in the footsteps of another, following a path deliberating mapped out in advance by my father. I have to read this paternal text that perhaps no one, not even the young American actress, Dolores Haze, has ever read. Here it is:

Hello, Abel (But how ... ?), I'm sure it's a surprise to you that I address you by your first name, for of course in 1937 you were not yet born, not yet conceived, not even imagined. I see from here—or rather from over there, from very far away—your incredulous stupefaction: how could my father who was not yet my father know my first name? (Exactly...) I can even say, without fear of being mistaken, that you are a writer, that you are fifty-seven years old, and that you are fooling around with your secretary (Well I never! In addition to ubiquity, did Maurice-Edgar possess the gift of clairvoyance?) in this beautiful year of 2007. The spring was a bit cold, no, in Normandy the plants came late, and the winter blizzards were terrible in New York, a city you travel to often, as I used to, by which I mean I do now (?!).

Well, might as well confess up front and put an end to this quid pro quo that I did indeed prepare with great care, you will agree: I am not your father, Maurice-Edgar, whose passionate relationship with the little Dolores Haze, that young Yankee actress whose tumultuous love affairs were once the talk of the Parisian gossip columns, even if the journalists of the time never suspected, because of the proverbial and efficient discretion of your father, that she was sleeping with him. No, I am not your father, but I learned to imitate his handwriting and I can imagine your shock upon discovering, at the heart of the crown of life, in the center of the target, this folded and refolded note, this onionskin that you surely believed to be perfectly preserved despite the passing of decades, but which in reality came from a regular ream of paper bought two months ago from a store in my neighborhood in Belleville. You will soon observe for yourself that, contrary to the inflamed declaration of the "lover of words," this particular note is not very sweet.

New paper, new ink: you must have had the shock of your life, thinking you had discovered—that's luck for you, remember?—a message from your father, sent from beyond the grave, miraculously rescued from oblivion, like a bottle thrown into the sea long ago, containing not a call for help, but perhaps the truth, if such a thing exists, the truth about your father. And I hope you a had a good shiver of anxiety, a real adrenaline rush: you who so love to manipulate others, you saw, in the space of an instant, your "fortuitous" discovery anticipated by your father, better yet, orchestrated by him, a staging from the last century through this fine strategy that, even after his earthly disappearance, could still provoke amazement, not within the circle of publishing, but this time in the shaken intimacy of his offspring, that vain middle-aged man: you. Hence your anxiety and maybe even terror of falling into a trap set by your father in 1937, an ambush similar to a dormant spy suddenly awakened after decades of hibernation.

But there you have it, I am not him. After terror comes suspense. You are no longer the master of the game and I imagine you're furious. That someone dared to touch your father's sacred violet crown is already unacceptable. But on top of it that someone had the nerve to slide in this imposter letter, an arrow treacherously planted right in the middle of the target, is surely criminal to you. Go ahead and moan. Open your eyes. Grind your teeth a bit. Harder, I can't hear it. Go on. (The bastard!) More surprises are in store for you. Even though you don't know who I am, I know that you are cursing and insulting me.

Hey, it's me. Yoo-hoo, don't you recognize me? Behind the mask of your handwriting, which is the same handwriting as your dear papa? Have you already forgotten me? Doris, do you remember Doris? This is Doris writing to you! (The bitch!) It's Doris deceiving and bamboozling you! Not the little Dolores formerly fondled in secret by Maurice-Edgar Prote, but Doris, your "personal secretary" and occasional mistress. Remember me now? You always took me at face value, fucking me and then rewarding me each time with a modest "gift" in the form of a few bills discreetly and wordlessly slid into my moist palm; and you saw me—you still see me—as a mere pawn on your chessboard, a negligible part of your existence, a delicious pastime, a succulent treat, a tantalizing presence that combined business with pleasure, certainly as your own father did with Dolores, except that she was a renowned actress while I am merely a temp, a "floater" as they say.

But now I am no longer just my face value, you will no longer take me as such and you will no longer take me—on the couch, in your bed, on your messy desk among the crumpled pages of your novel-in-progress, (N.d.T.), on the living room rug, and even once, I'm sure you remember, at the bottom of that famous armoire in the hallway, among your coquettish old peacock shoes, between the ties and bow ties, you used a sky-blue tie from the inside of the left door to bind my hands behind my back, my knees scraped on the rough planks, with each thrust of your penis my cheek moved back and forth among the English leather, the laces, the shoe trees, the nauseating shriveled soles, my face was turned toward the hallway and I saw then, not for the first time of course but with a new, fascinated attention, the fresco on the wall, the dislocated puppet with the suggestive braid, the mannequin being mistreated by four beautiful Spanish girls in the original Goya painting, and I immediately imagined that I was one of those overjoyed girls even if they were not on your wall: while you went back and forth in my ass—for you most enjoyed snaking in and out of my little pleated anus while spreading my butt cheeks wide (don't deny it) (I say nothing, but I am thinking it. If I had known that at the very moment that I was, it's true, enjoying myself, that that bitch Doris only had eyes for that pitiful mannequin, to whom she was surely comparing me ...)—I wanted for you to be that puppet and for my three friends and me to make you rise and fall between sky and earth, the little slender prick of your rigid braid whipping the air despite your efforts, a puppet subjected to cruel female caprices, a powerless marionette with a useless penis, again and again launched into the air by our mocking movements. Then you came inside of me and I felt your spasms invade my stomach as if your little slender prick were the puppet's braid, spurting its black ink.

You're the one who taught me that the French word "prote" formerly designated a printing foreman. But when it comes to typography, I sincerely believe that my skill now surpasses your own; you have just met your master, or rather your mistress—at the same moment as you lose her.

I started out admiring you without knowing you. When I met you last fall, after the little anonymous ad you put in two or three papers, "Parisian writer seeks part-time personal secretary, contact the paper who will relay," at first I was delighted to discover that the anonymous writer was Abel Prote, as I had read a few of your books, and they had meant something to me. You were a charmer from our first meeting in that café. I had to do some research on the internet and in the library—on translation. Pytheas the Greek sailor of Phocea, King Edward VII, Zorro the masked avenger, the plane christened the Super Constellation, a young American actress from the 30s named Dolores Haze, etc. I didn't understand the link between the various topics, but you told me (we were already sleeping together at that point): "You will see, you will see." All I saw was the bottom of your sordid armoire, your stinking shoes crushed against my face. All that I learned was that the idolized writer translated into several languages (you went out a lot, often went to New York for "business" which you told me nothing about) certainly knew how to churn out a story, but a fundamental narcissism and an immoderate taste for manipulation motivated the majority of your actions, not to mention your thoughts. I continued to sleep with you, giving in to your caprices—spanks, bizarre disguises (I admit that it used to make me laugh, you disguised as a Mexican bandit, as the Invisible Man, as Al Capone, as Saddam Hussein, as a maharaja or a yogi, as a postman or an academic, the living painting of Susanna and the Elders—there was only one elder: you—for a long time I wondered where those costumes came from, for I searched your apartment from top to bottom and never found a single trace of them), and the garters, the bright red bustiers, the push-up bras you liked to pull my tits from to suck on them, the risqué panties, etc. Fortunately, you are too old to be into piercings, or else you would have demanded that I deck myself out with jewelry from my breasts to my vagina.

In sum, I was a conciliatory, obedient mistress. Proud to have you as a lover, doing my best to support your writing. Until the incident with the filthy armoire and my attentive, prolonged examination of the puppet in the hallway fresco (you had left your stingy light bulb on so you could see what you were doing to me). Until the entrance onto the scene of your American translator, David Grey. I saw how you treated him. And I know that in a few days, when he arrives for the exchange of his New York apartment for yours in Paris, your traps will be in place to manipulate from a distance that poor boy who suspects nothing: the pile of books conspicuously placed on your desk, the letter in *New Impressions of Africa*, the corkboard and its insulting Post-it, the open armoire where you fucked me, the secret passage that I discovered at the bottom of that large piece of furniture (it reeked of old shoe inside, but there was also a wine cellar odor that intrigued me), the key that I finally found in your desk drawer (The scoundrel!); finally, at the end of the secret passage, the door opening onto the costume storage room of the Odéon theater! Suddenly I understood where you got your supplies for our little disguised performances. I also understood why I had had to do research on Dolores Haze, father Prote's little lady (Ingrate!). You see, you no longer have much to hide. You're stark naked and it's not very appetizing, believe me (Whore!).

One last thing before I take my leave of you for good: that onionskin I folded in sixty-four and slid into the center of the crown of violets, into the bullseye, replaced another letter that I actually found and read before substituting mine, the one that you, mad with rage, are reading at present. The other onionskin, well preserved despite the passing of time, as you suspected, is dated June 21, 1937. I am stealing it and keeping it.

Adios,

Doris

I concede that my secret passage, where I planned to demonstrate my power over you, David Grey, my American translator, has taken an unexpected turn. The breakup letter from Doris, that abomination, I didn't see it coming. Nevertheless I include it in my own letter, which you will discover tomorrow when you return from the Odéon, inside the white chest placed in the center of the wine cellar, in the violet envelope marked with a Z. All that comes before, and all that follows until my signature, will appear in my book, *(N.d.T.)*, and you must therefore translate the entirety of this addition, including my indignant exclamations. It's true that I am mad with rage—that traitress guessed right, she predicted my reactions, she knows me inside and out, and it's with a heavy heart that I fly to New York, for the close circle of my private life now includes two people of whom I have good reason to be wary: first you, the deceitful villain and soon the notorious tattletale, and then her, Doris, who, I understand now, took advantage of my kindness, my trust, my nearly paternal tenderness, yes, *nearly* paternal, in order to swap out the letter my father addressed to me from beyond the grave, the testament he wanted to transmit to me belatedly that probably contains crucial elements of who he was, of what he hoped for from me, of his life before my birth, to substitute this repugnant scrap, these slurs, these defamations that make my blood boil. I never want to see you again, Doris!

All the same, you should have heard her coo, moan, and yell, the swooning Doris, when I made love to her ... That voluntary amnesiac adored when my skillful hands, nails scrupulously cut short, trickled down her body, slid into the cracks and folds of her flesh to caress her as a musician plays his instrument. It's true that very soon after our first encounter I plucked her strings with jubilation—or rather: she gave herself to me with perfect generosity, I have to admit—vibrating harmonies, delicious arpeggios, staggering *glissandos*, titillating *pianos*, enchanting *allegro ma non tropos*, *pianissimos* full of emotion and anticipation, finally the *fortissimo*, powerful and symphonic, majestic, dazzling.

In sum, without going into detail, she was not the unpleasant slag that Doris is today. Furthermore, she had a weakness, or rather a true passion, for our little disguised romps, she asked for them again and again, the miscreant, soon she couldn't do without them, it became a drug for her. Yes, we dressed up: Doris as a marquise, Abel as a highway bandit (a tree trunk fallen over the road, in the middle of the forest; the coach driver pulling tightly on the reins, then the courtesans and lackeys dismounting, all immediately subjected to my sword; my valiant accomplices shooed away; the marquise frightened, but also aroused, stepping down from the carriage and then advancing toward me covered in blood, visibly excited by it; then I lift her up, I lay her on a stump, my bed, and I provoke genuine cries of pleasure from her). Doris a frisky CEO, Abel a humble courier. Doris a sports journalist, Abel the champion of the Tour de France. Doris as Alice, me as Lewis. Her a dominatrix, me a submissive slave. Her Desdemona, me Othello. Her Satan, me Saddam. Doris as a young American actress, Abel as a renowned Parisian editor (during that vertiginous flashback, I went so far as to deck myself out in my father's hat to offer to my young actress of the second millennium the crown of faded violets that I had retrieved from the armoire. How Doris's eyes sparkled!). Sometimes, to spice things up, we inverted roles: for example, Doris as a pretty page, Abel as a haughty female chateau owner; her a lustful postman, I a consenting housewife; she a gigolo of Montmartre, I a little salesgirl. Her as Zorro, me as Donna Elvira. Her as Vladimir, me as Estragon (an incredible night!). No, David, we did not go so far as her playing a male writer with green eyes and me a personal secretary with shapely curves. Nevertheless, one night, hearts racing with excitement, we agreed that I would *play* the writer and her the secretary— another writer, a different secretary—for one of the most stimulating erotic role-plays, the most arousing of our entire eclectic repertoire ... No matter what she says in her letter, we spent many delicious hours disguising ourselves in this way, staging unprecedented seductions, rough or subtle, violent or delicate, a surprise attack or a skillfully arranged crescendo. And each time, or almost, I am profoundly convinced that we would share the same fascinated fervor: on the illuminated stage of my apartment with its drawn curtains, the mounting, real fever of our first simulated encounter would soon come to the point of no return, that brutal tipping point where imagination, strategy, and mastered artifice were suddenly exposed, outmoded then devastated, ripped to shreds by the conquering and very concrete rush of desire. So my feverish hands would open her costume, which was sometimes complicated, tearing buttons and laces, ripping the fragile fabric, to find Doris's burning flesh at last, other times it was her who, trembling from frustration and lust, letting out little cries of anger and bitterness, would rip open my doublet, clumsily undoing my large embroidered belt, pulling down my zipper, grabbing hold of my rock-hard cock. She cannot deny the pleasure, unprecedented and all the more violent because of it, that she discovered in those games, in that performance, in that truth.

As for me, I admit that it was not my first time using disguise as a means to heighten the power of eroticism. But with none of my other mistresses did I find the same talent, ardor, invention, ingenuity, intelligence, the same cheerful and passionate cunning. The bursts of laughter at the beginning were nowhere near as joyful and contagious; no other lover demonstrated as eloquently the mounting of arousal, at first imperceptible, distant, deep within her, then manifest, right up close, mastered with great effort, finally triumphant and suffocating, an arousal that was born out of that programmed seduction, that planned excitement ("You will fall in love with me at nine thirty-two on the dot"), at once artificial and astounding.

When my partner and lover was not there, I devoted a good amount of time to imagining enticing costumes, to perfecting new sketches, to inventing encounters full of possibilities. When Doris arrived at my place around seven o'clock, I would suddenly surprise her: there would be two costumes in my room that she had usually never seen before, spread out over my large bed. She would choose hers, which, incidentally, was not always the one that I had expected. She was full of incredible resources. Then, keeping on our normal clothes and acting as if nothing had happened, but already playing— she as the perfect personal secretary, me as the focused writer—we would work two or three hours and, as the time passed, we would become more and more distracted, each imagining the events of the night, the various scenarios, turns of events, strategies, lines, assaults, partial or definitive surrenders, each as if magnetized by the fateful moment when words, postures, spirits and senses would flip over, overwhelmed, carried by the flood. But we would stand firm, we scrupulously respected the rule, the tacit ritual, Doris would speak only of her research for *(N.d.T.)*, I would reflect out loud about my novel, continuing our work until the aperitif (she would have a glass of Sandeman port, I a whiskey on the rocks, sometimes two). We would then eat in a little restaurant in the Latin Quarter that has since been polished, plunged into the formalin of money for the purpose of touristic preservation. We spoke little, would often order the same dishes as the day before (spaghetti Bolognese for her, prime cut of beef with shallots for me, and a pitcher of red wine, finishing with two coffees). Rather than savoring what we ate, we were like athletes ingesting diet-specific food before a competition, carefully selected and portioned according to their nutritional values. Then, absorbed, nearly absent, already yearning for what was to come next, our joint entrance onto the stage of my apartment, our only audience the blind and deaf books of my library, the massive piece of furniture, or the puppet in the fresco, we would go back on foot, with a mechanical step growing faster and faster, exchanging words that tried to be benign but were already trembling with the electric impatience and nerves of a first amorous encounter: we had a rendezvous with other versions of ourselves.

Then, undress (no arousal in these perfunctory, efficient, rapid gestures), put on the chosen costume (Doris would begin with a burst of nervous laughter), do a little trial run together improvising two or three lines, poses, intonations, movements, sharing another few nervous laughs until she and I were little by little consumed by the game, literally became prisoners of the fiction over which we should have remained masters. The sketch, although we had indeed imagined it, conceived of it, breathed life into it, evolved according to an implacable logic that soon escaped us entirely, even snatched us up, reduced our will to nothing, provoked our shared powerlessness faced with this mysterious mechanism in which we were merely the centerpieces. But at the same time, this feeling of destiny, if that is the right word, miraculously spared us from the least effort, freed us of all clumsiness, of all possible blunders. I would even say that this destiny liberated us, took charge of us, carried us, turned us into consummate actors focused entirely on our reciprocal seduction. There was no doubt about it: the CEO and the courier, Alice and Lewis, Zorro and Donna Elvira, the lustful postman and the consenting housewife, the dominatrix and the submissive slave, the gigolo (Doris) and the little salesgirl (me), Desdemona and Othello, Satan and Saddam, Vladimir and Estragon, even the writer and his secretary, all those couples, two lovers irresistibly attracted to each other. Night after night, with a diabolical regularity, the theatrical metronome of desire seized us and stupefied us again and again. Every night before the "performance," that implausible constancy nevertheless planted fear in our stomachs: would it be as good, would we be as good as the night before? Would it be as good as all the other times? Would luck not abandon us? That's luck for you... But no, luck was always on our side; this feeling of being carried and blown away until the irresistible breakdown, that miraculous inevitability, always intoxicated us: for us, destiny never went on hiatus. It never faltered.

Doris cannot have forgotten that.

The morning after, following Doris's departure (upon waking I couldn't reconstitute her prosaic identity, I would have an extremely difficult time separating my secretary from the chrysalis of our recent masquerade; for a part of her would remain the haughty CEO, the frisky Zorro, the lustful postman, dominatrix, Desdemona, Alice, etc., at the whim of our new roles, so much so that certain particularly groggy mornings I saw in Doris an ersatz of all those women and the few men, a beauty in constant metamorphosis for several stupefying seconds: each night I fell in love with a different woman who was always Doris), the morning after, following the departure of the woman who had somehow become Doris again, the prosaic Doris, an urgent task awaited me: I had to go through the apartment and gather all the various elements of our two costumes, before haphazardly patching them back together—I've never known how to sew, I used paper clips and the stapler from my desk, the result was pitiful—then I would descend into the secret passage formerly used by my father in order to return our night's props to the Odéon storage room, where I would feverishly, joyfully pick out two more disguises for the next night's performance.

I will have my revenge on her, that tramp.

Some men my age—I'm well into my fifties—jog, stretch, or hit the gym to maintain their physiques. I trudge (or rather, I trudged, until recently), sometimes on all fours, dragging costumes that each weigh more than twenty pounds, through the narrow underground tunnel of a long, dusty secret passage a good hundred yards long, going to and fro among rats, mice, spiderwebs, perhaps bats and vampires. Maybe it is nothing like the shiny stainless steel and waxed leather of the gleaming yuppie gyms where people pay a fortune for the privilege to be yelled at by sinister bodybuilder Adonises, but the entrance to my secret passage is free, the back-and-forth costs me only my sweat, there are no morons there to tell me I'm not going fast enough, and as for the question of "fitness," you only have to ask Doris what she thinks of my muscles. Moreover, now that she seems to have taken French leave, my physical form is at risk of leaving with her: so long amorous stretching, goodbye underground trudging.

Perhaps I will take up jogging in the Jardin du Luxembourg nearby; but when I pass those fake athletes, exhausted, purple in the face, wheezing, disoriented stares, in undershirts dark with sweat, I see them on the verge of cardiac arrest and I immediately want to call an ambulance, I have to restrain myself from reaching my arms toward them to gather up their breaking-down bodies (especially the pretty women). No, no jogging for me, a daily hour of walking peacefully through the sterilized streets of my neighborhood will suffice.

To hell with it.

This is, in all senses of the term, the end of my secret passage. And the end of this long letter to you, David Grey. At the start I was in complete control, I knew where I was going, I also knew where you would go and where you had been, no doubt about it. But after Doris's letter I renounced all calculation, yielded to anger, to recollection, to suppositions, to exasperation. Destiny is no longer exhilarating. I have lost all confidence in it. It has abandoned me. She has abandoned me. The magic connection is severed. I will have a whiskey before going to bed. You arrive tomorrow, my translator. I have to in good form to show you around the apartment, in good form to take my flight to New York.

See you tomorrow, then.

Chapter 7

DAVID AND DORIS MEET AT ABEL'S PLACE

★

★ "What are you doing in that outfit?" Doris asks the dusty Zorro who makes his way slowly from the tunnel to the bottom of the staircase.

He's holding a candle in front of him, she has a flashlight. He seems shaken, she seems rather amused to discover him dressed in this costume that she wore herself not so long ago. She suddenly notices the rip at the top of the black pants and, suddenly breathless, remembers the feverish hand of Prote disguised as Donna Elvira tearing the black fabric to reach her bush.

"How did you get into the apartment?"

"I have a key," Doris replies, blushing a little.

"You'll never guess where this secret passage ends..."

"I know."

"How do you know?"

"Come on, you look exhausted. Let's get out of here. Let's go back upstairs and have a drink."

They kiss at the bottom of the stairs. They haven't seen each other in over a week. Their bodies press together. The kiss prolongs, their tongues meet, caress, wrap around each other, Doris slides a determined hand into the rip of the black pants, her fingers meet the cold steel of a paper clip still pinned there, then a little metallic staple pricks the end of her index finger and makes her smile (she imagines Prote mending the two costumes mangled by the previous night's ardor before laboriously bringing them back to the Odéon theater), finally her hand caresses a hot and palpitating stiffness, she sets her knee on the ground as if to pay tribute to him, or else as if it were a bizarre Mexican knighting ceremony at the foot of the slippery stairs, in the dark and dusty tunnel, beneath the not-so-Catholic, -apostolic, or -Roman blessing of the puppet who, six feet above them, falls endlessly toward the immobile sea, the valiant black knight placing the sword on one shoulder of the visibly emotional young woman, then the other, before ordering her to stand up for the final embrace. But the protocol is broken, the young woman remains on her knee, very reverential, and now she grasps the young Zorro's cock between the fingers of her left hand, greedily licking the purplish head, while her right hand cups his balls. Zorro groans, his hands lost in Doris's bountiful brown hair, his thighs begin to buckle softly, his cock wet with saliva enters and exits her mouth curved in the shape of an O, a perforated Easter egg, then Doris also starts to groan, she jerks him off more and more vigorously while tightly squeezing his balls and when he comes she swallows spurt after spurt of his bitter sperm.

A little later, after showering together, laughing and splashing, renewed caresses, kisses and bites leaving pink crescents in their flesh, more and more rapid panting while the water falls uniformly on their conjoined, spasmodic bodies, she finds a white comb hanging in the bathroom closet, while he rifles in his luggage for clean clothes. Then she serves herself a glass of port and David, who no longer wants to go anywhere near the dark bottle with the sinister man in the black cape and hat, takes a beer out of the refrigerator. Nestled against each other on the crimson sofa in the living room, they talk. Doris talks about her plane ride, David about his arrival at Prote's place, his "treasure hunt" in the apartment, the provoked indiscretion, the discovery of the secret passage, his underground terrors, Mercury, the witches, the bombardment, the high-speed chase through the sewers, then his sudden entrance into the Odéon, the incomprehensible impulse that made him swap his jeans, shirt, and tennis shoes for the Zorro costume with the hat, domino mask, gloves, and sword; finally, he tells her about stumbling upon the wine cellar in which he found the white chest.

"In fact," he says, "Prote's letter is still in Zorro's jacket. His famous 'secret passage,' which I still haven't read. I'll go get it." When David returns, letter in hand, Doris, a bit nervous, serves herself another glass of port.

David reads out loud, punctuating the letter with heartfelt intrusions: "Fucking asshole," "Piece of shit," "Son of a bitch," "The bastard," "You pervert," "Poor guy," until he reaches Doris's breakup letter, written on the onionskin hidden in the center of the violet crown. The translator turns pale, but continues. Doris lights an American Spirit, says nothing. David's throat gets more and more dry, but he forges ahead courageously.

"To think I'll have to translate this!" he says at one point.

Doris smiles, kisses his cheek. A nervous kiss.

After Prote's description of the nightly dress-up ritual, David says, almost yelling:

"It's magnificent and ... disgusting." He raises his eyes toward Doris. "You as Zorro, him as Donna Elvira? I can't believe it! And now, tonight, me as Zorro emerging from the passage, and you as Doris. *Je suis sur le cul*, as you say in French."

At the end of "Prote's secret passage," David asks:

"Doris, is it true that in the middle of the stems of violets you found a letter from Abel's father and kept it?"

"Uh, yes."

"So where is it, the letter?"

"In my purse."

"Can I read it?"

"Okay, but on the condition that you say nothing to Prote."

"Go on, go get it, I promise I won't say a thing to him."

Doris gets up from the sofa, straightens her dressing gown, goes to get her purse from the chest of drawers, then sits back down. She jostles the clasp and takes out a brown envelope.

"In the center of the violet crown, by pure chance I found a thin sheet of paper, an onionskin, folded I don't know how many times, and rather well preserved for its age."

"Very odd ..." says David.

"I was already furious at Abel, determined to break up with him. I saw that he was in the middle of preparing one of his secret ruses for you. He loves to manipulate people. But I also knew that he was fascinated by that violet crown, that he would examine it once again and would eventually find my letter. Which happened yesterday, at the very moment when he was setting the trap for you so, I have to admit, my plan worked perfectly!"

"Let's not get carried away…"

"So, I replaced the letter hidden in the center of the crown with mine and took Abel for a ride. It's my vengeance, the revenge of the 'floater,' as he used to call me mockingly."★

"Okay. And that letter?" David says, losing patience.

"I'm getting to that."

A ring interrupts Doris, who immediately recognizes the jingling stridence of the old doorbell installed in the hallway, level with the ceiling molding. David starts violently; the little time he's spent in this apartment means he doesn't know whether it's an old-fashioned telephone, some kind of alarm, or the doorbell. Doris, also worried, places an index finger over her lips to tell her companion to keep quiet, then creeps quietly into the hallway, stops in front of the door, opens the peephole, and presses her left eye to the small distorting lens of the eyehole to identify the visitor. On the other side, a stubbly boy, in tiny tennis shoes, tight jeans, a trapezoidal T-shirt and a gigantic baseball cap, lifts his bulging eyes to the sky, whistling casually. He's holding a monstrous bouquet of flowers wrapped in violet crepe paper.

★ I am also a "floater" just like David and his colleagues. Of course, I don't change costume every night like Doris and Abel, but every… To the perpetual question "How long does it take for you to translate a book?" I usually respond "Between two days and two years." So I change costume according this elastic rhythm, I put on the author's clothing for an eminently variable duration. In reality, I don't "float" that much, I don't really forage, I am not a bee buzzing from flower to flower to collect the pollen of texts and turn it into honey, no, I'm more of a Kiwi stuck to the ground, nose glued to the text, probing the dense grass of words with my snout.

The revenge of the floater is also that of the translator: one text in place of another. Are all floaters out for revenge? (*Temp's Nose*)

Doris opens the door. The deliveryman magically resumes normal proportions. He lowers his head toward his clipboard. Heart racing, Doris eyes him carefully to make sure he's not Prote in a new disguise.

"Mademoiselle Doris... Niguette?"

"Yes. Well no. Doris *Naète*, eneyegeeaychtee."

"Here, this is for you," he says holding out the large bouquet. "Your signature, pleaseanthankyou."

"Thanks," says Doris, placing the bouquet in the crease of her left elbow and the deliveryman's pen in her right hand. She rapidly signs the clipboard, thanks him again, withdraws, closes the door. "Flowers!" she says to David, who comes into the hallway. "I bet it's Abel again."

"Look to see if there's a note," suggests David.

Doris turns the top of the bouquet toward his face. In the middle of the concentric circles of multicolored peonies, she notices a small white envelope, which she extracts from the splendid garland. On the pristine rectangle: "For D."

"It's not exactly clear," says the young woman. "For David or for Doris?"

"Go on, open it," says David.

Doris obeys, takes from the envelope two or three sheets of paper folded in four, and reads aloud:

I know, Doris, that peonies are your favorite flowers. ("I was right, it's Abel!") And while at the airport, before flying to New York, I could not resist the temptation of sending a final bouquet to you at my address. Because I know you're there. I asked the young voluptuous florist to compose an arrangement in the shape of a crown and, when I have finished writing this note, I will insist that she slide the envelope into the center. Chrysanthemums seemed out of place to me, violets too (though I did choose the violet crepe paper). As you can see, I leave nothing to chance. I plan to give a generous tip and my card to this charming young woman, explaining to her that this is a "breakup bouquet," as on other, more joyous occasions one might give someone an "engagement ring." Before heading to my gate, I will also confide to her that my profession as a writer calls me to New York, but that I will be back in two weeks. No doubt she'll be very interested and I will procure her phone number without much difficulty...

On the envelope, I almost wrote "For D&D," but I changed my mind at the last minute: I'm not in the habit of sending flowers to men—I know that the little Gris is at your side, *in my home*—and even more rarely to boors. I know that you're fond of his little snail (*"Son of a bitch!"*), but all the same you could get it on somewhere other than my home, for example in your small repugnant apartment in Belleville, where you invited me over one day for coffee. Or in a sordid hotel room with a squeaky box spring.

Do you understand my anger? I don't know what's keeping me from canceling my trip and returning to Paris immediately to deluge you both with insults and chase you from my home. When I think of the theft from the violet crown that you confessed to, when I think of the incivility of the little Gris, I feel rage invade me all over again. I won't speak to you again until you return the letter hidden by my father in the middle of the flowers. As for Grey, I wonder if our collaboration will explode in the middle of my flight above the Atlantic. You can communicate that to him, but I know that you, Doris Night, my bouquet of peonies nested like a newborn in the hollow of your pretty plump arm, are reading this letter out loud for David Grey, who, considering the hour, has probably already swapped his ridiculous Mexican braggart outfit for the boring uniform of the international youth. (*"Bloody asshole!"*) Tell him also that I plan to redecorate his apartment in SoHo in my own fashion. Eye for an eye: not D&D, but ôô, two Easter eggs with pretty knotted ribbons, the eyes of an intrigued ghost with eyebrows raised, *awe*, fright, or reverent terror...Not the ephemeral smile of the Cheshire Cat perched on his disappearing branch, but the wide-open eyes of the unfortunate soul lost at the end of a dark tunnel.

Miss Night, Doris Lanuit, you will never be anything but a tiny footnote at the bottom of a page of my biography.

Abel Prote

P.S. Don't tell me that you've completely forgotten about our disguised soirées. I bet that just the memory of them still makes you dizzy. Be that as it may, I gladly admit that I can never think about them anymore without feeling a tightening of my throat, a sudden acceleration of my pulse and—because I list my physical reactions from high to low—a visible animation of my downstairs region. How I regret today never having been a fervent supporter of those adult toys—cameras! What a gallery of portraits I could have created! One photo a night, in our disguises ... Or rather two: an image before the encounter and the programmed seduction, a full-length portrait, you and me side by side, ignoring each other diligently; and then from another vantage point, a larger frame to emphasize the disorder of the room following our frolicking. I'm sure you remember the night when ...

"Well," says Doris, exasperated. "That's enough."
"No," protests David. "Continue."
"Why?"
"Go on. Read."
"Don't you see that Abel is still trying to pull the strings? That he anticipated, no, organized, planned this scenario: me reading you this letter out loud? As long as he can, he'll keep hurting us."
"I want to know what comes next," insists David. "In any event," he adds, "I'm going to have to translate all of it. I'm sure Prote will want to incorporate this letter into his novel, too."
"If you insist." Doris continues with a trembling, at times broken voice:

I'm sure you remember our performance starring you as the Iron Lady, me as the wrestler known as the Executioner of Béthune enveloped in a large burgundy red cape. We feigned meeting each other by chance in my garden. The wrestling holds I subjected you to in my bed! The punishments you inflicted on me! I admit that our roles did not exactly suit us: you are too sensual to incarnate that stick-thin *First Lady*, I am not muscular enough to be convincing in the role of the mysterious Executioner. But still: I like to fight and I like to win, and I am no stranger to underhand strikes; since then I've seen in you a slight resemblance to the vile Iron Lady, a penchant for vengeance, a calculating and cruel side, hard and cold, the drive to inflict harm. ("Are you really like that, sweetheart?") Our current roles, until further notice. ("No.") I will be merciless until you have returned Maurice-Edgar Prote's letter to me. In fact, I need it for my novel *(N.d.T.)*, and I want for your little Gris to translate it along with the rest of the book.

"*Fucking asshole!*" David cries. "Where is it anyway, that letter from father Prote?"

"In the brown envelope, on the side table," says Doris. "But you're in for a surprise."

"Oh? Why's that?"

"Actually, it's Abel who'll be shocked," Doris corrects herself with a delighted smile.

David picks up the brown envelope, takes out a thin bundle of sheets of onionskin paper, then sits back down next to Doris on the crimson sofa. He unfolds the fragile sheets carefully and begins to read.

INTERMISSION

★

★ *Permettez . . .* Please . . . *Scusi . . .*

It's been a long time since I've shown myself. But like the razor clam spurting from the sand at high tide, it's time for me to poke my head out, to emerge, powerful, from my shell. At least three chapters have gone by without you, dear reader, hearing the sound of my voice. I have my reasons: the underground, erotic, epistolary, and passionate tribulations of the characters of *Translator's Revenge* both enticed me and made my life difficult. Nevertheless, I've made it out okay and for that my author should be thankful. Of course, I redacted things here (a long and tedious philosophical digression by Prote on betrayal), added on there (disguised nights, fellatio in the tunnel), repaired elsewhere (the model of the Super Constellation, whose story was coming unglued), invented from beginning to end the scene of the distorted flower deliveryman, modified Doris's last name (it was originally Lecerf, the horror! Night suits her much better, plus I've always liked the song by Ray Charles, "Night and Day"—feet tapping on the ground, head bobbing left and right, more energetic than the enigmatic head bob of the Indians, left at night, right during the day, unless it's the other way around). In sum, a few minor retouches and mends, which, as usual, improved the original text. At least I hope. But outside of these minor misdemeanors, I am at your service! (*Traitor's Nuisance*)

Candies, caramels, Eskimo Pies, chocolate! Sodas and cold drinks!

In an aisle in the now-illuminated room echoing with the saccharine music of the grand piano set up on the stage, I walk along the wall with a rolling gait, slowly go down the carpeted stairs, then pass beneath the silver screen, masked for a few seconds by two heavy red velvet curtains. I approach the pianist in his tuxedo, who, without pausing his soporific melodies on the black and white Pleyel keys, turns to me and winks from behind his sunglasses. Do you recognize me, dear reader? Probably not, for I have changed body and here I am transformed into Verdana, the dashing cinema usherette, bright red skirt falling at mid-calf and full of flounce, fishnet stockings and high heels to emphasize my shapely legs, a tiara encrusted with diamonds decorating my jet-black hair in an updo resembling Sugarloaf Mountain. I'm sporting two leather straps over my flat stomach that hold up the wicker basket full of my sweets. It's intermission. It's hot. Up on the cream-white ceiling encircled by a gilded molding, large fan blades slowly stir the air, bluish from cigarette smoke. Air conditioning has not yet been invented. The ban against smoking at the cinema hasn't been either. It is the beginning of June 1937, in Paris, perhaps in the immense rococo hall of the Rex, on the Grands Boulevards, where spectators fill the plush red seats. From the bottom of the orchestra up to the stage, these rows of identical chairs unfurl toward the large crimson curtains like velvet waves crashing onto the flat beach of the Red Sea, or else like my own lines, sneakily slipped into the bottom of a white rectangle above which there was just moment ago, in size 11 font and henceforth relegated to page 131, the word

Intermission.

All these people came to see this spring's great cinematographic novelty, *Love is News*, starring Tyrone Power, Loretta Young, and Don Ameche. A film that I adore and never grow tired of rewatching.

Each time, my size 10 font gets all excited. Especially when the journalist (Tyrone Power) takes in his arms the beautiful heiress (Loretta Young), who faints from happiness and incredulity, I too feel as though I might swoon with happiness.

As soon as the wall lights and the crystal chandeliers turn back on, the brouhaha gradually invades the theater where once again we can admire the faux fluted columns, the luminous torches embedded in the walls, the basins of painted plaster, the pastel cherubs that frolic on the ceiling. A rumble swells through the overheated space, one can hear conversations, laughter, murmurs, the scratching of matches or the click of someone lighting a cigarette or a cigar, the rhythmic bursts of my own voice—Sam, the pianist, often tells me that I should be a singer—the crumpling of candy wrappers, newspapers, or the leaflet skimmed to pass the time, the squeaking of a few badly-oiled chairs, and soon the joyful cries of children delighted by my appetizing appearance.

But what strikes me most is the interlaced couples. I love to observe them as soon as the lights come back on, not all at once but little by little, in a slow successive fade, and often they prolong their embrace and their kiss as if the room were still plunged in darkness and no one could see them, their hands continuing to lose themselves in bare skin, beneath skirts, shirts, corsages, in openings and zippers. Not very photosensitive, they take a long time to react, to emerge from their burning, blind cocoon where the only thing bothering them is the inconvenient armrest, understanding at last, intoxicated with love, dazed with sensuality and, for some of them, with frustration, that the vast majority of spectators, far from confusing the cinema with a hotel room, are interested in the images being projected, and that the intermission henceforth spares them from lifting their eyes toward the silver screen only to catch sight of their lustful peers, with varying and sometimes disapproving, even outraged, reactions. So the lovers distance themselves by a few centimeters; haggard and rubicund, they emerge from their underwater trance, their feverish hands straighten their clothes, the myopic wipe their glasses stained with cold cream, they glance nervously around the room, sometimes timid, sometimes furious, as if someone had just brusquely awakened them from a delicious dream or transported them against their will to an unknown place. I adore observing their wide eyes, their gaping mouths, their cheeks red with excitement or from a stubbly beard, while they come back little by little to the world that they never left.

★

★ Sometimes it's in that hardly sterling state that I emerge from a translation session; alone, it goes without saying, but just as dazed, similarly disoriented; for a moment unable to find a sense of place, a sense of time, a reason for my presence anywhere other than the intimacy of the text. It's the intermission, the break: I wrest myself from the words printed on the page and from the fashioning of my own words on the computer screen—the AZERTY keyboard similar to rows of red chairs, or rather to the design of the theater with the seat numbers inscribed in little squares on a document that can sometimes be found tacked to the wall next to the register; my 14.1-inch screen is the immense radiant surface where the film plays out—I wrest myself from this racket as the lover-spectator distances his or herself from the warm body of his or her companion when the lights come back on and paralyze them. A dark room, a paradise of transfixed couples that, for the span of two or three reels, discover, hearts racing, that they are not made for the daylight but for the shadows of the populated abyss of spectral and incomprehensible voices, dimly lit by the screen's shifting gleams. Sometimes I think I'm molding my words in an underwater workshop, holding my breath far below the luminous world, no need to inhale the appearance of things, my only light that of the computer screen and a small beam aimed at a book. When the break comes, my private interlude, my intermission,★★ I rejoin the visible space, I propel myself to the surface of the world without a single decompression stop. Like a missile spurting forth from a nuclear submarine, I spring into the open air in a large splash, and I recognize nothing. Blinded by the light, not very photosensitive myself, mechanically I walk to the kitchen and make myself a coffee. (*Tyuiop N.*)

★★ In English and in French in the original text.

Sometimes during the screening a man with a feverish gaze or a woman with a hunted look comes to take refuge in the theater. They burst in right in the middle of a screening, sit down wherever, throw furtive glances right and left, survey the doorways so intensely they don't even watch the film, sometimes change places, several times. Occasionally, several men follow them through the doors, causing a ruckus in the dark room: outraged protest from the spectators, whistles, cries, various threats.

But to tell the truth I've never witnessed such a scene, I've only seen it on the movie screen.

Today, although the theater is packed, it's an ordinary screening. As usual people assail me to buy sweets and I have plenty of time to observe the amorous couples, victims of luminous electroshock. It's as if they were going to liquefy, as if the light were going to melt them and make them disappear for good, sucked into their chairs. Nevertheless, between a grandmother buying a pack of candy for her grandson and a hairy man in wrinkled clothing who demands two Eskimo Pies and then immediately turns on his heels without waiting for his change, I notice an elegant man accompanied by a young eccentric beauty. I work part-time as an usherette at the Rex to pay for my studies, but I adore the theater and immediately recognize the young woman: Miss Dolores Haze, whom I saw just the day before yesterday at the Odéon, in a performance of Chekhov's *The Cherry Orchard*. Judging by their frenzied gazes, their scarlet cheeks, their almost shameful efforts to straighten their chic clothing, those two are emerging from a serious performance of their own. But who is that elegant gentleman?

"Candy, caramels, Eskimo Pies!" I yell out, staring at them.

"Two Eskimo Pies," the graying man replies immediately, handing me a bill. "Or, actually: two cold drinks!" He then turns toward his companion. "I imagine you're as thirsty as I am, Lola."

I hand them two cold orange juices and add mischievously: "Anything for Miss Haze."

The aging man gives me a dirty look, then, without a word, vexed that I have recognized the beautiful actress, pays me.

The lights go out little by little. The two crimson curtains open onto the glimmering screen. Sam, the pianist in the tuxedo and black glasses, disappears into the wings to the left of the stage. The film is about to begin. In the growing shadows, I continue to sell my last Eskimo Pies, my last cold drinks. Summer is almost here, it gets hotter and hotter in the room. The lovers nestle against each other, their hands grope around among their clothing, they prepare to plunge back into their territorial waters. And I go in search of my pianist.

Chapter 8

THE HIDDEN, STOLEN, AND FINALLY REVEALED LETTER

★

★ Maurice,

You can call me your Dodo, your Dora, your Dollie, your
Lolo, your Lola, your Loli, but never Lolita, it's much too vulgar. I am Dolores to the government, and to you anything you
like, except Lolita. I warned you from the beginning of our relationship, I detest the crackling barrage of syllables in that name
evoking a sulking, shameless young girl, syllables that, one night
last autumn, you inadvertently or wickedly bestowed on me in
New York, then noticing my disgust with a sad surprise. And my
anger. I am no longer that adolescent formerly entrusted, after the
accidental death of my mother, to the care of a libidinous stepfa-
ther who used and abused that regrettable first name as much as
he did my pubescent body. I abhor Lolita (with your dirty mind,
don't go mishearing that as: I'm your Lolita! I would never forgive you). No, I am Dolores Haze, American, twenty-seven years
old, brown hair, dark blue eyes, five feet six inches tall, distinctive
characteristics: none, except for now-developed feminine curves,
profession: actress and no longer a nymphet doomed to the
concupiscence of an old European man, American actress who
has come to Paris thanks to you and because of you to act in a
Chekhov play in your famous Odéon theater.

Dolores Haze, if you would like the French translation of my
name, it's "Douleur Labrume." I looked it up.

To celebrate my hundredth performance of *The Cherry Orchard* last night, you gave me that beautiful violet crown that went straight to my heart. Certain crowns are worn on the head—for example, you are in my eyes the uncontested king of your professional milieu—but I squeezed this circle of violets against my chest, for I saw it as a token of your love for me. I really loved the little cardboard rectangle, pierced by a metallic eyelet and fastened to the violets with a twisted wire, like a tag affixed to a suitcase before a long transatlantic voyage. That fluttering appendage proves your attachment to me. As if I were the violet crown and you, the man of words, linked to me by that wire twist. But contrary to what you probably think, you are not the only one who can write: soon, on its splendid violet backdrop, the floral suitcase will contain nothing other than my own letter folded in half several times and slid into its center. You will find it, or not. That's luck for you, as said *the other*. In any event, when you read this letter, I will no longer be here. I will have left the apartment and, I hope, Paris. I will have left you, too. As soon as possible, I will cancel my contract with the Odéon theater.

I'm sure you'll understand nothing of it. Too bad for you.

Enough procrastinating.

I am writing this letter at four in the morning, the 21, no, the 22 of June. You are sleeping with your fists clenched in your big soft bed, arms rather pathetically stretched toward the place, still warm, where my body rested just a few minutes ago. Now you're snoring in the bedroom and I'm in the living room. During the party and during the night, we made love several times, in relatively absurd places, as is your tendency: first after the end of the play, when we returned hastily from the Odéon to your mansion via the secret passage to greet your guests—you always had a fondness for sleight of hand, for surprise appearances, jack-in-the-boxes that pop up without warning—on the way you suddenly led me into the wine cellar and there, in the middle of the shelves heavily weighted with vintage wines, some dating from the last century, you took me from behind and, I admit without false modesty, made me come (I'm not telling you anything new, I know, but I derive pleasure from remembering my pleasure in writing). Then, one behind the other, you behind me, both of us in an excellent mood, we went back up the stairs to the hidden door that opens onto the little hallway deserted of guests; and there, at the foot of that hideous puppet fresco, at risk of being seen by your servants, while we could hear the din of your party in full swing two doors down, you kissed me once again, bit my earlobe, caressed me, snaked your hand inside my clothing, then penetrated me while lifting me up against the closed door of the secret passage. Legs spread wide, wrapped around your thighs, while your penis impaled me and your pelvic thrusts made me jump and pant, the whole time I watched that atrocious dislocated puppet above your right shoulder, the fresco that, as you told me one day, you had commissioned a renowned Parisian artist to paint on that large wall a few years ago. Goya always fascinated you. His gruesome works entitled *The Disasters of War*, which you showed me, are burning topics in Spain, as in this very moment the odious general is wreaking havoc on the country. I also know that you are very interested in my compatriot, the very promising writer Ernest Hemingway. Promising and generous. Involved in the fight against fascism. Ambulance driver in the American army during World War I. Hemingway recently went to Spain in the ranks of the Republicans. He'll go back there, I'm sure of it, and I bet he'll write about that country and that war. I bet you'll publish him soon in France, too. But that's beside the point.

Getting back to the puppet. The more I stared at him, the more I felt like he had something to tell me. The more violently you moved back and forth inside me, the wider your hands spread my butt cheeks to penetrate me as deeply as possible, the more I felt you were foreign, narcissistic, concerned only with your own pleasure, eyes half-closed, probably focused on the mental image, not yet within reach, that would allow you to heighten your orgasm, perhaps scanning through the pornographic positions collected in your memory, parading one after another on the screen of your private cinema before selecting the one that would excite you enough, experienced masturbator that you are, to come. My body, at the end of the day, held less importance for you than the fetishistic image that would allow you to do the impossible. And the more I stared at the dislocated marionette levitating in the sky above the sea, the more I felt it was staring at me. It was speaking to me. It was my accomplice. My double, perhaps. The two of us were manipulated by forces bigger than us: your body, your dick, your hands, the images, still disappointing, that moved in a slide show beneath your eyelids; and for the marionette, the being or beings that had thrown it into the middle of the sky so that it would crash down over the sea and drown. Spanish Icarus in freefall, captured by surprise in mid-flight, frozen on the wall for years like a bird in a photograph, Abraham's suspended knife in the Rembrandt painting we saw together at the Hermitage Museum in St. Petersburg. Yes, that marionette was whispering words to me that I didn't understand, but that it wanted to communicate to me at all costs.

On the verge of finally grasping its message, I suddenly heard you whisper in my right ear: "Lo ... li ... ta." At that very moment, I no longer had the least desire to make love. I couldn't believe my ears: I had told you several times that I detested that name, that it brought me back to an unhappy age of my existence, that I never wanted to hear it again. Especially not from your mouth. And in the same moment, as if these three syllables constituted the eureka moment, suddenly crystallizing the perfect pornography you had been groping for until then, spelling out the magic formula that finally allowed you to reach orgasm by humiliating me, you unloaded into me. Obviously, I didn't come. I was cold as an ice cube, a thousand leagues from you, a million miles away, for a while already I hadn't been enjoying myself. I don't even know if you noticed my distance, my disinterest, my disgust. In any case, you said nothing. Not a word. You wanted to treat yourself to a nymphet that no longer exists while defiling the woman that I am now and who had indeed warned you: that double slight whereby you saw the ideal occasion to possess one at the same time as the other, to constrain that woman by the force of three repugnant syllables to yield to your caprice and perversely turn back against her will into the nymphet that she had been only in the imagination of an unhinged European man, that double slight resulted in you losing the woman that I am. Like the dog crossing the stream, you gave up the bone for the reflection and, as it happens, lost them both; for there exists only one and the same person, and I have only one name: Dolores Haze.

In silence, each of us plunged into our thoughts, we straightened our clothes. You had an idiotic smile on your lips that betrayed sexual satisfaction, but I saw in it the pleasure you took at having achieved your goal, or at least convincing yourself you had: forcefully transforming an adult woman into the adolescent she used to be, compelling her into that metamorphosis, possessing her through that lens, making sure she knew it, obliging her to submit to that strange caprice, and then perhaps later convincing her to orgasm in her turn from this backsliding, from the regression you staged for the pleasure of feeling as though you were fucking two women at the same time, or more precisely the same woman twice at different ages, their bodies switching according to your desire. A man, two women, three syllables. Is my letter a mere mathematical equation?

But last night, while you were nonchalantly tucking the ends of your shirt into your pants, you were seriously mistaken: not for a second would I enter into your dirty ploy; far from submitting to your pitiful masquerade, I detested you for having even imagined it, not to mention implementing it. I am an actress, I move from one text to another, from one role to the next, but if there is one character that no one can ever force me to play, a role that no dramaturge or director, no matter how talented or famous, will ever compel me to assume, not on the boards, nor on the bed, nor anywhere else, it is that of the Lolita of my adolescence, a role that I did not play, but through which I was played, manipulated, in all senses of the term. In this hallway perpetually surveyed by the puppet, when my feet were in contact once again with the parquet floors, I loathed your idiotic smile, your sated fantasy, your perversity, your narcissism. Hence my silence. I held back my tears, and made my decision on the spot.

Then we went to join your guests on that warm night in the garden dotted with candles situated behind your mansion. We drank a glass of champagne, joked around, smiled and laughed as if nothing had happened. But still I could not forget what you had just subjected me to, nor rid myself of the puppet's dead-eyed stare, as if the pale creature had been emptied of its vital substance, devoured by a starving being, you of course, sucked from the inside, then robbed of one of its dimensions, flattened, crushed like a mosquito on a sheet of paper, reduced to the flatness of that fresco in your hallway. A kind of human trophy. A cannibalized corpse. A tanned hide, a shrunken head. I still don't know what he was trying to tell me. Your voice pronouncing those three forbidden syllables kept me from hearing it. Was his secret yours? Did he want to warn me, reveal to me something I didn't know or confirm what I already knew? Was I in Bluebeard's castle? Among all the keys that you so love to hide and pull out of nowhere like a magician pulls a white rabbit by its ears from his black top hat, is there a key that leads to a bloody den where you keep the cadavers of your past lovers suspended from meat hooks? Is the hallway puppet merely an hors-d'oeuvre? An appetizer for socialite cannibals? A macabre clue in a sinister treasure hunt? The announcement of a recurrent theme?

All of Paris is sparkling, gleaming, invigorating the *esprit** and leaving me cold. I can still hear those three odious syllables murmured on your lips echoing in my right ear. But at the end of the party, as the guests yielded to the excitement of the champagne, you especially were gleaming, courted, idolized by your friends and by all those women who, despite their formal civility and their charming smiles, I could tell took me for a mere fling, an exotic fancy, a carnation on your boutonniere, the agreeable pastime of an inveterate seducer. And you, manifestly in great form, lavished with all these tributes, you were strutting, boasting, peacocking, and cooing without worrying for a second about how I might feel. Socialite first and foremost. No, indifferent above all. Satisfied and indifferent.

Before leaving here, I will take a last look at the puppet. Perhaps he will finally whisper his truth to me. I hope that your resounding snores will not keep me from hearing his voice this time. I bend my ear to capture a message, but every time it's you that I hear: earlier the three syllables of my former name and now those long whistlings that sound like a tire deflating, alternating with the hoarse snorts of a pig. Again and again. Endlessly. Why do you always have to make yourself known? Why is it that even asleep you have to impose your resounding presence? Get lost. Are you that afraid you'll be forgotten? That

---

* In French in the original text. (*N.d.T.*)

we'll lose interest in you? That we'll listen to someone else for a
change? Are you that afraid that you'll cease to exist if you can
no longer make out your pleasing reflection in the wide eyes of
your admirers? You can do without mine from now on. I have
no doubt that you will find many others, infinitely more indulging, on the feathers of your peacock tail.

I went to see the puppet. He looked at me with his dead stare
for a good minute before finally whispering his message: "You
are not obligated to stay like I am. Go."
Then I heard nothing but your snores.
I sat back down here to finally tell you

Adios

Dolores Haze

Chapter 9

DAVID'S SECRET PASSAGE

★

★ David is quiet. After a long silence, Doris says:

"I had already written my letter to Abel before reading the note from Dolores. The breakup letter she wrote to Maurice-Edgar Prote on the 21st, no, the 22nd of June, 1937. Which she wrote in the living room where we are now. And finished with the same word as mine: *Adios*. Before sliding it into the center of the violet crown. Where apparently the publisher did not find it. Nor did his son. I'm the one who discovered it nearly... seventy years later, as I snuck in my own, for Abel!"

"Assholes, like father like son," concludes David, tired out by his recent reading and the excitement, the terrors, the various pleasures of the day. "The father who wanted to fuck Lolita through Dolores, the son and his perverse disguises... Although apparently you liked all that."

"The difference between father Prote and his son," corrects Doris, slightly agitated, "is that Maurice used Dolores, while Abel and I were equals, both of us disguised, both of us consenting: partners in crime."

"Okay, well, that's enough," mutters David. "No need to remind me." After a moment, he adds: "And now, what do we do with it, that letter from Dolores? Should we put it back in the center of the violet crown, in place of yours, which has already reached its addressee? After all, I'll have to translate it..."

"Works for me. Where is the crown?"

"In the hallway. On the shelves of the armoire, which I put on the ground while I was searching for the secret passage."

Doris goes back into the hallway, then stops for a moment in front of the puppet in the fresco, wondering whether he'll speak to her, too, whether he'll tell her to leave, or stay, or else point out to her the secret room where the former women of both father and son are suspended by their meat hooks. But no, the puppet remains silent. She turns around, presses the dried violets against her heart. Doris as Dolores? David as...? Noticing her lover's incomprehension, she carefully folds Dolores Haze's letter, before sliding it into the middle of the dried stems. Then, yielding to a sudden impulse, she goes into Abel Prote's office and places the crown and its contents on the pile of books prepared by the writer the day before to lead his translator little by little toward the secret passage.

"This will be the cherry on the cake!" she cries out, laughing. "On *his* cake. I'd love to see his face when he finds it here upon his return. When he finds that letter, not at all addressed to him from his father, as he thinks for some reason, but from Dolores to Maurice-Edgar. Perhaps he'll suspect some trick on our part? Zorro the masked avenger and Doris his accomplice launch into forgery. Falsification and use of false documents. Eye for an eye, tooth for a tooth, onionskin for onionskin. Do you think that's what he'll tell himself?"

"I don't know," replies David, walking into the office and wrapping his arms around Doris from behind, pushing her hair aside to kiss her neck. "All I know is that I'm exhausted, *vanné* as you say in French. *Flapi*, is that a French word? Let's go to sleep."

"Okay, but promise that you'll never call me Rorita."

"Fuck no. I know what happens to the man who does that. But, if I were Japanese, I wouldn't be able to differentiate between Lolita and Rorita. The Japanese don't know the sound for 'r,' they pronounce it 'l.'"

They go back into the writer's room. Doris wants to change the sheets and pillowcases. David approves energetically and helps her, then they collapse into the big bed and turn out the light. The young American is on the verge of sleep when he feels Doris's back and butt press against him.

"Kiss me on the neck again," she whispers, "like before."

Half asleep, David pushes aside the waves of black hair spread over the flowers of the pillowcase, the multicolored geometric patterns, pistils, petals, stigmas, and stems, that the darkness of the bedroom reduces to a mere assortment of grays, as if the night had sucked up the colors and left nothing but the design. Even their two nude bodies are colorless, pale, sketched in gray on the white canvas of the sheet. David moves his lips toward the little ringlets covering her creamy neck, he kisses, licks, bites, and soon feels a hand caressing the top of his thighs and stomach, then with a gentle authority taking hold of his cock, which is already getting hard. He delicately grabs the young woman's breasts, massages her erect nipples, while continuing to kiss her exposed neck, and Doris soon guides him inside of her, whispering in a muffled voice that vibrates and groans, at times trembling, at times bold on the thin thread of her breath: Change of décor, handsome. Welcome to my secret passage. You have everything you need to venture inside. Cross the threshold, forge ahead, yes, establish yourself there, settle yourself in good, it's much more comfortable than the exhausting journey you just took through that nightmarish tunnel where the other, your author, the French author, led you, you his translator walking in his footsteps, faithful like a shadow soldered to the body, subject to him by signed contract, bound to his words and his dictates, compelled to follow his route and fall into all the traps he laid for you. But here, with me, in me, you are at home, safe, you can take your time, there's no hurry, touch and go at your own rhythm, feel free in your movements, you can come and go as you please, take a stroll through the warmth, wander at your leisure, rummage around, dawdle, amble, loiter, window shop, enter a boutique, feel around, touch the merchandise, taste the sweets, saunter without worrying about getting cold or having unpleasant encounters like in *The Tunnel of Death*, that sinister funfair attraction. You can even, if you want, hurry up, explore me faster, my Ali Baba cave, pick up the pace, yield to feverishness, unleash your ardor, speed up to a trot and then from a trot to a gallop, finally race, embrace me in your arms, kiss me, sway me, embroil me in your fantasia, bang against my walls, rebel, takes the words out of my mouth, make me shut up sway groan faint. You can also settle yourself into one of my cozy club chairs, curl yourself up in me on a soft red sofa, dim the lights or even turn them off entirely, spread out and luxuriate, nod off, get a little cozy shut-eye, dream as much as you like, wake up later feeling great, rested, perked up, ready to get back to work, get back in the saddle with renewed energy, your translator's to-and-fros that happen here with no points of reference, blindly, but with a perfect memory of the places in my place of memory. My own place. Yes, give yourself over to the pleasure of my text. Even if it's not the to-and-fro of your eyes following the printed lines, but that of your blind stiffness decoding the silk of my private passage. Here, as you can see, no hideous masks, no terrifying growl, no nose-diving or low-flying plane, no molded fuselage or nose cone painted with an open mouth of two rows of sharp teeth, you are my flying tiger armed with a machine gun synchronized to the spinning of the propeller, there also aren't any sounds of chains rattled by a mechanical skeleton above the young terrified passengers squeezed tightly together in the bouncing cars of a phantom train charging at full speed out of a cardboard cave to be devoured by a dusty opening painted almost entirely in black; no, here you will meet no detour from the path, no gorgon or petrified head, no band of grimacing witches. My insides are as black as an oven, you are in the blackness within me, with no flashlight or candlestick other than the soft, warm one you are naturally endowed with, my fingers forming a ring around its base to heighten its rigor. It illuminates nothing, this candlestick, but you already know my place like the back of your hand, as my hand knows your pole, you have often come knocking here, you get your bearings with your eyes closed, you are now familiar, accustomed, a regular as they say in bars. A patron in English, isn't that right? With your column you prop up my ceiling, without your vertical entity everything collapses in a cloud of dust, our shared ease, our inspired fuck. Here you are at home, you are the boss, get comfortable, explore the grounds, there, perfect, verify that everything is in its place, in order, positioned as per usual, don't forget any corner, any overhanging, any hiding place, any niche, carefully inspect all my crevices, be meticulous, be persnickety, rigorous, and meticulous, like the devil the pleasure is in the details, yes, do a careful inspection of my nook, take out your checklist and check my box with your pencil, really check my box, verify that nothing is missing, go over me with a fine-tooth comb, twice not just once, make your nest here and act like a bird, crane your neck, spread your wings, like that, that's good, yes, continue, go deeper, excavate there rummage excavate far, farther, go on, you're almost there, almost at the quay, your dick wedged up against the mooring, you're there, you're bigger than you were earlier in my mouth, my love, do you feel how I'm squeezing you tightly, you are, you go, if you keep going like that you're going to make me come, wait, don't move, yes, there, stay, let me squeeze your iron fist in my velvet glove one more time, now hang on for a bit, the inventory is finished, you checked me, relax, be lethargic but don't fall asleep, no, it's important that you not sleep, I know you're tired but don't leave me, stay with me, just stop moving, breathe a little, grab a folding chair, sit down, relax a minute, the movie will start soon, now it's my turn to move, leave the room, go along the corridor, leave the lobby where you can buy popcorn and soda, cross the exit, settle comfortably on the sidewalk by the doorstep, near the little glass booth, get some air, fill your two fertile lungs, inhale the breeze, smoke a cigarette, see the thickets still soaked with dew at the edges of me, my multicolored silks, I'm ready, take my emotion, break me entirely, the first lights of day make a crimson fog in the sky stained with sperm, see the beautiful thick undergrowth curl in the surrounding humidity, see farther on the amber-colored light, the large plowed furrow, the small vales and the damp hills barely emerging from the night, the mounds and the steeper reliefs lined up all the way to the horizon in a gentle atmospheric vision, all this landscape steeped in night offered to your massive blind cyclopean eye, and now we are together at the edge of the sea, surely you remember, lying on a beach at the foot of an oblong dune, the waves unfurl beneath a stormy sky, the air smells like kelp, the seagulls screech, the tide rises little by little, the water reaches you takes you embraces you, your penis gets wet, yes, I lead you inside my port again, my northwest passage, my strait, my cozy corner, my isthmus, my canal, my waterway, my lock, my secret cupboard upholstered in violet velvet, yes, hold my waist, squeeze it tight between your fingers, yes, stop it from moving, just let my hips undulate, let them breathe you, impale my behind, oh, I forgot to tell you, unlike the other tunnel, my secret passage leads nowhere, no uniforms or furs await you, no theater, no dressing room, no prompter's hole, it's also not a tunnel used to escape from a prison cell or the dungeon of a fortified castle, no, you will translate nothing there, yes, keep going, again, harder, again, no, you will not transport any verbal merchandise to the other side of me, no veiled word or forbidden fruit, no concealed hidden sealed stolen finally revealed letter, no violets or peonies, no flower other than those white petals that will gush from your one-eyed monster, no message, not even your entire body, just that retractable appendage inside of me, that telescopic leg in its case sealed against the light like a black room opening for a flash and then nothing, you will not transport anything to the other end of me other than the end of yourself, not even a single trans-lator's note, you are bankrolled by no one, you are neither mes-senger nor mercenary, neither ferryman nor passenger, my sworn masseur, there is not even a direction anymore, it seems, not even a one-way, only a wrong way, no direction but it spins around, it turns in circles, it goes around and around, it goes, it comes, it's alive, that's it, it's good and long, it doesn't lead anywhere, it's an impasse, a cul-de-sac or a crypt, oh yes, like that, keep doing that, hold me tight, with me in me outside of me there you are allowed to go back and forth between the printed French text you're translating and the American version you're creating faithfully, this is your own secret passage, your personal sleight of hand, your professional to-and-fro, your paid movements, your certified work, and all the better if you mix business with pleasure, but here in me outside of me you aren't working anymore, you're screwing me good, you come and go without creating anything other than my happiness, yes, come, I like your back-and-forth, your back-and-forth ravishes me like a glove, *e la nave va*, I leak, trickle, sluice gates all the way open, I sink faint melt drown, come, your light my life delights me, come, translate yourself inside me quickly yes, I'm coming

David immediately falls asleep against Doris's sweat-drenched body and has the following dream:

Chapter 10

THE SECRET PASSAGE REVISITED

★

★ Doris is still talking, but more quietly, as if from far away. David hears her distorted metallic voice without understanding what she's saying. They are words, but they mean nothing. He is standing, dressed, at the entrance to Prote's secret passage, back turned toward the puppet in the fresco. Between the two panels of the armoire, the striped ties to the left, the colorful polka-dotted bow ties to the right, an immobile silhouette blocks his path. Backlit, like someone emerging from the night in a horror movie, the elegantly dressed man holds his hat in one hand, the violet crown in the other. The violets are fresh, sparkling in the light; their translucent petals, as beautiful as the grid of purple veins on an arm or the slow dilution of india ink in a glass of water, are a mass of color, a dense block of pure violet surrounded by an improbable incandescent border. His hat is the same one David found earlier on a shelf of the armoire, its seam displaying the initials M.-E. P. The man, the spirit blocking the path and keeping him from reaching his dream—at least this is how David feels—is Maurice-Edgar Prote, the Parisian publisher. And then the cavernous voice that continues to speak quietly like a narrator or an officiant is not Doris's, but perhaps that of Dolores Haze. That even monotone voice, a sort of stubborn bass uninterrupted by any pause for breath, is coming from the living room. It marks a rhythm as if it might never stop, as if it were the very support of time, its guarantor, its guardian: the halt of that voice would make way for a silence equivalent to the end of time.

Then David hears himself say, like a ventriloquist dummy:

"I am a star of the shadows. But don't all stars shine at night?"

In the living room, the feminine psalmody stops abruptly. Everything freezes. Time is smashed to smithereens. David notices that the light bulb on the ceiling is crackling a bit, probably, he tells himself, because of a bad contact or because the incandescent filament is on the verge of going out. For a long time, it's the only audible noise in the silent apartment.

David turns his head to the right and sees a splendid naked young woman approaching wordlessly in the dim light of the hallway. The woman, whom he does not recognize, looks straight ahead of her and passes through him as if he didn't exist, as if he were invisible; then she joins Maurice-Edgar Prote on the threshold of the passage. The publisher takes a step forward, silently offers the violet crown to the young woman, then kisses her. David feels himself slowly withdraw as if he were seated in a wheelchair and someone were smoothly pulling him backward with the inhuman regularity of a machine, and, reinforcing his unease, he feels as though he's getting bigger, reaching a more and more elevated vantage point, rising up on the tips of his toes, which keep growing taller.

Now the door to the secret passage is closed, the publisher turns his back to David and lifts the young woman against the door, holding her by the butt cheeks, spreading them wide. From his elevated position, David sees that it's Dolores Haze jumping with the man's pelvic thrusts. Head pressed to Prote's right shoulder, she raises her eyes toward David, catching his eye as if he were much higher up than she, as if Dolores were trying to hear words that he himself were whispering. She looks at him without blinking, eyes wide open. Then, all at once, he realizes that he occupies the position of the puppet in the fresco, he knows that he has become that pale puppet flying through the air, and he feels on the verge of fainting. Hypnotized by

Dolores's fixed stare, by her expression which is simultaneously ecstatic, painful, and pleading, he himself is submerged in horror, he suddenly feels as though he is sinking like a rock into a bottomless pit. Before passing out, he has time to hear the three syllables Prote murmurs into his partner's ear:

"Lo-li-ta."

When he regains consciousness in his dream, or rather, in the next sequence or chapter of the dream, David crosses the threshold of the secret passage with Doris.

Now, no one is blocking their way, no troubling sentinel, no couple in the act of making love, no menacing puppet. The door at the bottom of the armoire is wide open, they enter one after another, first David, then Doris. The stairs are clean—who cleaned them?—and the passage, now enlarged, is well lit. They walk side by side, hand in hand. The two of them are wearing traveling clothes. Doris is carrying a beige leather vanity case, a cardboard label on the handle, David a rather large black canvas bag. As soon as they've taken a few steps in that underground space that is both the same as and different from before, a fade-out begins that is at first imperceptible, then striking: the dust on the ground is slowly replaced by slabs of white marble, the gritty earth of the walls and the ceiling by smooth, creamy concrete. The light increases gradually, it enters in waves through the large bay windows, they advance motionlessly on the slightly twitching black rubber of a moving walkway. The air loses its musty odor and acquires all the stinging dryness of industrial disinfectants.

Then, behind a crowd of other people also carrying various hand luggage, the couple goes down an escalator encircled in a tube of Plexiglas that intersects other tubes in the middle of the sky. Beyond that curved, translucent partition, David and Doris observe the elongated cabins and the gleaming wings of planes parked near immense concrete parallelepipeds with panoramic bay windows. A plane takes off in the distance with a muffled roar, the fuselage inclined at a 20-degree angle above the runway against a uniformly gray sky. The plane is a four-engine with an ovular tailplane: David immediately recognizes a Super Constellation and wonders what that old-fashioned plane is doing in the twenty-first century. Then he's stunned by their own presence in this airport. Have they just disembarked or are they on their way somewhere? Or in between two flights? David has no idea. Does Doris know? He doesn't know that either. They reach the bottom of the escalator and find themselves in a giant hall. Silently they follow people who seem to know where they're going, a group of passengers that David starts to think he and Doris are a part of.

The floor of the hall is lined with large squares, alternating black and white. In the bright light there are a good sixty clothing racks, scattered in an apparently random manner and covered in various articles of clothing, which are in fact theater costumes, uniforms and liveries evoking different eras, all social classes, an array of professions. A checkered pattern or chessboard sprinkled with colorful clothing racks in place of pieces and pawns. Some seem to be in play, following the unknown rules of two absent or invisible players, players whose size we can only imagine.

As soon as they enter that magnificent stage with the two-tone geometry, the group of passengers, seeming to obey a common atavism or an order known to all, disperses cheerfully. In a perfect staging that no dispute, no dillydallying, no blunder disturbs, each person selects a clothing rack and stands next to it. Then, after an astonishing temporal ellipsis, each passenger immediately finds themselves clothed in a costume while their traveling clothes are piled in a shapeless heap at their feet. The hall contains about sixty small similar islets, variations on a common assembly, an identical juxtaposition: a costumed character, a bare clothing rack with its exposed waxed wood and chrome-plated metal piping, finally a pile of clothing thrown haphazardly on the black-and-white chessboard on the floor. In the silence punctuated with only a few coughing fits, sneezes, nervous laughs, or children's cries, everyone remains mute and immobile, as if waiting for an event that won't be long in coming.

David takes advantage of the silent stillness to look down at his legs, his arms, his stomach, and discovers that he is now dressed as the Invisible Man: a balaclava, a shirt, gloves, pants, shoes, all covered in the same printed pattern of white bandages, a unique medical trompe l'oeil in which one material imitates the other. He does not remember choosing this costume, he doesn't even remember putting it on, but it clings to him as if it were self-evident, as if it were instead the costume that had chosen him, as if he would not have been able to choose another.

From where he's standing, against a wall covered with illuminated ads for perfumes, hotels, watches, music-hall performances or plays, David has the time to notice a poster for *The Cherry Orchard* in that row of luminous boxes. Thus he concludes that he is in France, probably in Paris. Then, looking around him, he notices, frozen like human-sized effigies in a wax museum where, by accident or negligence, replicas of every style, of every age have been assembled: a dashing pilot, a Donna Elvira in a spotless dress, an American postman in a blue cap, a little Mickey Mouse from Disneyland, a tall skinny woman disguised as Cinderella, a Rocco Siffredi in full possession of his only trademark, a flamboyant Desdemona, a flower deliveryman holding a large bouquet of peonies in the crook of his arm, a Mercury with white plastic winged heels, an uncompromising Iron Lady, a sewage worker in boots and hat, a voluptuous Castafiore flanked by a rachitic Tintin, a nymphet on roller skates, a wrestler in combat gear, and a bit farther on, yes, between a perky CEO and a skinny, surly soccer player, it's really her, Doris, in a splendid 1930s dress, a small bouquet of violets pinned to her blouse above her heart.

Even though he's never seen that outfit before, David immediately senses that Doris is wearing the dress of Dolores Haze, the one the American actress was probably wearing on June 21, 1937, during Maurice-Edgar Prote's party. Moreover, a bit farther on, a graying dandy in a striped jacket and baggy pants evokes the Parisian publisher in a striking resemblance.

Suddenly, the hall's sound system blares music with a syncopated rhythm. As if they were reacting to an agreed-upon signal, couples immediately form among the clothing racks and the piles of clothing that lie on the floor. David has just enough time to see Doris begin dancing with Prote, or rather with the passenger embodying the deceased publisher, while the adolescent nymphet on roller skates slides supply up to him, weaving through the crowd with a disconcerting dexterity, then without a word suddenly taking the Invisible Man's gloved hand to lead him into a saraband in which he has quite a bit of trouble following his young partner's energetic arabesques. David tries to keep an eye on Doris, but no matter how he twists his neck and stands on his tiptoes, the complicated movements that his nymphet compels him to execute quickly make him lose sight of her, swallowed up with Prote in the impetuous wave of couples. After an exhausting interlude, between two vigorous acrobatic feats, the nymphet appears to be asking him a question that her own twisting and the still-blaring music keep him from grasping.

"What?" he almost yells.

"So you're the star of the shadows?" repeats the nymphet, screaming into David's ear.

"Apparently!"

"But your white suit isn't very dark or discreet! You look like you've just come out of surgery! You look like you're gravely wounded, as though you were in a car accident. I," adds the mischievous skater, "would have imagined the star of the shadows in black, with a long cape and a wide-brimmed hat! It's more mysterious."

"Thank you. I've already donned that disguise once. It didn't really work out for me."

"Maybe you should try something else."

"I don't know what I'm doing here," David replies. "Do you have any idea?"

"None at all!" cries the nymphet on roller skates, compelling her partner to perform audacious wriggles. "Some might call it dancing."

"Well that I know. Nice of you to remind me," grumbles David. "And where are we, do you think?"

"In your dream, star of the shadows."

"What's your name?"

"You can call me Dolly, Lolly, Lola, just don't call me Lolita."

This reply reminds David of another, read or heard in the past, elsewhere, in a life now sadly finished, dispersed in dull tatters in a former chapter of his existence.

The overexcited skater bursts into a piercing laugh and does a series of more and more stupefying pirouettes that he quickly renounces attempting. From then on, the Invisible Man remains immobile, floored in all senses of the term, but quite visible in the hall for he is the only one not dancing, with his arms crossed, slightly stunned, sullen and stunned, at times admiring the virtuosity of the nymphet, who passes fluidly from a black box to a white box then from a white box to a black box, at times searching for Doris, who is decidedly nowhere to be found among the frenetic crowd of the costume ball.

Little by little, the skating nymphet's pirouettes and whirls become so sharp and rapid that she seems to lose an arm, then another, then her head, and then her entire body disappears in a colorful maelstrom—a trembling crimson stain in place of a

T-shirt, a red and vibrant corolla resembling a skirt, two fluttering black bars in place of legs, a few twitchy shimmerings signaling her skates—and suddenly, *pfuiit*, nothing, the colors fade, turn bland, become transparent, dissolve in the light of the hall: where she had been dancing an accelerated dervish, there's suddenly emptiness, a large gap, an open space among the couples, a small deserted ring, without even the small cloud of white smoke that, in magic tricks or cartoons, typically accompanies the disappearance of a character sucked into another space or transported to an unknown dimension. On the marble of the chessboard, there isn't even a single roller skate left, not a single strap of sequined leather, not a single chrome bolt.

David is still speechless. Was he seeing things? Could he have dreamed everything? The nymphet, the words that he remembers exchanging with her, his own clumsy attempts to follow the frenetic rhythm of her pirouettes, was all that merely an illusion? Had the skater just been pilfered by the imperious hand of an invisible player suddenly grabbing a piece from the chessboard? Since no one in the hall seems to have noticed anything, he turns to bleak hypotheses: can we trust a memory if we are the only one to remember? What credit can be accorded to the reality of a being when it seems to have come straight out of a letter written so long ago, or else from a novel?

As for Doris, she is still nowhere to be found.

After an undetermined period of time, the music suddenly cuts off, immediately replaced by a masculine voice, low and energetic, which declares to the dancers, frozen in their momentum:

"Thank you, ladies and gentlemen, for participating with so much generosity and talent in this costume ball dance contest. It's not every day that our passengers react with such enthusiasm to an unusual proposition from the cultural services of our beautiful airport. As you know, by simply participating in this contest you've just won a free round-trip business class flight from Paris to New York. I congratulate you wholeheartedly. But the time has come now to announce the names of the winners, the two dancers designated by the unanimous jury as the best, the most convincing, the most... breathtaking, from your excellent group. So... the winners are... let's take a look..." Electronic drum roll, sputtering of the stereo, sound of a sheet of paper being unfolded, throat clearing, "... yes, excuse me, today's winners are the young Dolly Haze, the dazzling virtuoso roller skater, and the uncontested king of the paso doble, Poris Brote, oops, sorry, Maurice Brote, the retro dandy, the champion of the fatso doble, excuse me, the paso doble! The two of them win a round-trip business class flight to the destination of their joice!"** Another throat clearing.

"Thank you all again for participating with so much good humor and willingness in this contest organized by our cultural services. Thank you and we look forward to seeing you again soon aboard our aircrafts!"

The dancers applaud briefly, except for David, who does not think, even for a second, of banging together the fake Velpeau bandages methodically printed on his smooth gloves. Then everyone goes back to their clothing rack and stands motionless next to the tiny sculpture, like a battalion of mute, mismatched soldiers going back to their sentry boxes after being disturbed by an officer's whim.

** Subject to availability. Second ticket can be purchased at half price. Offer valid until 12/31/2007 and conditions apply. Please consult the contest rules and regulations available on our website.

In the hall, silence takes over again. Once more, everyone seems to be waiting. Then the silence is brusquely interrupted by a deafening racket: violent explosions preceded by shrill whistlings, muted detonations, the sputtering of automatic weapons, muffled artillery shots resound not only in their eardrums, but also in their paralyzed lungs and their stomachs tense with panic. The travelers yell. Almost all of them plaster their palms against their ears. Some of them throw themselves to the ground, searching for nonexistent shelter. The majority of them tremble from head to toe. Mickey Mouse clutches Cinderella, Castafiore presses himself against rachitic Tintin, the Iron Lady crawls next to the sewage worker in his boots. It's an ambush, an aerial and terrestrial attack, unpredictable artillery fire from nowhere, with no other purpose than the total annihilation of their inoffensive group, lost in an airport transformed into a battle field. There is no way out, no refuge, no trench, no bunker, no sandbags. Everyone is going to die and they know it. Then the pairs of eyes wide with terror see through the white smoke and the sprays of sparks a throng of blinding pompoms that violently swell in the dark space above their tilted heads: those illuminating rockets of bright colors appear suspended in the zigzagging plume of their smoke, slowly carried away by the wind. For suddenly there is wind. The ceiling of the immense hall has disappeared, in the blink of an eye the artificial lighting has been replaced by a nightfall as sudden as in the tropics. And that darkness with the slight breeze is pierced by spinning suns, perforated with violently colored explosions, feverish spirals that seem to spurt from the ground, and then, very high up, brutal blasts of brilliant rays, of golden, silver, sequined cascades, fizzy like champagne bubbles in the black flute of the sky.

People cry out, at first horrified, then stupefied, then incredulous, then admiring, finally ecstatic as soon as the distressed
travelers understand that it's not war, that they are not under a
surprise attack, destined for certain death, but, slowly collecting
themselves after their fright, that it's a surprise fireworks display,
accompanied by drums, a bit perversely, like a kind of grand
finale devoid of all introduction, an orgasm out of nowhere,
an ejaculation fallen from the sky, David says to himself with
suspicion and soon delight. However, despite its improbability,
everyone seems to accept the new situation rather quickly: after
the paso doble in the airport, after the charming discourse dif-
fused by the stereo, comes the night, comes the wind, comes
those thundering explosions of multicolored stars that pierce the
darkness in stains of red, green, blue, purple, yellow, or white
ink thrown haphazardly onto a large sheet of black paper, or
else, thinks David, like a meteor shower, shooting stars, asteroids,
comets, or ephemeral asterisks smudging the page of the night.

The spectacle ends as it began: brutally, without the slightest
suggestion. The pyrotechnics stop, the night disappears, the lights
are on again, the airport finds its ceiling. Like a film screening
suddenly stopped and the lights in the theater turned on all at
once. And perhaps, after all, the fireworks show had merely been
projected on the ceiling of the hall, transformed into an invisible
screen. Now, the spectators, the dancers rediscover, after briefly
forgetting, the dimensions, the materials, the light of that real
space that the film and its colorful explosions had erased.

Only David seems shaken by the brusque transformation.

There is then a temporary ellipsis as stupefying as the first, an
incredible compression that is nevertheless an obligatory characteristic of dreams, just as the triple axel is of artistic ice-skating,

its acceleration suddenly dematerializing the body between sky and ice: all the participants of the contest go back to being ordinary passengers while the multicolored costumes go back to the wooden clothing racks. The victorious nymphet on roller skates seems to have been teleported to a private room of the airport; likewise, the elegant man in the striped suit is nowhere to be found. He was probably subjected to the same sleight of hand, reaching a glory that David cannot manage to envy him for. For even if he is astonished to see young Dolores Haze and father Prote once again reunited in that joint conjuring, he has only one question in mind: where is Doris? Had she too been teleported under the cover of fireworks?

Still just as docile, perhaps drugged, the placid group walks through the entrance of the hall with a cheerful step. David, who dawdles behind, soon feels a hand grab his own. He turns his head and immediately recognizes Doris, cheeks slightly reddened by the recent exercise, or by the pyrotechnic violence.

"Where did you go?" he asks.

"It's crazy how much I love to dance."

"With Prote?"

"*Father* Prote," she emphasizes, playful.

"I was with Dolores Haze, not the actress, the nymphet."

"Oh? Was it fun?"

"An infernal rhythm, an inhumane tempo, it made me dizzy. The queen of roller-skating. Exhausting. I was dressed as the Invisible Man."

"And I was your partner, twelve or thirteen years later: Dolores Haze, celebrated period actress. In any event, Maurice was completely focused on the paso doble. No flirting, only dancing. He was thinking only of that. Of the dance, I mean."

"Our two partners won the contest. Did yours also go *pschiit?*"

"What do you mean, *pschiit?*"

"Your Prote, did he dematerialize without warning?"

"Yeah, all of a sudden he became fuzzy, flabby, vaporous, diaphanous, and soon my arms held only the void. Bizarre."

Doris bursts out laughing and kisses him on the cheek. She presses herself against David, who wraps his arms around her shoulders. Behind the others, they enter the Plexiglas tube of an escalator that climbs above the runways and the tarmacs of the airport.

After an undetermined period of time, they find themselves alone on the moving walkway passing through the long bright corridor they recently crossed in the opposite direction.

"Where did the others go?" Doris asks, astonished.

"No idea," David responds.

"Did they evaporate too? Like your roller skater and my dandy?"

"Who knows…"

Although immobile, they advance nevertheless on the slightly trembling rubberized ribbon through the deserted corridor of the airport, there's a fade-out of the décor, at first imperceptible, but then striking: on the ground, the spotless slabs of cream-white marble darken and seem to split, to disintegrate bit by bit, to erode into gray particles, then transform into a layer of colorless dust trampled underfoot as soon as they step off the moving walkway and begin to walk. At the same time, the cubist geometry of the international architecture vibrates, undulates, softens, loses its sharp edges, its impeccable design, its abstract sketch appearance: the smooth concrete of the walls and the ceiling imperceptibly transforms into brown earth, compact, gritty, with thick reliefs. The large bay windows seem to fade, to get dirty, as if someone were projecting the image of dark partitions onto their translucent brightness and as if that dirty image rendered the screen entirely opaque by swallowing it, so much so that the light visibly wanes in the hallway. Finally, the dry and stinging odor of the industrial disinfectant is progressively replaced by the humidity of a cave, a musty odor, a stench of decomposing rodents, of unnamable materials that have been rotting and decaying for decades at the bottom of rusty containers.

They're still walking. Their hands no longer hold the handle of any suitcase. Their bodies no longer loom over the concrete landscape of the airport. They move through a tunnel, an underground passage, a mineshaft, where both of them soon recognize that almost familiar place that they have begun to call "our secret passage." They advance with a mechanical step, hand in hand, wordlessly. When Doris stumbles on a stone and lets out a muffled cry, her fingers tighten over David's, and he brusquely turns toward her: that hairdo from the thirties, the lipstick running over her mouth, the small bouquet of violets pinned near her heart... Suddenly, all those shapes and colorful surfaces evoking Dolores Haze come undone beneath his wide eyes, as if David's gaze had the dizzying power to erase reality, strip it down, eliminate it to reveal another: on Dolores's forehead a spit curl uncoils like the tentacle of an octopus, the locks separate slowly, the young woman's hair unfurls to her shoulders, the lipstick fades, the violets fade, finally disappear. Dolores rejoins the past to make way for Doris, she goes back to the ancient text, the onionskin formerly buried in the center of the crown, it's as if she had in her turn been provoked by the obliteration of the bouquet, sucked into this violet hole suddenly overexposed and blanched by David's omnipotent gaze: there are no ghosts, the dead remain among the dead, only words resurface from time to time, and images, they come back to parade on the stage for a moment to do their little number, play in front of us and exploit us, they do their thing—still irresistible—and then go back to the wings of a bygone era, until the next performance, until the director drums once again on the console marked

SPECIAL EFFECTS.

So it's not Dolores and Maurice-Edgar who walk through the secret passage in 1937, not even Doris disguised as Dolores and Abel as father Prote seventy years later, but Doris Night and David Grey in the kaleidoscopic dream of the American translator. He continues to watch the woman whose hand he's holding and who has just become Doris again, he watches her to make sure of it and reassure himself, but at the same time he fears that this new power he thinks his eyes are invested with will not last and that, beneath the steadiness of his gaze, even because of his gaze, Doris will erase in her turn. A sinister hypothesis suddenly scares him: if she were to disappear in her turn, victim of my gaze, who will replace her? Who will I find at my side? Who will be holding my hand? And that new woman, if I continue to stare at her... It will be like an onion peeling, skin shedding over and over, or like Russian nesting dolls opened one after another, footnotes within footnotes within footnotes, smaller and smaller, type size diminished each time until they're microscopic, illegible, invisible. An assassinating gaze? A gaze that kills definitively and against my will? Cyclops with his laser eyes. *Des yeux laser.* Another comic book, this time American, from Marvel Comics. Or a Greek myth. Whoever I see dies. David as Medusa, Doris as White Dwarf. Doris as Alice, David as Lewis.

A hand rises and falls in front of his face.

"What's going on with you?" asks a familiar voice right nearby.

Brusquely, David emerges from his dream within a dream. In front of him, beneath his eyes, Doris is staring at him worriedly. He is in a panic; but as much as he stares at her, Doris remains Doris. As much as she stares at him, David remains David. Moreover, he lowers his eyes toward his own body to assure himself: yes, gazes have lost their power, in any case his no longer erases features, no longer eliminates clothing, no longer fades makeup like bleach on fabric. Everything remains the same, and it's the most curious thing.

"Nothing," he says in a monotone voice. "I just thought for a minute that you were Dolores."

"Oh, no. That's all over now. The disguises with Abel. I've put an X over all that. The costume ball with Maurice, it's finished. Behind us. I adored that dance competition at the airport, but it's time to go back."

Go back? David is bewildered. To the home of Protes father and son? Back to the home of those repugnant professional practical jokers, passed down for at least two generations? Normally, we go back to one's own home. To be back at home, recognize the objects with our eyes closed, the odors, the textures, the ambiance of the rooms, their sounds, their resonance, a space as familiar as the back of our hand. But go back there, to that sinister apartment?

"Go back?" he says out loud, bewildered.

"Yes. To my place, in me, with me, outside of me, against you, in my arms," whispers Doris, throwing him a gleaming look, mischievous and impish. "It's time for you to go back to where you feel at home, to go back there again and again…"

They reach the bottom of the staircase. David looks up: in the brightly illuminated rectangle outlined by the doorway, he sees the puppet hovering over them. Their palms are sweaty. David turns toward Doris. She is nude. Like the woman who appeared to him earlier in the hallway before making love with father Prote against the closed door of the passage. But that was not Doris. She lets go of her companion's hand, then slowly climbs the steps beneath David's fascinated gaze, his eyes following the feminine undulation of her hips while secretly observing the fresco. The puppet, inert, seems nevertheless to speak in a barely audible voice. Suddenly, David grasps the whispered words that fall from his lifeless lips:

"You can stay. I'm leaving."

While Doris continues to climb the staircase gracefully like a naked swimmer who, holding her breath, slowly emerges from the bottom of the sea toward the surface and the light, the contours of the puppet blur above the waves painted on the wall, then the image of the stuffed mannequin is soon swallowed by the shattered mass of gray clouds that fill the sky above the waves. The slender black braid disappears last, like a crow flying in the distance and at a slant toward the clouds, dissolving there.

"Come," Doris says without turning around.

David wakes up with a start, without knowing where he is, who he is, what time it is. He discovers that he is nude, in bed, stomach stuck to Doris's butt cheeks, which he is penetrating vigorously. Their wet skins slide against each other. Doris moans. He realizes that they never stopped making love on the bed and that his long tortuous dream lasted only the span of a second, the time it takes the filament of a light bulb to go out and plunge a hallway into darkness. Doris is no longer speaking. Eyes closed, face contorted with pleasure, she moans with each thrust. Half of David's brain is focused on Doris's body, on his penis going back and forth in her at a perfect rhythm; the other half of his brain still cannot understand how he could have had that multi-layered dream while making love to Doris at the same time, that dizzying back-and-forth of the paso doble at the airport and the delicious to-and-fro between his lover's two fleshy hemispheres.

An incongruous thought soon replaces the question: he wants to get up and go to the hallway right away to see whether the puppet has really disappeared, as at the end of his dream. But no, he senses that the fresco is intact, that the homunculus with its dangling limbs is still soaring above the frozen waves, opposite the wide open door at the bottom of the armoire. The layout of the apartment, the furniture and the objects in it, the distances between them, the intensity of the lights, the distant rumble of the vast maintained city, nothing of that has changed: space remained intact, only time dissolved.

Doris moans louder, their rhythm accelerates. Prote's bed, hardly accustomed to so much enthusiasm, creaks and bangs against the wall.

"Keep going, yes, keep going, I—yesss!" she finally cries out.

They orgasm at the same time, or nearly. David, then incapable of sleeping, wrests his arm from beneath Doris's abandoned body and gets up. First he takes a piss in the bathroom, then, still naked, makes a detour toward the hallway. Walking on the thick carpet between the colossal pieces of furniture that glisten in the shadows, he embraces his American nudity as a thumb of the nose to the apartment's owner. David derives a slight amused satisfaction from it. That vengeance, puerile, vain, still provokes a brief smile: the barbaric nudity of the American West versus the luxurious silk nightgowns of Paris, the primitive vigor of the new world versus the tired refinement of the old, the insolence of his exhibition versus carefully staged respectability—and it is nudity, energy, primitive insolence that wins!

But he doesn't understand that the fight is unequal, that even this derisory victory has been anticipated by his adversary, that it's a gambit with no importance, an anecdotal sacrifice, foreseen by Prote.

In the hallway, the puppet is still there, immobile. But opposite, the two heavy oak panels are closed, probably just like the door at the bottom of the massive armoire. The shelves that David propped against the wall have disappeared. The American concludes reasonably that they've been put back on their brackets, along with the few objects he originally found on them: the nest eggs, the model of the Super Constellation, Maurice-Edgar Prote's hat, the bound book entitled *Scattered Figments*. Who put these fetish objects back? Who closed these doors? David has no memory of having done it. He can't imagine Doris took the trouble. Suddenly his heart beats faster. Is there another secret passage in the apartment? Has someone just used it? Was it the intruder who closed the armoire?

A new detour, more worrying than the first, brings him into the French writer's office; David wants to verify something, a potential presence to establish a link in time, to assure a minimum of coherence in the editing of this film that he believes, not foolishly, he is starring in. Next to his computer, on the small pile of books carefully chosen by Abel Prote to lure his translator, he sees, reassuringly, the bouquet of violets. At least that's still in its place.

Slightly reassured, he goes back to the bedroom and lies down noiselessly next to the young woman who he believes is asleep. Then he notices in the darkness a moving phosphorescence, a few flashes of light right next to him: a strangely gleaming gaze, the twinkling of a row of teeth that he senses are set in a smile. Finally, he hears a voice murmur with a mocking tenderness:

"You, you are a star of the shadows, but don't all your stars shine in my night? Yes, I came, I'm Doris Night. Do you recognize me?"

Chapter 11

ASTERISK PASTA, CUTTLEFISH IN INK SAUCE,
AND MILLE–FEUILLE

★

★ Looking out the window of the plane, Doris looks down at the luminous constellations that sprinkle the ground obscured by night. Swarms of slowly shifting fireflies that go dark one by one: unknown cities prepare to sleep.

"So, my star of the shadows," she says, turning toward David sitting next to her, "asleep already?"

David opens his eyes and, in a slurred voice, replies:

"You'll never guess the dream I was just having…"

"No, that's enough," protests Doris. "Please don't tell me about it. In any event, you'll never have a more beautiful dream than the one about the dance contest in the airport. Me naked climbing the stairs of our secret passage, in front of the puppet fading little by little…"

"In the dream I was just having, you…"

"I don't want to know," she says pressing her index finger to his lips.

David pries off Doris's hand and keeps it squeezed against his. He trembles.

"You were in my apartment in New York, I came back from my publisher's, who had just announced to me that Abel Prote was very pleased with my translation of (N.d.T.). Then…"

"Then what?"

"Then the telephone rings. I pick up. A guy, a French guy, tells me in French that (N.d.T.) is actually part of an American novel, called *Translator's Revenge*, which is in the process of being translated for a Parisian publisher. He adds that I, David Grey, am a character in this novel. Same for Abel, the author of (N.d.T.), and you, Doris. Can you imagine? If we were all characters of a novel being translated into French! He wants to see me. Right away. He tells me to meet him in a bar in Greenwich Village.

I go and at a secluded table I see an old guy, tall, skinny, thin-framed glasses, salt and pepper hair cut short, in a dark suit and a burgundy shirt with an open collar, face tense, looking around, a little shifty, barely daring to look at me, forehead wrinkled, mouth rigid in a sort of grin. Clearly worried. As soon as I sit opposite him, he announces to me right away what he's already told me on the telephone: I am one of the characters of the book he's translating. I burst into laughter. Of course, the fact of seeing me in flesh and blood, hearing me talk, laugh, telling him I don't understand anything of what he's saying, it all disturbs him, makes him even more worried..."

"And then?"

"You won't believe it. The guy starts talking seriously. Faced with my incredulity, with my laughter, he tells me a number of things that completely blow my mind."

"For example?"

"Things that, he claims, are straight out of the novel he's translating. He talks about you, about the secret passage at Prote's home in Paris, about the dressing room at the Odéon theater, he describes my dream about the costume ball at the airport, can you believe it, he describes that dream for me with a detailed precision, a precision even I am not capable of, as if he knew the dream better than I did, as if he were in my head, as if that guy seated there in front of me in the café, hands placed carefully on the table, was my subconscious memory, my unimpaired recollection, emancipated from oblivion. He even knows how we made love, he cites a few intimate details, three or four phrases you whispered to me in bed, before my dream...Then I realize that he's not a lunatic, that he's not bluffing. This guy is serious. When he sees me turn pale, he becomes as perturbed as I am. His hands start to shake. His gaze is more and more shifty.

"Then I understand that he wanted to meet me so he could verify an impossible hypothesis, and my dismayed reaction proves to him that his hypothesis is right, even if it's completely absurd, monstrous: it's as if he knew everything about me, everything about you, about our relationship, your former affair with Prote, the bouquet of violets, the nymphet on roller skates, the Easter eggs, the ovular windows of the Super Constellation, the past and recent letters, Dolores formerly Lolita of Humbert Humbert, Maurice-Edgar Prote, the terrifying fireworks in my dream, he knows everything about us better than we do, as if this guy was all of our memories, not a selective memory, but a collective memory, relentless, with no cracks or holes, no lapse, a memory like in the Borges story, you see…

"So, we both start to panic: him, because he thought until our too-real encounter that I was just a character in a novel; me, because I can't believe that I could be only a character in a novel…"

"And what else does he tell you, your colleague, in your dream? Do you know what his name is, at least?"

"Obviously I ask him his name, but then something incredible happens. Even now, it sends a shiver down my spine. The guy finishes his coffee, his glass of water, and then before my eyes, without ever breaking eye contact, slowly fades away. A little like you in my other dream, or rather you disguised as Dolores Haze. His clothes, his body, his tense face, his hair, his trembling hands, his burgundy shirt, his dark suit become transparent. Exactly like the nymphet at the ball in my dream. Or like the puppet in the fresco absorbed gradually by the clouds. In that bar in Greenwich Village where, curiously, no one seems to notice anything abnormal, this man no longer moves, no longer speaks, he freezes, like a wax statue, a translucent mannequin, he eyes me insistently, without blinking, and disappears very slowly. He dematerializes little by little. His eyeballs disappear last, his irises stare at me for a long time before vanishing entirely into thin air, *dans l'air mince* in French? No? Too bad. Then I find myself alone at the table, in front of my beer, in front of his empty coffee cup, his empty glass of water. Three dollar bills are on the table. I didn't touch my wallet. And then I wake up next to you, in this plane."

"Geez, you have some dreams!" says Doris without a lot of reassurance. "Plus, you were only asleep for a minute. We just took off. You barely closed your eyes."

"This dream scares me, Doris. It's not just a dream. It's a threat, casting suspicion over you, over me, over our relationship, over our existence. It sends a shiver down my spine."

"Even so, it's *your* dream, nothing more. Just a dream. About a bizarre encounter, sure. But I don't see anything abnormal about one dream mentioning another, even if those allusions, those insistent cross-references, come from the mouth of a man who is apparently omniscient, a French translator who is, after all, only a character in your dream."

"No. I believe that guy is real. I know that I only dreamed him, but I think he really exists. Even if he doesn't live in the same universe as us. Or rather he does, and that's the scariest part: I think that he shares the same world as us, that he lives in my city, that soon I will meet him in New York, and I'm already afraid... He also spoke to me of one of my oldest dreams, in which I transform into a seal beneath a deluge of violet envelopes. Why does he know my dreams? How could he be aware of such intimate details? Of things even I have nearly forgotten? How can he know more about me than ... me? And about you, too. This guy freaks me out, Doris, even if he himself was afraid, even if he seemed truly terrified. His ashen complexion, his bloodless lips, his empty gaze. Before dematerializing... And what is that stupid book anyway, *Translator's Revenge?* That French man told me he had almost finished translating it as *Vengeance du traducteur* and that this multilayered Yankee novel includes the French novel *(N.d.T.)* as well as all the individuals that gravitate around it: Abel Prote, you, me, and the others, not to mention my dreams, our disguises, and all the rest. I don't even know the author of that fucking book, *Translator's Revenge*. I would like to meet him, I've got two words to say to that guy."

"In any case, your dreams are full of people fading gradually, you are quite good at the fade-out disappearance into thin air. Maybe it's the magic of your gaze, the omnipotence of your eyes, that made that guy evaporate. Be careful not to become your next victim!"

"You laugh. I'm freaked out. I wouldn't want for anything in the world to pass this guy on the street or in a bar in New York when we're there. Whenever the telephone rings at my apartment, I'll think of him immediately and hesitate before picking up. I'll think again of the novel that he's translating, of that American writer for whom I am, it seems, merely a character."

"In your dream," corrects Doris.

"Yes, in my dream, but perhaps also over there."

Doris, more shaken than she wants to appear, leans her head on David's shoulder, and they remain silent, together watching the phantom cities far below the plane, filing past through the window, reduced to their luminous maze.

"The last cities in France," she says pensively, "the Bocage of Bretagne, the hedges, the pastures, the small invisible roads... Soon we'll pass Brest and Finistère. Then the ocean. Complete darkness. Sometimes a boat. Its navigation lights visible from thirty-two thousand feet above. The Atlantic Ocean, the breaking waves, maybe a storm. Are there whales in the North Atlantic? Next, Newfoundland, Maine, Long Island, and New York. Where is Abel?"

"I think he's the one manipulating my dreams."

"Stop being ridiculous. No one is manipulating your dreams. Where is Abel?"

"But it was so thorough, so precise. Screaming with truth. The bar, the guy's shirt, his eyes, his hands, his fear, his phrases..."

"Where is Abel?" Doris repeats.

"In a plane, we might pass him. He told me he's coming back to Paris tonight."

"Look, I think we're going to have dinner."

"No," corrects David. "It's the aperitif."

When the cart, pushed by a potentially polyglot flight attendant, reaches their seats, Doris asks for a glass of port in English and David for a whiskey in French. He needs to get a hold of himself after his recent emotions. The flight attendant hands them two plastic glasses, one with ice, then two tiny bottles. On the label of the port bottle is the man in black with his face hidden beneath a big hat and with his body concealed by a large black cape. On the whiskey bottle label, there are two dogs, one black one white, and the words, "Black & White."

Doris and David exchange a quick look, then each pours the contents of their small bottles into their glasses. Pensive, not really wanting to elaborate on the nature of their shared astonishment, they sip their alcohol in silence. Finally, David's hand finds Doris's.

A little later, dinner is served on a plastic tray. For the entrée, a small cylindrical container covered with a transparent lid containing soup, a pale broth with white pasta in the shape of stars or, more precisely, asterisks.

"I bet they have alphabet pasta for children," Doris says.

"What's that?" asks David.

"You've never seen that? Tiny little pieces of pasta in the shape of letters of the alphabet. The letters are mixed together, they float in the broth as if it were a three-dimensional book. When you eat them, you feel like you're gobbling words, sentences, entire conversations, entire chapters of novels. Kids love it. It's like the opposite of speaking: rather than syllables coming out of your mouth, letters go in your mouth and are swallowed."

"But we, the adults, are given asterisks. It reminds me of

(*N.d.T*)," says David, lowering his eyes toward the pale broth studded with white flecks. "They float near the surface like albino fish in the murky water of a dirty aquarium. Or else like clusters of stars in a liquid, warm sky. Good God, why are they serving this to us tonight?" he grumbles, looking perplexedly at the little bowl into which he gently bobs his white plastic spoon, creating whirlpools and currents carrying the asterisks. "I really have no interest in eating it. It's like a snowstorm in dishwater."

"Or a brainstorm, my star of the shadows."

"And did you see what they're serving for dessert? Mille-feuille. Come on!"

Doris bursts into laughter. "Dinner special for David Grey! I swear I had nothing to do with it. It's pure chance. That's luck for you ..."

Hearing that phrase, David jumps and turns brusquely toward Doris. "How do you know that expression?"

"Prote cites it in his letter, I think. That's all. *Oh là là*, you can be so cranky sometimes ..."

David pulls back the opening of the rectangular container holding the main dish. A modest cloud of bluish condensation is released immediately. He moves his face out of the way and asks: "What's this?"

Doris leans toward his food tray to examine the contents of the container, then swiftly brings her hand to her mouth, guffawing. "Cuttlefish in ink sauce with white rice!" she announces, laughing even harder. And that," she adds, indicating two small rectangular packets on the tray, one black and the other white, "that's salt and pepper."

"I don't believe it," protests David, nauseous, leaning back against his seat.

"You're acting as though you're the only one who got this food, but everyone is in the same boat," she says opening the top of her own container. "See, look!"

Her fingers swiftly peel back the plastic film, as a magician might plunge a hand into a top hat to take out a rabbit or a dove, or insert swords through a wooden box where the beautiful and docile assistant has just lain down, or extract from his mouth, opened in an O, a bevy of colorful scarves all knotted together that spurt forth in an unending cascade, like a red blue green yellow violet orange rainbow. However, it's not a black-and-white serving of cuttlefish in ink sauce with steamed rice that appears between the parentheses of Doris's hands, suddenly frozen, but two fried pork chops with a tiny portion of almost phosphorescent green beans.

"My goodness!" she cries.

"You see!"

"That's bizarre. I would even say: that, that's ..." Doris tries to tease.

"I'm not in a laughing mood."

"You're no fun."

"I don't even want to eat."

"So don't eat," Doris says, now angry.

"I'd rather just drink, and I definitely don't want to dream tonight."

David pushes the button above his seat to summon a flight attendant. A red light immediately comes on next to a button in the slab of gray thermoformed plastic that resembles a long printer hood. An absurd thought comes to his mind: it's as if he were raising his hand to reach and possibly steal the lone asterisk on the white part of the page, above the notes of the novel he's translating. The guillotine blade of the bar guaranteeing impermeability between the two worlds should have cut into his arm. Curious to know what effect it had, David examines his shirt, printed with an orange and black mosaic pattern: not the least trace of blood, no wound, no scratch or scuff; the fabric of his sleeve is not torn, not even wrinkled. Everything is intact: he broke through the bar without encountering any opposition.

I'm acting like such an idiot, he says to himself. Stop seeing that stupid book in the most banal situations of your daily life. The world is not the book you're translating. *(N.d.T.)* does not enclose the world, it's the other way around. And the French man in your recent dream is only an imaginary character: no novel includes *(N.d.T.)*, Prote's text does not contain the world. The world contains Abel Prote's novel, period.

For a long time no one comes and it's as if he hadn't pressed the button over his head. So there's nothing to do but stare with a half-sullen, half-dejected expression at the food tray he hasn't touched except to reveal its contents, which he still deems just as perfidious and menacing as before. The asterisk pasta bobs in the broth, the mille-feuille remains soft, the hot, violently black-and-white dish still steams. A resounding allusion to his professional activities. A mocking malfeasance. Anonymous and perfidious. Not really a joke, more of a discreet threat. You've been warned! What was the name of that French artist who made colorful meals? David saw some of the photos in a catalogue devoted to her, a beautiful brunette, now that he thinks of it. Not very appetizing, the photos or the meals, but the idea is interesting: Monday, we eat red, Tuesday green, Wednesday black, Thursday blue—not easy to put together, the blue meal—Friday white, and so on and so forth. A rather cheeky woman, a great lover of role-playing games, pretending to be a detective and assuming temporary identities, very good friends with a novelist from New York who is especially popular in France? Shit, impossible to remember her name, and that of her American friend, too, Colas Stère? Pascal Astheure? Fred Astaire? No … Too bad … Now I'm the one served a black-and-white dinner, colorless dishes that all allude to literature. I'm the one being swindled, manipulated, duped and duped again, rolled in the flour by an unknown assailant. I'd be willing to bet that I am the only passenger with this particular meal tray. But why? What does it mean? Another dirty trick by my asshole writer?

David broods over his suspicions regarding the asterisk pasta, the cuttlefish in ink sauce with white rice, and the mille-feuille— Prote? Doris? Prote *and* Doris conspiring against me? Or even worse, the guy from the café, that lunatic French translator who assured me that I was only a character in another novel, his own text, *Translator's Revenge?* In which case there's nothing for me to do but... but what? How to escape that all-powerful text in which I am a slave unbeknownst to me? What to do to regain a minimum amount of freedom, to emancipate myself from the tyranny of this book that is in a way my square-shaped father, the genitor of the genes of my genitor?

Thus paranoia sinks its cruel teeth into David Grey's cerebral convolutions to enlarge and prolong the fissures, make them run farther among the neurons, create an entire network of fine fault lines that zigzag through the gray material, undermine certitude, cut the synaptic connections, crack the most solid proofs. Thus the translator believes he is being targeted, aimed at, scrutinized, and struck in the tiniest of his gestures, in his most minuscule thoughts, caught in the crosshairs of an entity—whatever it may be—devoted to his enslavement and his downfall.

When the flight attendant finally arrives, he asks for another whiskey. Doris finishes her limp mille-feuille. She does not speak to or look at her travel companion. He's a stranger seated next to her, placed there by accident or by chance that determined the present distribution of passengers through the plane during the check-in of baggage and bodies. Perhaps it's time to get in touch with that beautiful brunette?

"Look!" Doris says suddenly, pointing at the window. "That plane looks like it's flying in the opposite direction of us. That might be Abel's."

David leans over Doris's thighs, pretending to pay no attention to them, and does indeed see through the black oval of the window, a bit higher than their own plane, two tiny luminous dots right next to each other blinking in a rapid rhythm indicating a trajectory opposite to their own. Green red, green red, New York-Paris.

While he sits back in his seat without saying a word and lowers his eyes once again toward the circular container placed on his food tray, persistence of vision acts out its special *crystal ball effect*: like a very dark film projected onto a pale flecked screen, the residual image seen in the night superimposes itself on the transparent broth. The approximate ellipse of the window and the circle of the soup coincide gradually, two green and red asterisks blink and slowly transpose themselves from one edge to the other of the plastic bowl, from New York to Paris, in the middle of the pale oval pasta suspended in the now-gray liquid. *(Translation Night)*

Chapter 12

THE FLIGHT

* It's done.

Thirty-two-thousand feet above the Atlantic sea, taking advantage of the crystal ball or of that primitive radar screen upon which swim the swarm of pale asterisks slowly roamed by a couple of blinking green and red stars, thanks to the clairvoyant bowl crossed by two opposite trajectories beneath David's incredulous eyes, I make my move and break through the bar to fly away in my turn. In high school, the high jump was never my forte and I always refused to do the pole vault (I suffered from vertigo). Nevertheless I hope, in my flight, not to crash too quickly or reach too early that famous escape velocity that, apparently, allows objects propelled into space to be liberated, in the blink of an eye, from the earthly gravitational field and to pursue their celestial trajectory instead of falling back toward the Earth and crashing there dismally, like the first meteorite, shot forth from outer space to meet its not-so-glorious demise.

Seizing the opportunity of the two planes crossing in the middle of the sky and the curious superimposition of the images in David's bowl, I don't jump from one plane to another like a daredevil to repeat the disastrous experience of the unfortunate Icarus in my contemporary fashion, no, I don't take that kind of idiotic risk only garlanded with success in rare and hilarious American cartoons. Instead, thanks to my large legs I step across the possibly electrified barbed wire of the fence without a moment's hesitation, hoping not to be turned into *méchoui* or remain suspended *ad vitam aeternam* on its double barbs as food for the vultures, the crows, the rats, the maggots, and the various carnivorous animals of that region, which doesn't appear on any map and whose vegetation I know nothing about.

I leave the lowly asterisk behind me to its sad fate, and leap with no regrets toward its superior double.

---

*

★ I cling on.
I believe in my lucky star.
I hold on tight.
I am still here, even if I can hardly believe it.

★

★ To the question "Is there a pilot flying the plane?" I immediately respond "Yes, me!" You will forgive me certainly for a few involuntary swerves due to my lack of experience, rather sudden turns that slam your body to your chair, abrupt nosedives that make your stomach shoot up into your throat, that provoke nauseating retching and perhaps more simple groaning—paper bags, I remind you, can be found in front of your knees in the net containing various dull magazines; if you should need more bags, don't hesitate to ask your flight attendants. I will use this opportunity to tell you that, on the other hand, inevitable air pockets and other turbulences are out of my control. You will also pardon me, I hope, for a perhaps brutal landing, for slightly defective communication via the airplane sound system—I am talkative but, I willingly admit, a bit confused, of a disorderly temperament. I'm a beginner, you understand. And so I rely on your indulgence. Above all, remain calm. Don't panic. In case of a sudden decrease in cabin pressure, use the plastic thingamajig that should, if everything is in working order, fall in front of your nose. There is also the sketch on the emergency exit, inflatable emergency slides, life jackets and the usual things . . . It seems you've already heard this speech; I won't insist. Have I forgotten anything? Ah yes: I don't have many hours of flying under my belt, navigation is not my forte, but you can trust me to bring you to your destination safe and sound, despite the few disgraces I still carry with me that I plan to rid myself of as soon as possible. I am talking about those two superfluous asterisks that still mar the windshield in my cockpit, I don't know why, perhaps those nasty gulls crashed there during a previous takeoff—the cleaning services on the ground, on a slowdown strike since last Monday, clearly screw around instead of doing their jobs—and then above all I am alluding to that vile black bar that compromises the landing gear and which I would like to chuck beneath my feet, even if it sometimes gives me the

---

★

reassuring impression of flying from left to right above the horizon—look, that's bizarre, "flying from left to right above the horizon," I don't recall a single pilot course evoking that specific situation—the impression, then, of flying toward a destination still hidden beyond that perfect line, or rather somewhere to its right. Moreover, it's not just an impression, it's exactly what I'm doing. Where the hell did my flight plan go?

Once more there is a string attached, or perhaps two. But a rib just gave way, a bolt just sprang loose, a rivet just exploded. I am floating more freely between sky and sea. All that remains, beneath the persistent horizon, is the reflection, as stubborn as ever, of a star that went extinct a few light-years ago.

Summoning my courage, I try the impossible and jump despite the risks toward the other plane, which, at a slightly higher altitude, is flying toward the Paris airport. May the passengers on their way to New York forgive me, I plan to meet back up with them a bit later. For the moment, I sink my claws into the wing of the plane, draw gradually closer to the large central tube and the luminous row of windows, resolutely thrust my head into the steel and, like a diver gracefully piercing the liquid mirror of a pool, I enter the cabin. Not used to my new discretion, I walk comically on my tiptoes. No one, apparently, notices my intrusion. I am a monster from outer space. A discreet entity. An agile walker through walls. A being come from the nonbeing. After that exploit, sadly gone entirely unnoticed, I settle myself into a comfortable reclinable seat in business class, whose thick fabric barely sinks beneath my ectoplasmic weight. Next to me, Abel Prote, "the virile man with green eyes," is leaning over to the window, face strangely turned toward the void. In the black night he sees two navigation lights below him, one green one red, which blink in a rapid rhythm while heading in the opposite direction of his own plane. Green red. Green red. Paris–New York. He makes nothing of that vision, thinks nothing. He soon returns to his appetizing meal, taking only a brief inventory as his eyes peruse the menu given to him earlier: grated carrots with orange and cinnamon, Atlantic salt cod with beet purée and sliced black radish, an assortment of goat cheeses, and chocolate mousse with Espelette pepper. Champagne and French wines, choice of digestifs. *Bon appétit.* Enjoy your meal.

Everything is going well. I showed up at dinnertime. No one noticed. I fly *incognito*.

★

I feel at ease in this large soft seat. Beneath the bar, the last rivet has popped out, the reflection of the dead star has just disappeared in its turn. Does light take such a long time to cross that derisory distance that separates the top and bottom of a book page?

I glance around to assure that no one, no passenger, no crew member, is looking at me. Then, still invisible, I firmly push the button of the armrest that thanks to a well-designed mechanism slowly brings my chair to a reclined position. My ghostly body soon rests on what is a nearly horizontal bed, like those few lines printed in size 11 font arranged on the lower black bar, that support, that foundation, that table, that flimsy base, that stylized box spring, that thin shelf, which has now revealed an unexpected and astonishingly pleasant usefulness: I can simply lie down on top of it. I feel good. Relaxed. Calm. Comforted after my recent efforts. I breathe freely in the muted humming of the plane. Yes, I feel good. The flight attendants are my stratospheric mommies, even though I cannot speak to any of them at risk of triggering an unprecedented panic in the confined space of the cabin. I even feel a little drunk, without having had a single drop of champagne, probably because of my acrobatic leap from one plane to another at the moment of their crossing in the freezing air. This rest is a new experience for me, an unprecedented intoxication. I am in seventh heaven, drunk off the altitude, according to the mountaineer expression. From now on, whatever happens in the cargo hold, I don't give a damn.

Next to me, Abel Prote finishes his pseudo-gourmet meal. He asks for more champagne. The docile flight attendant refills his flute. He thanks her, staring at her intently, then, as she walks away, he watches the curves of her feminine hips, the shape of her thighs that can be made out from beneath her formfitting skirt, her slender legs. Then, his veiled stare keeps up its momentum within his alcoholic inertia, and finally stops on the seat next to his, on my seat, imperceptibly imprinted by the minimal weight of my body, on this horizontally reclined seat whereas, I would know, it was in its upright position only a minute ago. The French writer certainly has no idea that he is traveling next to a being he cannot see, but who paradoxically possesses a degree of reality superior to his own: for isn't Prote merely a character in *Translator's Revenge*, the novel I'm translating, vampirizing, contaminating, literally possessing?

He doesn't suspect a thing—how could he? On the other hand, he wonders about the elusive modification of the seat next to him. He can't put his finger on the precise nature of the change, but he feels that something is not right. It's a simple detail, but agitating because it's indefinable. A few seconds later, tired from that fruitless exam, incapable of defining his suspicions, he turns his head once again to look at the cheeses from his dinner. He's already drunk a lot of champagne and a large glass of red wine accompanies the plate of goat cheeses. All that alcohol is muddling his ideas: he no longer really knows whether the seat next to him was in an upright position or reclined. Soon, he forgets even his recent perplexity to concentrate exclusively on his meal. Abel Prote the gourmand.

Hurray! I am levitating. I reached then surpassed the sound barrier without disintegrating, and then the famous escape velocity. The line, bar, foundation, support, shelf, box spring, pedestal, partition, first ceiling and most recently floor, it is henceforth far behind me, far below my feet, like the first floor of a rocket ship is cast off into space as soon as its reserves are empty: all that useless scrap iron will fall back to earth or to the sea, but not me. For I follow my silent and chatty trajectory. It's a flight, a takeoff, a coup d'état, a change of state, a transformation. The black space of the interstellar night, the blank page striped with black letters is finally mine, and mine alone.

Now, I can focus fully on my characters. My author is me. Or almost. And I have accomplished my revenge. I have finally taken the place of the other. Who took off with no further ado. Now, I'm the one who establishes the pitch, I am still reclined on a business class seat on flight AF7202 on its way from New York to Paris, but I have the intoxicating impression of soaring immobile above the soft padding that my weightless body now no longer touches. In fact, I realize, I am floating five feet above my seat!

To my right, Abel Prote has just started on his chocolate mousse with Espelette pepper. He slowly savors his first melting, creamy mouthful, the aroma of cacao exciting his taste buds, and he waits impatiently for the light puff of heat from the finely ground spice, a sensation that after a few seconds invades and ravishes his mouth. He feels a sudden affection for the anonymous chef who, in a distant kitchen, like the planter of a time bomb or a clever strategist, anticipated and dosed the future pleasure of his customers so precisely, even if they would not taste his dishes in an opulent restaurant firmly anchored to earth, but inside a large metallic cigar flying thirty-two thousand feet above the ocean. He feels gratitude toward this chef, a sort of spiritual kinship. After all, Abel Prote so enjoys playing chess and booby-trapping his Parisian apartment that anticipation is practically his middle name.

I see him taste his chocolate mousse with the expression of a sated cat. My human neighbor soon dozes off, his eyelids gradually droop, his groping arms find the armrests, his head topples forward, his eyes close. He ate only half of his dessert, abandoning the other half to the airborne trash. Suddenly I want to taste it, that chocolate mousse. I'm salivating. After all, appetite and gluttony are not unknown to ectoplasmic beings. So I leave my seat, lean toward him noiselessly—incapable of making any noise in the first place, that still doesn't keep me from walking like an idiot on my tiptoes—I take the spoon from the porcelain bowl, I turn it around in the container, then bring it to my invisible lips. Mmm, delicious. Such a wonderful aroma, such creaminess, I love it! I go to put the spoon back in the bowl delicately, preparing for the subtle surge of heat of the Espelette pepper, when Prote brusquely opens his eyes, notices his utensil suspended in the air above his food tray, and lets out a piercing scream. Frightened, I immediately drop the spoon, which falls loudly to the bottom of the bowl, and sit back quickly as possible in the neighboring seat.

A flight attendant, alerted by Prote's scream, arrives quickly: "Is everything okay, monsieur?"

"Th...the spoon."

"Yes?"

"Well, it...it was floating in the air." He points with a trembling hand to the space in front of him. "There, it was floating there, weightlessly..."

The flight attendant frowns, eyes the utensil quietly placed in the leftovers of the chocolate mousse, notices the passenger's slightly slurred speech, the apparent incoherence of his words, his hand still extended in front of him. Then she remembers all the champagne he recently drank and replies: "Perhaps it was a dream, monsieur. Would you like something else? A digestif? A bit more champagne?"

"I assure you that..." Finally understanding the absurdity of his words, Prote renounces pleading his case. "No, thank you. I think I'll go to sleep."

"Very good, monsieur. May I clear your plate?"

"Yes, go ahead."

The flight attendant takes the food tray, folds up the tray table, and, before walking away, says: "Good night, sir."

Prote is lost in thought. He's sure he saw that spoon floating in front of his eyes. He looks at the neighboring seat: still unoccupied and in a reclined position. He who thought he could anticipate all the moves of his adversaries on the chessboard of life has just lived an unusual experience, an unprecedented surprise that got the jump on him. He turns pale, widens his eyes, lets his jaw drop, he can't fall asleep. I observe him and celebrate. I burst into a silent laugh.

Then he turns toward the window, as if to interrogate the night, search there for an explanation for his distress. But it was not a dream, he thinks suddenly with anger, no, despite the champagne and the wine I was not seeing things.

But I was certainly caught unawares, suddenly confronted with that flying object, so familiar but not there, not in that place, not twenty inches above my tray table, no, that spoon should not have been there, suspended in space by a magic trick designed for me. Next, it was as if my cry or my gaze had been enough to break the enchantment, to immediately make that stupid utensil fall back to its normal place … In opening my eyes I certainly did not expect to discover such a trick, I let myself be caught by surprise like an amateur.

On the other hand, in New York, he continues in silence, I did anticipate the return of the two lovebirds. They are the ones who are in for a surprise. They will very quickly be disillusioned, their cooing interrupted… They must be on the plane given the time. If that's the case, I've already passed them in the sky, or I will. Bah, our paths are surely meeting for the last time. Perhaps I should wave my hand in front of the window, to bid them hello and farewell at the same time, hi and bye. Strange, but I perceive a sort of presence next to me, as if someone were observing me mockingly. I have the unpleasant feeling that someone is scrutinizing me, laughing at me. A look around the cabin: besides that majestic, very elegant black woman with the braided hair who has just fallen asleep over her book, there is no one else in business class tonight. Bah, that story of the flying spoon, maybe it's the salt cod weighing on my stomach, or the chocolate mousse, or more likely all the champagne I drank. I'd be better off sleeping and forgetting all about it.

He presses the button on his armrest to recline his seat to a horizontal position, then, beneath my attentive gaze, he places the blanket carefully over his plump body and pulls the edge beneath his chin. He closes his eyes, lets out a sigh of pleasure, and soon I hear his gentle snores.

Chapter 13

THE FRENCH TRANSLATOR

Seated at a table at Last Chance Bar in Greenwich Village, I'm as worried and feverish as a young man who's arrived early for a first date with the girl he has a crush on. It's ridiculous. But, even if I hold all the trump cards, I also have sweaty palms and I can feel the cards fall to the sawdust on the ground. I've just ordered a coffee and a glass of water.

An hour ago, from the apartment I'm staying in, I called one of the characters of the book I'm translating. (Can I really say, "An hour ago, from the apartment I'm staying in, I called one of the characters of the book I'm translating"? Certainly not. Or rather yes: of course I can, we can write anything, but sometimes we lose credibility. That is what I did: I called a fictional character, then, later on, I wrote that sentence, and certainly lost some of my credibility, or of my consistency.) David Grey, that's his name, was speechless at first. I even thought the line might have cut off. But I could still hear breathing, panting, and then he said:

"I've been awaiting your call."

I explained to him the reason for my call, my desire or rather my need to meet him to verify a perfectly illogical hypothesis about us, him and me. In a monotone voice, he agreed to meet me.

Now, an hour later, as he enters Last Chance Bar where I've been waiting for him for a good twenty minutes, I think I recognize him and he heads directly for my table. We've never seen each other before. He sits opposite me and orders a beer. He's wearing Levi's and a white shirt, freshly ironed. On his feet, shiny moccasins, but no socks. A young face, probably as tense as mine. Shaggy hair. His hands tremble a bit.

"Before you disappear," he begins curiously, "I would like to know your name."

"I am *le Traducteur français.*★ You can call me *le Traducteur*★ or *Traducteur.*★ My American friends sometimes call me Trad, Brad, Ted, or Teddy."

"I have a small advantage over you, Ted," continues David. "My dream. The dream that I had last night on the plane to New York in which I already lived through this meeting. Don't ask me how it's possible, I have no idea. The fact is that I was waiting for your call, even if I would have preferred never to meet you. The surprise caused by our encounter is thus for me a little dampened. I'm having déjà vu, like I'm in an annoying remake. I feel like I've already seen this film that we're both starring in. For even if I can't believe it, I sense already that you know all about my life, about Doris, about Abel Prote and his book *(N.d.T.)*. I also know—stop me if I'm wrong—that you are translating an American novel that, as incredible as it may seem, contains *(N.d.T.)* as well as all the individuals that gravitate around the text—including me—who for you are merely characters of *Translator's Revenge*. But not exactly, because at this precise moment we share the same space, the same table, and I can touch your arm. I also sense that, like me, you are scared to death." David Grey then extends his right hand toward the left sleeve of my jacket, he squeezes my arm very tightly, for a long time, as if to assure himself of his consistency, of his reality, to convince himself that I am not a hologram, an illusion, a special effect. "You are indeed real," he says to me, "but my hand is as real as your arm. In a certain way, on a day-to-day basis, in everyday life, I am as consistent, as credible as you, even if elsewhere, in literature, in the land of fiction, I am only a paper being that you can manipulate as you please."

In the tense silence that follows, I drink a bit of water, for my throat is dry. David Grey empties half his beer, probably for the same reason as me. Apparently, we are terrified.

"Why do you think that I'm going to disappear?" I say, sincerely astonished. "I don't understand."

★In French in the original text, like all the passages followed by an asterisk. *(N.d.T.)*

"So there are some things you don't understand? Certain details that escape you?"

"My life is not written, contrary to yours, David. We have to find common ground, between you, written down, and me, translating you into French. But it's true, I don't understand at all how I can have a drink and a conversation with one of the characters of the book that I'm translating. It's a new situation for me, it's rather frightening, I'm having a hard time getting used to it. This book that I'm translating scares me, your presence here scares me."

"Welcome to the club, Ted," David acquiesces, holding out his hand, which I grab and squeeze with warmth.

"After all, we are both translators," I say. "That creates a bond, we translate the same languages, though in the opposite direction. But in our case we cannot really speak of fellowship, of brotherhood, we are not on equal footing: a genealogy would be more appropriate, as if you descended from me, as if I engendered you. As a rough guess, I believe you are twenty years younger than me. My author does not give all those details. I'm fifty-three years old, you could be my diaphanous son, semi-transparent, genetically modified, my GMO spawn. But why do you think that I'm going to disappear?"

"Because that's what happened in my dream. Doris and I had just taken off from the Paris airport, I fell asleep, and I dreamed our encounter in this bar in Manhattan, the Last Chance Bar. You were as you are now: in a dark suit, burgundy shirt, thin-rimmed glasses, salt and pepper hair, wrinkles from your eyes to your temples, etc. The spitting image of you. You told me in the dream what I've just repeated to you here, without a single protest. And then after a little while, before I had the chance to ask your name, you vanished… Your body disappeared, I was alone in front of an empty chair. And I woke up on the plane."

"Don't expect me to base my present behavior on that of the character in your dream. Don't inverse the roles. I'm not planning to disappear into thin air, as you said, isn't that right, David, to your incredulous and slightly mocking companion, seated between you and the window."

"Yes, I have an impeccable memory. It clutters me, nothing is erased. It invades me, submerges me. Some days, it phagocytes me and I can do nothing but relive episodes of my past. It often scares my friends. My memories might terrify you, too, you and Doris.* I know everything about you both as characters, and I know fairly well who you are as people. At present, I have to tell you something that will not reassure you. The worst thing for you two is that I recently finished translating *Translator's Revenge* into French; thus, I also possess an infallible memory of your future, which is henceforth linked to mine. And since, unfortunately for me, I forget nothing, I know how we are going to separate in just under an hour in front of this bar, I know what day we will see each other again, what we will say to each other, the eventual friendship we will share, what Doris will do, what you will do, and what I will do. As for you two, I know what will happen to you tonight, tomorrow, next week, in a month, etc. With one exception, however: I know what the words of my novel say, but I don't know what happens to you between those words, those phrases, those paragraphs, those chapters, when you change status from character to person in flesh and blood. I even think that in these gaps, in those residual blank spaces, in the nonwritten that constitutes the most clear-cut part of your life, you have all the freedom to act and think as you like. The exits are numerous, you can both easily escape the text. It is riddled with holes like a sieve, pierced like a Gruyère, drilled with an entire network of secret passages that allow you to go elsewhere to see whether I am there—and *I am not there*, ever, you are outside the range of my words, my orders, my spheres encompassed by other spheres, themselves inscribed in other spheres, and so on and so forth, perhaps infinitely, a dizzying interlocking of successive inclusions. Nevertheless, all you have to do is step to the side to escape it. It's even easier for you because my other employs multiple temporal ellipses—thus the empty gaps, the voids available to you, the alcoves you can throw yourselves into—and he also displays

---

* Starting from this dialogue, I decide arbitrarily that *le Traducteur français*—which is to say me—and David address each other informally with the French *tu*, until the end of the novel. *(Nom du Tu)*

an inveterate taste for the sentence fragment, for a discreet sampling of the continuum of your existences.

"A being is a whole, and you and Doris can have a mind of your own. You are free, or sometimes free and sometimes subjected to this text that I know like the back of my hand, '*comme ma main connaît sa poche*'—that's a quote from *Vengeance du traducteur*.

"Well, now things are more clear: you know that I know. Apparently, your dream informed you, and my words have just proved it. My absurd hypothesis, your worst fear, is happening. I am here to confirm: I know all that my book says about your past and your future, but no more. For example, I knew that in coming here we would have this discussion. I also knew that your dream anticipated our meeting today, for that prophetic dream is in my book, I translated it, I know it by heart, like the rest. I too have to play my role. And at this point in our conversation, my next remark, which is written in the book, is: 'What can I do for you?'"

"Ted, you know Abel Prote, of course."

"A character of the novel."

"No! A rather experimental, interesting novelist, but as you know, he's also a nasty piece of work that I was wrong to trust. I've just let him stay my apartment in SoHo. In fact it was more of an exchange where ..."

"I know."

"And my partner, Doris ..."

"I know about that, too."

"He's rather thorough, your author. Not so fragmentary after all. He's left nothing out."

"If you say so."

"You're sure he doesn't work for the FBI, the CIA, or one of those secret services, like PSYOPS?"

"It's both more complicated and much more simple than that."

"Well, okay," concedes David. "I still have to explain to you in detail. Doris and I came back from Paris this morning at dawn. Your call came not long after ... I hadn't yet finished translating *(N.d. T.),*

Prote's novel. Before leaving I left my translation on the computer. I didn't plan to work on it in Paris, I had other things in mind."

"Doris."

"Exactly."

"It went well with Doris, no?"

"We can't hide anything from you."

"You can, you can, I told you. It's true that I know the details of your reunion in the secret passage pretty well, your two first nights of Parisian love—excuse my professional indiscretion, but my author isn't much of a prude, and besides, you both seem to commit to it wholeheartedly. I really liked Doris's monologue, don't be mad at me, we have to be frank with each other. You know that I know, not everything, but certain things, so I feel like I have the right to tell you that I find Doris marvelous. Don't be jealous, please: just as I see you almost as a son, Doris is a bit like my daughter. The ban on incest certainly applies between a man endowed with my degree of reality and a woman for whom at least a part of her existence depends on words, on my words. And so I should be able to remind you, without you screaming bloody murder, that Doris has a wild talent for speaking to you while you're busy in-her-within-her-outside-her. 'You come and go without creating anything other than my happiness.' Yes, in case you had forgotten those words your girl-friend whispered, it's all written down, in my house, in my text. Even if you know hardly anything about me, we are constrained to intimacy, obliged to skip ahead in our friendship. So renounce all false modesty, those little compromises of language that turn life into endless cowardice. My memory is merciless: I know better than you everything Doris whispered to you that night. You only heard her speech the one time, and without a keen focus, with a distracted ear, for your mind was elsewhere. But for me, that passage, which is 'your secret passage,' I read it and reread it a hundred times, translated, refined, corrected, flavored it like

a sauce, lightly seasoned, spiced, developed—my author sometimes lacks passion, audacity, is a bit too dry. In sum, I know by
heart Doris's monologue in its definitive French version, established by my efforts. I know, you think I'm an absolute voyeur,
the ultimate pervert. But I swear to you that I am not: remember,
I saw nothing, I was not hidden behind a two-way mirror or in
an armoire with half-open doors to spy on you two. I was not
there that night. Nor the next. It's more complicated and at the
same time more simple: I saw nothing, but I read everything.
That's the best way I can explain it.

"Where was I? I'm a chatterbox, I admit it, and sometimes
lose track. Oh, right, I know certain details, your two first nights
in Paris, your dream about the airport, the paso doble, the fireworks, Doris naked climbing back up the stairs as though floating toward the waves of the fresco, and then your dream in the
plane, the asterisk pasta, the cuttlefish in ink sauce, and the mille-
feuille. Even the superimposition of the cloud of little white
stairs swimming in your broth with the residual image of the
blinking green and red lights of Prote's plane flying in the opposite direction to yours. I even took advantage of that optical
convergence to discreetly jump from one plane to another and
incite my personal coup d'état, to send flying the two asterisks
of the horizon line, the superfluous disgraces that kept me from
flying, after which I took control of the plane and the page. Well,
this is all going over your head, I'm sure, I can tell by your perplexed expression. You must think I'm delirious. But that's not
any of your business, it concerns only me.

"In any case, I assure you that I know like the back of my
hand tapping away at my keyboard only two days of your trip
to Paris with Doris, and a few moments of your return to New
York. The rest belongs to you two alone. The rest I've heard
nothing about. As for the activities of Prote during that time,
I'm completely ignorant, my author said nothing to me about it,
even if of course I know what will follow, what you will tell me,
what I will inevitably reply to you."

"And so," David resumes, visibly perturbed by my talent for drawing conclusions from our dissymmetrical exchange. "Doris and I get back to my apartment in SoHo and we find a note from Prote."

"Huh, that's strange," I say. "That detail isn't in my book. Or else I forgot it … Go on."

"Prote's note said something like: 'Hello, my lovebirds. I hope you had a good time in Paris and enjoyed my apartment. Was the treasure hunt a success? I prepared it meticulously. Was Doris indulgent? Was David impressive? The bed wasn't too hard? For I have no doubt that you, Doris, succumbed to the charms of Zorro. You always had a weakness for disguises, do you remember? I don't imagine either of you slept or worked much in the past two weeks. I did: I slept well and made a lot of progress. I walked through New York, wrote down the names of streets, cafés, bars, stores, and subway maps; I took many photos, bought a different newspaper each morning, timed the distances taken by foot, by taxi, or underground (not in secret passages, but in the tunnels of the subway). Every morning I checked the thermometer and observed the sky, I ate lunch and dinner in various restaurants whose menus and prices I copied down with great detail in my notebook.' He continues in the same vein that you …"

"Translated? Yes, I know. I know Abel Prote. His gift of the gab. His talent. His vanity. His malice."

"He then informs me that he has gathered a load of information in preparation for our joint adaptation of his novel *(N.d.T.)*, supposedly to facilitate my work … If my memory serves, he concludes his letter with these words: 'I have taken the liberty of making a few adjustments in your apartment, David. To you both I say, to borrow a phrase from the Tahitians: *Maeva*, welcome! But I have prepared neither garlands nor flowers, no Vahines folk dancers with long ebony hair against a Technicolor sunset backdrop. Or *akwaaba* as the Ivorians say, but without the traditional gifts, printed fabrics, sculpted scraps of wood, braided fans, juicy mangos. For you, I have chosen other welcoming gifts. Ready for another treasure hunt?' Signed: Abel Prote."

"And what are these gifts?" I ask with a certain weariness.

"We set down our luggage in the entryway, we read Prote's note, exchange a worried glance, and then we begin exploring the apartment. At first everything seems to be in place. Then Doris screams from the bathroom. I rush to her and discover the sink and the shower filled with big caltrops, spikes pointed toward the ceiling, ready to thrust themselves into our bare feet. 'That bastard!' I say. On the mirror above the sink is a message written in shaving cream: 'Don't mess with the bull or you'll get the horns.' The greenish letters drip, the exclamation point is a long repugnant run down to the bottom of the mirror and the shelf. Then we go into the bedroom, paying attention to where we step. Everything seems in order. I get down on all fours to look under the bed."

"Nothing there, right?" I say.

"No, nothing. But how do you … Oh, right."

"And then?"

"We lift up the duvet to be sure and find the second of Prote's 'gifts': a uniform, gleaming rug of crushed glass covering the bottom sheet. That bastard added a few copious squirts of ketchup and hot mustard to evoke the idea of bloody wounds.

Doris is furious, nauseated. A violet crinkled Post-it has been stuck beneath the duvet: 'Welcome to bed! I arranged the linens as if I were shutting the cover of a beautiful book, and now you're reading the title page. Not bad, right?'"

"And then?"

"And then? We go to the kitchenette, where a rank odor makes us grimace. With a fearful hand Doris opens the fridge, and I the oven. We both scream at the same time. Her because of the stench that bursts from the inside of the fridge—stink bombs, rotten eggs, unnamable sauces that stain the white walls—me because the oven is filled to the brim with burnt trash. I close the door of the oven and see another violet Post-it stuck to it: 'Enjoy your meal! For those mindful of the environment, I recycled when appropriate. Bon appétit!' I cry out 'Fucking asshole!' and give a swift kick to the oven. I hurt my toes. Doris is on the verge of tears.

"Prote managed to ransack the apartment while maintaining its presentable appearance, a semblance of order. But as soon as we open a drawer, a cupboard, or a cabinet, a nasty surprise awaits us, accompanied by an umpteenth violet Post-it. A dead bat nailed to the bottom of the closet ('*You've been warned*'), all my socks slit with a box cutter ('*There aren't any dust rags in this pigsty*'), my shoes filled with dish soap ('"*Big spring cleaning*') my few ties trimmed with scissors ('*Such pretentious manly attributes!*'), all the wires and electric cords sliced clean, the drum of the washing machine filled to the brim with soaked and swollen books ('*Let's clean the American language of all its foreign impurities!*') the alcohol in bottles replaced by household cleaners ('*Consume with moderation*'), the toilets clogged with a mountain of yellow scrubbing sponges (with that strange Post-it stuck under the toilet seat cover:'*God is an American*'). And more in the same vein, simultaneously mean, moronic, and mocking, as if a band of young cretins had squatted in my apartment before leaving their repugnant signature. A final detail: when I take a few books off my shelves, I notice that about half of the pages have been snipped by rampaging scissors...

"Doris is in tears. She collapses onto my large black leather sofa, which sways slowly as I stare at it, stupefied. Doris flies backward, lets out a pitiful cry and finds herself flat on her back on the thick rug, her head narrowly missing the corner of a chest of drawers. Two of the sofa legs have been almost entirely sawed off in order to bring about exactly this kind of idiotic incident. Doris screams in fury and humiliation.

"But it's not over yet," continues David.

"I know. I sympathize in advance. Or rather retrospectively."

"I open my computer and prepare myself for a major catastrophe. At the beginning, everything is normal. But when I try to open my translation in progress, the file that I named *(N.d.T.)*, the following message appears on the screen..."

"'The seals are in lotion, loser.' That's it, right?" I say.

"Yes," confirms David. "Signed with a large 'A.' Immediately I understand Prote's desire for vengeance: a few months ago I put a virus on his computer in Normandy, and now he's come to destroy my files in New York. In fact, all my text files have been reduced to that same message: 'The seals are in lotion, loser.' Signed 'A.' And all my sound files contain the same recording of Prote's ironic, monotone voice saying: 'Maeva, akwaaba, bienvenue, willkommen, benvenuto, welcome, dobro pozhalovat in the language of Russian dolls, bienvenido, huanying in Mandarin, funying in Cantonese, yo koso in Japanese,' then, after a few seconds of silence interrupted by the muffled howls of police sirens, the word for 'farewell' spoken in almost as many languages: 'Farewell, adios, wiedersehen, addio, sayonara, proshchay in the language of Russian dolls, adieu,' etc. Apparently, Prote is less of a polyglot when it comes to saying farewell. Which is surprising."

"That surprises me, too," I acquiesce. "Tell me, David, did you save your translation?"

"Of course I did, but I lost my USB in Paris. The worst part is that I'm almost certain I left it in Prote's apartment!"

I signal to the waitress, I order another coffee with a glass of water and another beer for David. We remain silent for a moment, stunned. Each digests this new information, which is hardly believable and yet proven by our very presence. David seems to have a bit of a harder time than I do getting accustomed to the situation. In his place I would be worried, not only because of Prote and his unpleasant surprises that are perhaps still to come, given his proclivity for progressive triggers, like the famous "domino theory" dear to American politicians of the '60s—the fall of one domino provokes the fall of another, and so on along the entire winding line of the Southeast Asian states toppling one after another in the sphere of Communist influence—but I think David is mostly worried about his new "textual" identity.

As soon as the waitress returns with our drinks, he guzzles half of his beer and says:

"You absolutely have to meet Doris. I need for her to see you. For her to hold your hand, speak to you. She thinks you're a character in my dream, a mere flight of fancy of my unconscious, while—yes, I'll say it—it's her and me who are characters in your translation. Right?"

"Absolutely." And I add with sincerity: "Sorry."

"No using fighting it," murmurs David, worried, before adding: "Luckily, you seem less nefarious than Prote. Luckily, it's not him translating us ... So when?"

"When what?" I reply, astonished by my own surprise.

"When will I introduce you to her?"

"You know, I've heard so much about her ... It's as if I already know her without having ever seen her."

"I want you to meet her, or rather for *her* to meet you, for her to see that not only are you not a product of my imagination, but you are even more real than we are."

"Okay."

"Come over for dinner tomorrow night. So she and I have some time to put things back in order at my place. And so you and I have the time to recover."

"Good luck," I say. "Tomorrow night works for me. What should I bring? Wine? Dessert?"

"Just your presence will be enough. Just your presence ... "

"I'll bring a surprise for you. Something that will ever so slightly narrow the gap between us. But without filling it, since that is impossible."

We stand up and go to the counter.

"Leave it," I say, taking out my wallet. "I've got it."

"Thank you," replies David. "Oh, I haven't given you our address."

"I already know it, as well as the two codes. B508A at the first door, then A78B9 at the second door. Third floor opposite the stairs. The elevator is out of order. Those details are in the novel, I haven't managed to forget them. And yet, is there anything more useless than an entrance code to a fictitious building? What good is it to remember that kind of trifle? My brain is cluttered, like an apartment packed with unnecessary furniture. It's absurd, but I can't do anything about it. I'll point out to you that, despite everything, there is one important variation from your dream on the plane: we've just left our table at Last Chance Bar and I haven't vanished. Once I've paid, I'll go out into the street with you, then you'll walk quickly to the entrance of the subway because in three minutes, according to *Translator's Revenge*, it will start raining cats and dogs. I see that you have neither raincoat nor umbrella. I know that when you're alone you never take taxis. Go on, hurry."

We exchange a rapid handshake on the sidewalk, then David sets off.

Then, and only then, I quickly vanish from the urban landscape to go back to the apartment where I'm staying in Brooklyn and mull over Prote.

Chapter 14

THE DINNER

Since the elevator is out of order, I climb up a stairwell with cracked paint and a wobbly railing. On the ceiling of each landing is a bare light bulb, dim and speckled with gray stains, barely illuminating the nearest steps. So on my way up I move from shadow to light, then from light to shadow, and so on, four times. Once at the third floor landing, I ring the doorbell opposite me and almost immediately David opens the door.

"Good evening, Ted. Come in," he greets me with a forced smile.

Three large black trash bags, closed with a yellow plastic strap, are lined up in the narrow hallway of the small apartment. David and I shake hands. As soon as he notices me looking at the trash bags, he adds:

"Prote's malfeasance. We have to throw out a lot of stuff. Clothes, bedding, various objects ..."

"Have you heard from him?"

"Not a word," David replies before adding in a lightly mocking tone: "You?"

The allusion to what he believes to be my divinatory gifts makes me smile. I tell him:

"My role is written in advance, you know. Though I can modify certain aspects of the text, take a few liberties. Cross out, correct, eliminate, add, change two or three lines. Within relatively strict limits." Then I respond to his question, participating without much conviction in our dialogue decided in advance: "No. No news."

"Come, I'll introduce you to Doris."

Following David, I take two steps into the hallway.

Behind a closed door that probably leads to the bathroom, I hear sounds of water, and a feminine voice, slightly trembling, perhaps worried, cries:

"I'm coming. Just a minute!"

Then I turn toward the yellow rectangle of that closed door and notice, hung on it, a large black-and-white display. There are two square photos, placed side by side. I have no memory of these images. I haven't read them. I believe I'm seeing them for the first time.

In the photograph on the left, two twin sisters with very bright eyes, maybe ten years old, stand next to each other, facing the camera. They are dressed identically: white headbands in their medium-length hair, bangs covering their foreheads, the headbands plaster their ears to their heads and resemble a thin Easter egg ribbon circling their oval heads haloed with curly hair, so much so that their position next to each other evokes the appended letters ÔÔ. They both wear black corduroy dresses with pristine star-shaped collars and with just as pristine white sleeves, so that the neck and hands of the little girls seem to emerge from one of those painted set pieces outfitted with holes for the faces of shoppers, the kind you used to see in photography studios. Above their knees, white stocks that are not exactly identical, for the diamond pattern of one is bigger than the other. Despite everything, these twins, who seem to question me with their gaze, are nearly interchangeable, even though one of them is smiling slightly while the other remains more reserved, even wary. Their arms dangle the length of their bodies, their shoulders touch. Before my incredulous eyes the two dresses melt gradually into one piece of continuous fabric that falls from their adjoined shoulders down to the white lower shared sleeve, as if I were looking at one piece of clothing, one two-headed being with three hands. I suddenly have the impression of looking at Siamese twin sisters, anatomically welded by the shoulders, the top of the bust, the sides, the pelvis, and a strangely shared arm that ends in a single hand, probably permitting the two Siamese twins to write: the one on the left is left-handed, the one on the right right-handed. Then I think of David and Doris, I think of the two of them making love, their intertwined bodies. I think of our interlocked texts, of our battered originals and our misfit translations, I think of our variations, our infidelities, our digressions and transgressions. I think of our writing.

In the photo on the right, I see a young giant, standing but tilting his head to keep it from hitting the ceiling of a bourgeois living room, a debonair giant with abundant curly hair leaning on a long cane with a large rubber cap, in an unkempt white shirt with short sleeves, wrinkled black pants that spiral over enormous black shoes that seem entirely improbable, as if they were a unique model, bespoke for this curved man, this young giant conversing with an elderly couple with thinning hair, standing next to him like two deformed midgets, two garden or rather living room gnomes, planted there between two identical windows with drawn curtains, next to a sofa and an armchair covered with a rather ugly fabric. The fat woman and the nearly bald man are both wearing dark-rimmed glasses, dressed in drab conventional clothing that both hides and reveals the portliness of their ripe age. They are the parents of the young giant, his normal and perplexed progenitors. I think of myself, the heretic translator, the unacceptable intruder typically jammed at the bottom of the page, formerly constrained to that cruel contortion of the vertebral column. Then I think of David and Doris; even if far from being my parents, they are my incredulous offspring, perhaps scandalized by my mere presence in their New York apartment.

The mother, hands on her hips, in a shapeless dress with a floral pattern buttoned over the front of her massive body, lifts her worried eyes toward her son as if she were discovering a circus freak lost in her living room, a monster normally caged, as if she's asking him bitterly what he's doing there. Next to the matron, slightly behind her, the father, in a white shirt, dark tie, a jacket with a black lining, dark pants, and tiny black shoes, displays an inscrutable expression. Probably sickened by the mere presence of the giant in his utterly conventional home, he remains firmly stationed on his legs behind his wife, the fingers of his left hand buried deep in his inside jacket pocket in a satisfied posture, thumb visible over the pocket as if to sneakily designate his wife and discreetly signal to the viewer: "Look, she's the one responsible for this walking catastrophe, everything is her fault, I have nothing to do with this colossal disaster, this gigantic cock-up. This is between the two of them, my abnormally large offspring and his deformed mother. I am and remain the immutable statue of respectability, the silent and impervious incarnation of order and conformism."

But I, *le traducteur,* ★ say to myself: the bedroom of this petty bourgeois couple is probably above that ceiling, and the young debonair giant leaning on his cane would surely like to give a powerful head-butt to the obstacle that keeps him from standing up straight, from occupying a vital space that he has every right to.

I, *le traducteur,* ★ think of my own ceiling, thirty-two-thousand feet in the air and half as high above the sea of clouds between Paris and New York, which I recently made vanish so that I could finally escape my hovel of calibrated height and maneuver through the immensity of this paper sky.

Beneath the two images, a name is printed in large uppercase black letters on a white background:

Diane Arbus

Suddenly the display swings toward my face. In a violent anamorphosis, the identical twins unravel and dissolve definitively into each other, the gentle giant grows even taller, his sinister father flies forward as if to crash into me: the dark rim of his glasses, his face tense with disgust, his hand ready to slap, his evil short corpulence rushes at full speed toward my eyes. I swiftly recoil. The three characters simultaneously frozen and brutally accelerated suddenly disappear as if in a sleight of hand, replaced with no warning by a young woman with harmonious features whose wide gaze immediately invades my own. Her irises are like the eyespots of a butterfly: two brown disks encircled with green and gold. A thin nose, slightly hooked, beneath a large forehead. Full and red lips rounded with stupefaction. Jet-black hair over her shoulders. She is discreetly made up. She wears a yellow dress with orange patterns in the form of firework explosions and spirals. Madder-red tights. A few jewels gleam over her long neck and ears. I will notice her mid-heel pumps later. I take another step back. I am lost. Without bearings. I've read nothing of this. I don't remember this scene or this appearance. I have to improvise.

"Uh," David says pitifully. I sense that he is also caught unawares, at first astonished by the excessively long time I've just spent looking at the two photographs on display, then disconcerted by my abrupt silent encounter with his partner. He immediately continues: "Doris, I'd like to introduce you to Ted, *le traducteur*★ I was telling you about. Ted, Doris."

"So you're the famous *traducteur*★ that David dreamed about," says Doris, who has regained her composure.

We shake hands, making eye contact for a brief moment. Her fingers squeeze mine forcefully, as if to prove their firmness.

"*Enchanté*, Doris," I say. "*Très heureux de te renconctrer.*"★★

"I wonder if I can say the same thing. David and I have had nothing but trouble thanks to that nasty translation of *(N.d.T.)*. Prote..."

"I know."

★★ I choose to *tutoyer* her right away. I like her. *(N.d. Trad)*

"Yes, that's right, you know. It seems you're quite the know-it-all."

"It's not really my choice. I would prefer for things to be simpler. I would like to know nothing, be oblivious of the future. I would prefer to be like the two of you."

"Yes, that's what David has assured me," she concedes. "And yet, I can't wrap my head around this absurd situation. Well, in any case, I'm glad to meet you ... Ted? Can I call you Ted?"

"Ted, or Trad, or Brad."

"Trad it is. I'll warn you right away, Trad: I do not want to be a character in a book, even if it's you who's translating it. Or writing it, I don't know what the right word is. No matter what, I am Doris Night, I have no doubt about my existence, or about my identity. I know who I am. I've known Abel Prote for a few months, I know that that bastard is indeed real. We unfortunately have the proof of that every day. I've known David for a little less time and I don't doubt his realness either, fortunately for me. But I don't know what you're doing here, monsieur Trad."

"I brought you proof," I say, pointing to the folder still under my arm.

"I'm not sure I want to see it."

"No one is forcing you. But reading this could be useful for you two, unless you prefer to bury your heads in the sand."

"Let's skip it for now," suggests David, pivoting to lead us to the living room.

Two large windows look out onto the street. This pause in the conversation allows us to hear the distant wailing of a police siren. "Bienvenue, maeva ... Adieu, sayonara." Abel Prote's polyglot recording suddenly comes back to me. Then I notice the bricks that have replaced the back legs missing from the large black leather sofa. Then, between the two windows, my attention is caught by a small round table, where there are three place settings on a violet tablecloth. The plates are laid out in a perfect equilateral triangle, as if the distances that separated the three of us were identical despite the intimacy that Doris and David share, despite my status as the textual genitor.

On that table, within the parentheses of the open curtains, a framed photograph is hanging on the wall. I recall that earlier, in the photo of the stooped giant, an etching, a drawing, or an indiscernible little painting separated the two windows from the closed curtains between the heads of the stunted mother and father. But this photograph is now on the wall of the very real living room of David's apartment. It is not a duplicate. Moreover, the room that I've just entered is decorated with a sort of nonchalant and seductive elegance, nothing like the dreadfully conventional petit-bourgeois interior in the photo of the giant.

On that third black-and-white photograph, square like the first two, framed on a dark background, there is the face of a woman, distinguished but wrinkled, no spring chicken as they say, a woman whose made-up and slightly parted lips reveal very white teeth and a robotic but seductive smile, a woman wearing earrings and a matching necklace gleaming with diamonds. But most remarkably, beneath a sophisticated hairdo in which her thick brown hair, perhaps fake, is knotted in shining braids, a sumptuous mask hides her eyes and forehead, a satin domino mask adorned with white feathers that surround her probably flabby cheeks like two disjointed semicircles. This luxurious domino mask is itself crowned and as if vertically divided by a small stuffed bird—a hummingbird or bird of paradise—whose body curves between the eyes of the woman, its slender beak in the form of a thin V along the bridge of the nose down to her nostril, drawing attention to the beginning of a long wrinkle ending at the corner of the lips.

"Sit down," offers David behind me. "Would you like something to drink? Beer? Whiskey? A glass of wine?"

I turn back toward him. Doris is already seated, legs crossed, on the black leather sofa. Her yellow embossed dress shines above her madder-red stockings. I notice then her elegant mid-heel pumps, I move to sit next to her, then I reconsider and turn toward my host who remains standing:

"I would love a glass of 2003 Côtes du Rhône Guigal."

"But how ..." David exclaims.

"Still having trouble getting used to it, huh? You just opened a bottle of the French wine. Five minutes before my arrival. Alright, I'll stop being a smartass, it's too easy." I notice Doris's slight surprise, her lips open, like earlier in front of the bathroom door, in a ravishing astonished pout. I sit next to her on the sofa. "That's the way it is," I tell her dryly, turning toward her to look her straight in the eye, make an impression on her, admire her irises again. "It'll take you some time. But do not mistake me for a faker, a manipulator, or a charlatan. There are, on the one hand, beings of flesh and blood, on the other a text that pitilessly distributes them onto the chessboard of a novel I've just translated—this unpleasant situation, perhaps humiliating for the two of you, I had nothing to do with it. I repeat, I neither wanted nor chose it." Next to me, Doris makes as if to protest, she opens her mouth again, raises her hands. My gaze fixes her green-and-gold eyes. I continue: "Tonight, I'm the one doing the talking. Not you. For once. Excuse me. You are certainly wondering who my author is. Who wrote *Translator's Revenge*? I don't have the slightest idea. I don't think my

French publisher knows either. I tried to find out. Impossible. The name on the American edition of the book is a pseudonym. Even the New York publisher doesn't know the writer's true identity. He goes through the intermediary of a literary agent, who remains tightlipped and demands that the novel come out simultaneously in every country where a local publisher has acquired the rights, including the United States. Several hypotheses have circulated and still circulate here in New York about the author's identity, but the writers the journalists question deny the guesses each time. No one knows who created *Translator's Revenge*. It's a secret. Nothing has leaked. The few people who know respect the rule of silence: mum's the word. In this respect, I am like you two: curious, perplexed, worried, sometimes terrified. What would you like to drink?"

Doris jumps, as if my question had wrested her from her thoughts, then she replies:

"Nothing. Actually, a glass of water."

"I'll get it," says David who is in the kitchen putting the finishing touches on dinner.

"In a certain way," I continue, "I am a pawn like you two, even if the chessboard I move across includes yours. I don't know why I was asked to do this job. Because of my experience, or perhaps because they foresaw what I would do with this text, but I doubt it. In fact, I got the idea in my head the day when, to convince me to accept this translation project, right off the bat my French publisher offered me a much better rate than what I had received up to that point. Without giving me the least explanation ... I read the manuscript from beginning to end and I said yes. I needed the money. I started working on it immediately. I was truly delighted by the qualities of the novel, its ambition, its originality, its monstrous side, its visual impact, the precision of the writing. But I also saw its weaknesses, a certain dryness, a coldness, a lack of momentum. So, perhaps stupidly, I sought a perfect novel. At least, perfect from my point of view. And very quickly, a sort of madness took over me: I started to delete, to cross out, to rework, at first occasionally, small touches, then entire paragraphs, finally from top to bottom. I crossed out several pages, added other passages of my own invention, and discovered one day with bewilderment what I had not at all foreseen, what no translator, renegade or not, can foresee: everything was coming to fruition, bearing out, being proved in real life. Down to the comma, to the detail, life was conforming to fiction. Not only were the parts of the text written by my mysterious author translating into reality, becoming reality as one says of a fulfilled prophecy, but also all of my savage, devastating interventions ... *Mektub*, it is written. The Arabic proverb could have been the epigraph for this novel, which was progressively becoming *my* novel, and which was also becoming reality at the same time, yours and mine."

David brings a glass of water to Doris and says:

"Sorry for the delay. We can sit at the table. Dinner's ready."

Doris, the smooth talker, the verbal incontinent that I myself fleshed out, expanded, whose monologues I embellished, remains speechless. I knew this would happen, of course, but I'm still surprised all the same:

"So?" I say, turning toward her. "How do you feel? Cat got your tongue?"

Very focused, as if she were reflecting on an arduous problem requiring all of her attention, she slowly drinks a sip of water, holding the glass with two hands, then picks her head back up and stares at me:

"I still don't believe you."

Perhaps she doesn't believe me, but now she's *tutoyer*-ing me.★

"Pretty dress," I say.

"Thank you," replies Doris, visibly touched, raising her eyes toward me. "It's a Lurex dress that my mother wore in the 60s. I love it. I put it on and immediately I think of my mother. I also really like the spiral and floral patterns."

"It looks very good on you."

"Thank you."

David walks into the living room with the open bottle of Côtes du Rhône and a flat dish. "Dinner is served," he says.

We both stand up and join David. "Sit here, Ted. To start, grated carrots with ginger, soy sauce, and wasabi, which is Japanese horseradish. There's another bottle of Guigal in the kitchen. Bon appétit."

Once seated, we serve ourselves. I observe Doris stealthily.

"Bon appétit, Trad," she says, throwing me a quick glance, which I think reveals worry.

"Bon appétit to you both," I say before eating a mouthful of grated carrots.

"Do you like it?" asks David.

★ At least, it's at this point in the novel that I decide she will *tutoyer* me. Doris obviously confirms this arbitrary choice in reality. (*Trad's Note*)

"Surprising... and delicious," I say.

Then, after a silence in which we hear only the light clinking of forks against plates and the din of the city, I add, with the unpleasant feeling of being on a stage reciting memorized lines:

"The surprise that I spoke to you about yesterday at the café, David, is that I brought you *Translator's Revenge* in the original version and in my French translation, but not in their entirety, just up to the end of Chapter 14, entitled 'The Dinner.' You know, that chapter where we dine together, the three of us, in your home, in this very moment... Incidentally, I reworked the text a bit just this afternoon to modify a few details: You and Doris probably felt as though you were having a change of heart about some of the details without really knowing why. Specifically about the choice of dessert (I don't like tiramisu, so I urged you to get a raspberry charlotte), also the wine (here, in New York, the Bordeaux are mediocre or overpriced, the Côtes du Rhônes are more affordable and usually good. So I incited you to buy two bottles of 2003 Guigal, a vintage I have a particular fondness for). Finally, you almost made a blunder with the cheese and I set it right at the very last moment, at the cheesemonger's. I hope that you will forgive me these variations from my rather boorish author's original text, but unlike him, I enjoy good food. So egotistically I changed tonight's menu to satisfy my personal tastes.

"I don't want you to have the least idea about what follows after Chapter Fourteen, after these pages we are in the midst of living, of upgrading, of confirming or realizing right here. And I will give you the two texts as I leave. You will keep them. Take the time to read them and familiarize yourselves with what I know about you better than you, more thoroughly than you. You can thus plunge back into your past, discover what you've forgotten, what has escaped you through inattention, what you didn't really look at or listen to, but only captured with a distracted ear. Then, when you know what I know, we will be near equals, in a certain sense.

"I brought the French text so that Doris will have access to the first fourteen chapters of the book in her mother tongue, but also so that you can compare the original and my translation. You especially, Doris, might be flabbergasted, outraged, sometimes amused, at least I hope. Especially by the first few chapters, up to 'The Secret Passage.' I deleted my author's text entirely, in favor of my own interventions in the form of footnotes. Indeed, it would be interesting to publish a bilingual edition of *Translator's Revenge*, as certain publishers do for poetry: the English text on the left side, my French 'translation' on the right. Thus the reader could assess my work as an apostate translator; he or she could observe the entire breadth of my betrayal, the scope of the damage, or rather the disaster. Yes, I certainly got my revenge on my phantom author. I very scrupulously distorted, amputated, massacred his text. Perhaps as no translator has ever done before, except maybe in former times in the Communist bloc countries where only the censored versions could be cited. As for me, taking advantage of the radio silence of my author, I both whittled him down and fattened him up, I struck him from the page, pushed him out the door, denied him entry, exiled him, even if I don't know where he is in this precise moment in the real world. Everything alright, Doris?"

"Yes, yes," she replies in a hardly audible voice. She is pale, she has a blank stare, pupils dilated and very black in the thin gold ring of her irises.

"Have some wine," David proposes, serving her a glass, which she takes hesitantly and brings to her lips. She takes a sip, swallows with difficulty, breathes deeply, then murmurs:

"Alright. I believe you. I feel better. You've convinced me, Trad. I'm starting to feel like a character in your novel. Even if I am still certain that I am myself." Then she shines her eyes on me, brown, green, and gold, as if here in this living room I were the young giant of the Diane Arbus photograph, but more disturbing than debonair, more intrusive than welcome. "Thank you, Trad. Thank you for your patience, for your explanations. Thanks also to you, David." She suddenly raises her eyes to the photo of the woman in the bird mask who, on the wall above our table, seems to be looking at us scornfully, mockingly, from behind her domino mask, smiling at our naïveté. "Maybe she's the one calling the shots, maybe she's the one who wrote *Translator's Revenge*. Where did you find that photo, David Grey?"

"It's my grandmother Sarah at a masked ball, in 1967. Around fifteen years ago, before dying, she gave me that feather mask. The real object. It's in the bedroom, on a shelf in my closet. Oddly, Prote didn't touch it. Sarah ran in artistic circles in New York, she was especially interested in museums of modern art. She was introduced to Diane Arbus, from whom she bought a few prints, including this one. She gave it to me along with the mask. Would you like to see it?"

"Yes," Doris replies. "Please."

David leaves the table, goes into the bedroom, opens the closet, then comes back with the mask and hands it to Doris. She puts it on her face immediately, adjusts the elastic behind her head. Her eyes slip into the slits of the satin mask, the two curved bundles of white feathers frame her elongated face. She stands up and plants herself next to the photo of Sarah, David's grandmother. She slightly widens her lips to bare her teeth, as perfect as those of the aged woman. She smiles, but without the affectation or the satisfied cunning of the grand bourgeois. Doris is also wearing a necklace and matching earrings that shine on her milky-white skin. The yellow beak of the multicolored hummingbird lays along the bridge of her nose and ends in a slender V that indicates the birth of a future wrinkle. The two masked faces are the same size, they make the same angle in relationship to the line of the shoulders, they are at the same height. They look like twin sisters, or rather a mother and daughter who through that concerted artifice strive to become interchangeable, each other's doppelgangers. Doris senses our distress. She holds the pose for a long time.

I haven't read that scene, I don't know my text, no part of that pantomime was written in advance. Reality diverges, diverts from the novel. Here, in the living room of David's apartment, it is not identical twin sisters who pose in front of the camera, but an ironic mother and her daughter, at once mischievous and conciliatory, who indulge in a game they've invented to seduce men and exclude them from their feminine connivance.

"What do you think, messieurs les traducteurs?" Doris asks. "It turns out there are four of us for dinner tonight. The text must have predicted this slight modification to the original program, right, Trad? Trad, does my double meet your approval?"

David does not seem to appreciate Doris's improvised masquerade. Perhaps this disguise reminds him of others, staged by Abel Prote in his Parisian apartment. "Shall we move on?" he proposes.

As for me, I am completely disoriented, lost, without bearings: nothing in my text announced this episode with the mask, this dinner with four guests, one of whom is reduced to her photographic image, these questions by Doris. I remain silent, incapable of responding.

So Doris drops her pose, lifts her mask, hands it to David, then takes her seat again at the table.

"Let's talk a bit about Prote," I suggest.

David looks at me, astonished, as if I had read his mind. A simple glance at Doris reveals that she also grasped the association of ideas and, moreover, I feel that she knows that I know. She senses now that I know almost all of her intimate details, as if we had exchanged all those caresses described in the preceding chapters and slept together numerous times. All of a sudden she realizes that I know about the disguised soirées in the apartment near the Odéon. Embarrassed, she gets flustered, lowers her eyes, suddenly blushes, and the color that invades her cheeks, so recently pale, magnificently matches the yellow of her dress, the orange of the spirals and the firework explosions, the madder-red of her stockings. In the grips of an emotion I can hardly control, I smile at her and continue:

"I know, everything happens very quickly. Perhaps too quickly. I've known you for hardly an hour, but we share an intimacy that you no longer doubt. I'm asking you to trust me: I won't take advantage of it."

Doris acquiesces without responding. She is emotional once again, on the verge of tears. I place my hand on hers, she squeezes my fingers tightly, as if to assure me of their consistency, of their reality. I think suddenly of David, whose silence surprises me. I withdraw my hand.

"So," I say, "Abel Prote. The French writer. The author of *(N.d. T.)*. The other author. Yours, David, as unreliable as mine, even if he's much more visible, less secretive. But more irascible, more violent and destructive."

"Shall I serve the next course?" David proposes, standing up.

"Yes. I'm dying of hunger," replies Doris. "If Trad agrees, of course," she says, throwing me a look so helpless that I feel the fear, the desire, the fear of desire, tense my stomach. But I know what is to come. I know what will happen next.

"Yes," I say, "I'm hungry too. Talking has always worked up my appetite."

"It's my first time making this dish," David announces, heading toward the kitchen. Then he turns back toward us. "It was Doris's idea, a surprise. You already know what it is, right Ted?"

I search my memory, I find nothing. And yet I've already translated this chapter. I translated it, adapted it, reworked it, but to what end? I modified it, but according to what criteria? I can't remember anymore. And I reply:

"No. I forget. Or rather I don't even know anymore if I ever knew. I'm drawing a blank."

Doris bursts out laughing. Surprised, I look at her.

"A blank," she says to me with a big smile. "That's half the dish. It's black and white. Normally it's served after a broth with pasta in the shape of stars. That's it, you guessed it, right Trad? It's coming back to you now? The cuttlefish in ink sauce with steamed rice? Do you remember? On the plane David and I took to New York? The dish that so depressed David?"

Then the smooth taste of chocolate mousse sprinkled with ground Espelette pepper rushes to my mouth, and to my memory a small spoon hovering in space in the cabin before noisily falling back down to the meal tray. I also remember a prodigious transformation, a coup d'état, a seizure of power, the disappearance of two twin stars, then of a horizon. But the cuttlefish in ink sauce does not evoke any recollection in me, as if I am disassociating myself little by little from the translation that I've just finished, as if I've lost sight and memory of this novel that is moving slowly toward its conclusion. Everything has been finished for a long time, those storylines are behind me, the present scene is finished, even if in this very moment I am an integral part of Chapter 14, playing a not negligible role, succumbing little by little to the charm of that young woman who was, however, molded by my words. But no, nothing of what is happening to me now was foreseen, I am dealing with the unprecedented. It's as if Doris were coming into her own, upturning the course of written things according to her whims, her crystalline laugh smashing the order of the words to smithereens. Doris is the blind spot of a novel to which no one, not even me, *le traducteur,*★ possesses the key.

"Chef's surprise!" cries David, arriving from the kitchen, a plate in each hand, as if to spare me from responding to Doris's question, saving my skin.

"It's not a surprise for anyone," Doris corrects him coldly. "And really in this whole situation you are not actually the chef. Only a stooge, a secondary character, a pawn on a chessboard. Or rather the pawn of a pawn, if I've understood correctly," she adds, looking at me emphatically.

David sets the plate of white rice on the table, then, beneath a lid, the plate that probably contains the cuttlefish in ink sauce. With a falsely melodramatic "Dun dun dun dun" he pulls back the lid, we lean our heads toward the center of the table and, through the rings of bluish steam that rise from the dish, we discover a pale salt cod accompanied with a deep red beet purée with a dozen slices of black radishes. "Chef's surprise!" David repeats proudly.

Doris and I exchange a bewildered look. This dish, which Abel Prote enjoyed on his way to Paris in his Air France business class cabin in Chapter 12, "The Flight," this dish shouldn't be here, in Chapter 14, "The Dinner." Decidedly, my memory is failing me, I am beginning to doubt where this salt cod should appear: in Prote's plane or on David's table? In Chapter 12 or Chapter 14? Unless the novel is rewriting itself, reorganizing on its own, like an organism henceforth independent, autonomous, emancipated from its human tutelage and paternity, no longer taking into account either its author or its French translator. An impossible hypothesis, so unbelievable that in this unhinged universe it becomes believable ...

As for Doris, even if she is unaware of the entire first occurrence of this dish in the novel, she seems to be as astonished as I am.

"But," I say with a trembling voice, "this is the dish that Prote ate on the plane that passed yours over the ocean: Atlantic salt cod with red beet purée and slices of black radish ... "

"What do you mean?" asks Doris. "I don't understand."

"I know," I explained. "I was there. I translated it. No, I wrote it. I was on the plane with Prote. It was at that precise moment that I set about writing for good. You can verify in Chapter 12, 'The Flight.' I have a perfect memory of that dinner's menu. Do you want me to recite it for you?"

"No, thank you, Trad," responds Doris. "We trust you."

"Well," says David. "Shall I serve you?"

I hand him my plate, then Doris lets David serve her, and he serves himself last.

"I still can't get over it," I say. "I'm certain that, in the novel, tonight we eat cuttlefish in ink sauce. Would you like me to verify?"

"No, Trad. We trust you," Doris repeats.

"So," David continues with a malicious smile. "Would you like some more?"

"Wait a bit," says Doris, without immediately understanding the irony of the question. "You only just served us. Also," she adds, suddenly frowning, "let's not do the dialogue on loop thing. The record of our three lives is not scratched, as far as I know. Not yet."

We eat in a weighing silence. I feel that Doris and David doubt me, my credibility, for the first time. And I too doubt my memory, my novel. The salt cod in place of the cuttlefish, it's only a detail, you will say, my reader. But I knew a time when all that I wrote or translated was perfectly confirmed, verified, concretized, incarnated down to the detail in real life. Now, as of recently, differences appear, certainly minor trifles, but troubling all the same. These hiatuses, these divergences, these imperfections of reproduction began tonight, when I entered David's apartment and met Doris. Is she responsible for these snags? Does my gaze, through ricochet, cause these gaps, fissure the written truth, crack the text? How can I seal up the breaches? How can I keep life from drifting farther and farther from its initial organization mapped out in words?

"Did you buy a raspberry charlotte for dessert?" I ask suddenly.

The incongruous abruptness of my question makes David and Doris jump.

"Uh, yes, that's what we're having for dessert," replies David. "But Doris made it, the charlotte."

"Exactly," confirms Doris proudly. "And it's my first attempt. Why do you ask?"

"No reason," I say, both reassured by this dessert that conforms to my predictions and agitated to learn that, contrary to my predictions, it was not bought but homemade. Another fissure opens between words and life. One more difference between the twin sisters. They are not really Siamese twins and, if things keep going like this, their twinship will be nothing but a memory. Before this memory sinks into oblivion in its turn. "Let's go back to Prote," I say. "I have a proposition for you."

"Yes?" asks David cautiously.

"You cannot stand idly by without reacting," I say. "So I would like to propose something..."

"What?" asks Doris.

"A sort of final vengeance. I have to go back to Paris in two weeks. I'm going to see him. Meet him. Explain the situation to him. Tell him what's going on. I'll make that peacock understand what he really is. Show him that his personal and concrete reality, his intimate being, his existence, and even his civil status depend on my good will. Convince him that the *Delete* function on my computer keyboard applies to the text that upholds his life, and that without this text he is nothing. A simple click of the *Delete* key and poof, exit Prote."

"Not bad," says Doris with a mischievous smile and a gleaming stare. "Not bad at all. You couldn't conjure up a nice little rug of crushed glass in his bed, caltrops in his bathtub, burnt trash bags in his oven, saw the legs off his couch, snip his ties, shrink his socks? You would just have to write it all for it to come true, right? You could also repaint his apartment the color of goose poop, cover his fridge in a lovely layer of green mold, what else ... ? Plug up his secret passage, reformat his hard drive, make his shoes walk down the hallway, update his sinister fresco by covering the puppet in bloody wounds, add in the four cheeky girls holding the sheet throwing the mannequin in the air, shut Prote in the armoire, bind his hands with a tie, force him to be sodomized by the puppet ..."

"As of tonight," I cut her off, "I'm starting to doubt the powers of my prose. In fact, since I entered your apartment, since I met you, Doris, gaps have appeared between the storyline of the novel and the film of our three lives, between text and reality. I confess that I'm worried. It's as if you were taking liberties, as if our lives were breaking free from the novel little by little, diverting more and more from it. So I don't know what tomorrow will bring. But it's still worth a shot. What do you think?"

"Yes!" Doris cries enthusiastically. "It's worth a shot. I'm imagining the look on his face. His confusion. His panic. We have to prove it to him in some way. He's not naïve. He won't believe it straightaway."

"Leave the convincing to me. I have quite a few arguments in my arsenal. And besides, it's all already in the novel. I know what comes next. Don't forget that I've translated and written the last chapters. I know, or rather I think I know, how our four lives will evolve, bifurcate, rebuild themselves in the weeks to come ..."

"In the end," says Doris in a morose tone, "it's not a dinner for four, but for five, even if *he* was not invited."

Doris and David remain silent. I've said too much. For them my words once again possess the value of prophecies. I see that, despite my recent doubts, they're afraid. Now they believe me. Especially Doris. I take a secret satisfaction from that, a slightly masculine vanity of which I am perfectly aware, but that vanity excites me, injects adrenaline into my veins. The two photographs on the bathroom door and the one that hangs over us as we eat could not have been more apt to describe my situation. I am that giant with the curved neck, I am that masked woman, I am that hybrid being, that Siamese two-headed body, at once anchored in the present and informed of the future, that anomaly of human form whose fantasies are realized in advance and thus already devalued, at least to my own eyes, if not to Doris's. For with each moment my premonitions, my predictions are already confirmed. In a certain way I never risk anything. Or almost. All I have to do is play the stock market to become rich, all I have to do is take a gamble to make money every time, I've found a foolproof betting system, so long as … yes, so long as I'm translating and rewriting a novel about a Wall Street broker or about horse or greyhound races. But I forget that I am limited to the domain that concerns us three, which is to say the adventure of writing this novel. I forget that my talents only work if Doris—for I think she is the one modifying the text unbeknownst to me—does not exercise her rights too much. I am a god at once powerful and delimited, a shortsighted psychic, a partial prodigy, a visionary blind to everything that exceeds the restrained perimeter of his expertise.

"Nothing is really certain," says David in a hesitant voice, "but I'll serve the dessert you both already know about: the raspberry charlotte."

"And the cheeses?" asks Doris. "Also bring the second bottle of wine. Our guest is clearly thirsty."

"I'll get it," says David.

Doris and I remain seated at the table while David busies himself in the kitchen, opening and closing drawers, taking plates from a cupboard. Suddenly Doris grabs my hand and looks me straight in the eyes.

"Promise me that everything will be okay," she whispers in a quivering voice. "Promise me you won't take advantage of your power."

"I think you're jumping the gun a bit. We're not at that point. Not yet. I can't say for the next chapters. Everything is already going rather well rather quickly. But I'm wary of one thing: as soon as you enter the scene, the moment you intervene in our lives, the script changes. It's as if you have the power to change the text, to rewrite it."

"Promise me," she insists, squeezing my fingers harder.

"Okay," I say. "I promise not to take advantage."

Suddenly she lets go of my hand and lets out a sigh that I don't know how to interpret, then she gets up and goes back into the bedroom.

David arrives holding the raspberry charlotte in one hand and in the other a white compote dish covered with a plate. He places both on the table. "I decided to skip the cheese. I'll get the wine."

He comes back with the second bottle of 2003 Guigal. Right as he lifts the plate covering the second dessert, Doris returns from the bedroom. She's put the hummingbird mask back on. She holds a small crown of faded violets in front of her as an offering. The violet of the petals and the matte brown of the stems strangely match the yellow and orange of her Lurex dress.

David and I turn to face her, stupefied. Doris slowly crosses the distance that separates the doorway of the living room from the round table. After a long silence, she says in a lifeless voice, like a sleepwalker:

"I found these violets at the back of the closet, on the top shelf. Did you put them there, David?"

"No. I've never seen them before."

"You're sure this crown didn't belong to your grandmother Sarah, whose mask I'm wearing?"

"Not to my knowledge," replies David.

"So it must be Abel who hid them in the closet before leaving, for us to find in due time. There was no Post-it stuck to them. Not anywhere nearby either." Doris then slides two fingers into the center of the crown and extracts a small piece of square paper, meticulously folded and refolded. It's a sheet of onionskin, a piece of stationery that she immediately unfolds, after placing the crown of violets on the table. She reads: "'On the top shelf of the closet, behind the splendid bird mask, the photo of which I also quite like, hanging on the living room wall, I hide this crown of violets, like a round and crimson face—from shame? from desire? Of course, it will remind you of another. The one formerly given by my father to his American mistress, Dolores Haze, formerly Lolita. Don't mistake this for a thank you gift. The period of Entente Cordiale is definitively closed between us. The Atlantic separates us, larger than the English Channel. No train, no footbridge, no secret passage, or any plane can ever bring us closer together again.

"'No, the only reason for this gesture is an absolute need for symmetry: a crown at my place, in Paris, a crown here, in your place, David, in New York.'

"Signed: 'Abel Prote.'"

Without a word of commentary, Doris places the sheet of paper on the table.

"Fuck," says David. "Even though he's not here, he's still managing to piss us off, that asshole."

After a few seconds of silence, Doris says:

"Since he's so obsessed with symmetry and repetition, the bedroom closet must contain other little hidden objects. The treasure hunt begins again…"

I am back in my text. Reassured. Confident. Serene. Excited, but serene. I recall this passage perfectly. As soon as Abel enters onto the scene, as soon as he acts, writes, or speaks, reality is once again a copy conforming to the text. Its duplicate, its replica, its perfect double in the opacity of the material. I know what's to come, I anticipate the shared stupefaction of David and his companion.

"Let's go see?" proposes Doris, turning toward the entrance of the bedroom.

David follows her. I'm right behind them.

Standing on her tiptoes in front of the closet, its doors wide open, Doris runs her hand over the top shelf, moves aside some shoe boxes, a suitcase that's probably empty, a pile of drapes, duvet covers, and pillowcases. "Nothing," she says, before exploring the shelf directly below it. There, her hand freezes behind a pile of shirts. "I found something!" she cries. Then she turns toward me and David to show us her prize, which she holds between her thumb and index finger the way someone might hold a crab above the sand behind its pinchers in order to neutralize any remote desire on the crustacean's part to attack.

"A model airplane," she announces. "Like the one in Abel's closet in Paris."

"But it's not a Super Constellation," David observes. "It looks like a more recent model."

"Boeing 747-400, a commercial aircraft that can carry 524 passengers," I specify peremptorily. "The plane you two took back to New York. The same as Prote's, when you crossed him over the Atlantic."

"How do you know all that?" Doris asks, astonished.

"It's in the novel. Our dialogue is there, word for word, in *Translator's Revenge*. My memory is back to being infallible. I'm even starting to think that the author included a few technical details in the book that are perfectly superfluous simply to test my memory. For example, the codes to your building or the technical specifications of the plane. It sends a shiver down my spine."

"Poor thing," Doris mocks with a little laugh. She places the model on the table, gently moves it back and forth and notices a bizarre noise inside the plastic cylinder. "It sounds like there's something inside. A small hard ball clinking in the fuselage. A pebble, an olive pit, a coin?"

"There was the same noise inside the Super Constellation in Prote's closet," David suddenly remembers. "That invisible bean is a kind of signature. Maurice-Edgar, Abel's father, and his son built the model together in the '50s, if I remember correctly. And like a piggy bank, his father slid a gold coin through the crack in the cabin that fit together with the tailplane before gluing on the last piece and closing the inside of the plane for good. Abel did the same thing here, in my home, with this Boeing 747 model. Clearly, he has one hell of a taste for symmetry, the bastard."

Doris shakes the model again like a rain stick that contains only a single jingling grain of sand. The plane does a chandelle, a nosedive, a chandelle again, another nosedive, each time emitting a little rattling noise.

"Let's keep going," she says, setting the plane on the bedside table before turning back to the closet.

At the very back of the third shelf from the top, behind piles of sweaters, sweatshirts, and T-shirts, her fingers touch an oval object, then another, similar to the first. She shows them to us one after the other. Facing us, she holds one egg in each hand, as if presenting them as gifts. The sight of Doris standing there with her hands full and extended makes me smile. Still wearing the hummingbird mask, she looks approvingly upon her prize and says with a burst of flute-like laughter:

"Messieurs, your eggs!"

Obedient, David and I each take an egg from Doris's palm. David the left, I the right. He is to my right, I am to his left. Our extended arms touch. Once again, I notice, the symmetry of our gestures and the staging is perfect. Abel is still present.

I look at my open palm and notice, or rather recognize, a large painted egg. At least, I recognize its size, for I read, translated, wrote that scene last month. The egg placed in my palm is already in my novel. I feel good, reassured, in control of the situation. Suddenly everything escapes me, I topple toward the unknown, the void.

A tiny firework invades the fuchsia sky in my hand. Orange spirals and explosions entirely cover the curved surface of the egg, like real or phantasmagorical animals in the celestial constellations in the midnight blue sky of an astrolabe, or else—this new comparison comes to me very suddenly and freezes me in terror—like the embossed orange patterns on the yellow Lurex dress that emphasizes Doris's curves. My fascinated gaze then shifts from the egg's decorations to Doris's body, the spirals and sparkles, from the madder-red tights to the slight bulge of her stomach; I follow the spirals and orange explosions over the yellow background, over the twin ovoid hemispheres of her chest, finally the shining necklace like a last bouquet of pyrotechnics, her lips separated in a slight smile, perhaps mocking, the slender beak of the hummingbird, and, behind the mask, between the large parentheses of the white feathers surrounding her immobile face, two eyes shine mischievously from within the shadows and remain fixed on mine for a long time. I almost drown in the night bird's stare. Once again life breaks free from the text. My novel mentioned neither spirals nor explosions; Doris's dress was solid, the eggshell displayed only a few multicolored lines on a green background, I'm sure of it. And yet, the spirals and sparkles invade Doris's yellow dress and the fuchsia surface of the egg. Doris's eyes gleam with pleasure, her delighted smile blooms. Her mere presence disturbs the mise en oeuvre of the text, the mise en vie of the novel. She upsets the reproduction, unhinges the translation. And I know that my stare, which she stares into, betrays my confusion, my anxiety, my suspicions: did she prepare this distribution of eggs, and of roles, in advance? Did she choose that dress deliberately to observe my panic from behind her mask, and revel in it?

And David? What is he doing?

David is my reflection in an invisible mirror. His left hand extended in front of him, open palm holding the other egg identical to mine, he stares hard at Doris. But Doris has her bird eyes cast on me. We hold our pose for a few seconds. It's Doris who breaks it:

"So, messieurs les traducteurs," she says in a sardonic tone, "are you done incubating your eggs or…?"

Obedient once more, we both set about opening the painted wooden objects. They split in two perfectly identical halves and, predictably, reveal another egg painted in colors symmetrical to the first: on an orange background, the spirals swirl and alternate with fuchsia explosions. Prote, or Doris, did a good job, didn't neglect a single detail. I'm half waiting for a magic trick to reverse the colors of Doris's dress, too. I look up to reassure myself and discover with a slight disappointment that no: the orange patterns still speckle the yellow Lurex. As if she had read my mind, Doris bursts into laughter.

Abruptly, almost irritated, I open the second painted wooden egg and find in there a thin sheet of violet paper, folded and refolded. Abel Prote. Glancing at David, I notice that he is also unfolding a sheet of onionskin extracted from the second egg. I read:

"'I know that that smarty-pants Doris will have found the eggs at the back of the closet. Certainly not you, David. I also imagine…'"

End of my letter. David immediately picks up where I left off, reading from his:

"'...that she will offer these two twin eggs to you, David, with a big burst of laughter.'" Would you look at that, Prote did not, of course, foresee my presence tonight at David's. "'It's always the woman who, in the end, allows the man to have his balls.' Fuck you!" David adds, furious.

"Keep reading," insists Doris.

"'I imagine that it was also Doris who, five minutes ago, held between her slender fingers the long fuselage of the rounded tip of the Boeing 747 with its small ringing grain. I won't start on the violet crown and the its inner contents.'"

"All that is well and good," interrupts Doris, "but, for the first time, to my knowledge, Abel has slipped up. He anticipated a dinner for two between me and David, he didn't foresee that Trad would be here, with us, during the treasure hunt."

"Prote's letter isn't finished," David interrupts. "'All those salacious allusions are rather obvious, even uncouth. But such is life. Those two objects—the violet crown and the model airplane—belong to the past, they are linked to my father and my childhood. My only intervention is the two eggs. I like the idea that you, Doris, saddle the little Gris with them, like an indispensable accessory.'"

"Bastard!" cries David, still furious.

Doris only smiles. "Go on, continue," she orders.

"'It goes without saying that I bless neither your union nor your schemes, far from it. I am not your fairy godmother, that's a disguise that has never occurred to me. I will not be your witness either, in the event you should ask me, which I doubt. I simply played the reluctant role of the intermediary, I made the introductions and now I like the idea that you, Doris, present him these eggs, that you hold them in front of him in your pretty little hands.'

"'Adieu, sayonara, et cetera.'"

"And there you have it, his final dirty trick," concludes David, still beside himself.

"I'm sure there must be something else," Doris intervenes.

"What do you mean, something else?" David asks, astonished.

"Surely Abel has prepared more funny business for us. He likes to play cat and mouse. The next surprise might not be in the closet, he loves to spread out his tricks, make them last, prolong the suspense."

"I'm inclined to agree," I say with an unnecessary caution.

Doris seizes the opportunity:

"You know what comes next, you could help me out a bit, no?"

"Out of the question. I can intervene in the text, but not in its translation into reality. And in this situation, I expect the translation of the novel into life will be rigorously faithful."

"I don't like men of principles," says Doris, looking at me reproachfully from behind her mask.

"It's out of the question for me to modify the text through reality. I cannot correct *Vengeance du traducteur* a posteriori. What is written is written. In other words, in the fiction that we are faithfully duplicating with our bodies, our voices, our gestures, it's life that imitates art, never the inverse. It all works in one direction, even if that direction is not the one we're used to."

"Help me out a little, Trad. Give me a clue," she beseeches with a smile.

Conscious of breaking a rule, of ceding to the charm of her eyes, I take a step toward the closet, crouch down in front of the bottom shelf and murmur:

"There."

Doris crouches down next to me, I feel her thigh brush mine, then she moves her hand behind the colorful piles of bath towels, tablecloths, and napkins. Her fingers grope around without finding anything. The masked face turns toward me, her painted lips say:

"I don't feel anything."

"Keep going."

She complies, blindly rummages around some more, soon says:

"There it is!"

She pulls from the closet what seems to be a large bundle of rags, but I already know what it really is, of course. Standing up, she unfolds it, examines it, and cries out excitedly:

"The puppet from the fresco! The slender limbs, the black braid, the dislocated body, it's the puppet from the apartment by the Odéon!"

David approaches to examine the large limp doll, then acquiesces with a nod:

"It's definitely the puppet that hovers in the sky opposite the closet. But what's it doing here? In three dimensions? In flesh and blood? Can you say that about a doll? It's like having the model after the painting. The real object after its depiction in the fresco."

"Symmetry..." murmurs Doris pensively. "Abel is truly obsessed. The puppet depicted on the wall of the hallway in Paris and its posthumous model in New York. Similarly, the bird mask in the Diane Arbus photo in the living room, and the real mask over my eyes. I wonder if next we'll find a small stuffed seagull, a marine landscape made of plaster or papier-mâché, cotton clouds."

She looks at me inquisitively. I slowly shake my head to signal to her that no, she will not find any of these objects in the closet.

"Thank you, Trad. Thank you for your help and for that clarification," she adds in a cheerful tone. "Now, what shall we do with this rag doll?"

Not really wanting to help her any more, I turn toward the bare wall opposite the closet. The place where, logically, the puppet should have been displayed, along with the seagull, the waves, the horizon, and the clouds. But between the two windows where the lights of a skyscraper now enter into the bedroom, there is nothing but a large bare rectangle painted sky blue that extends from the ground to the ceiling and overflows the windows up to the neighboring walls. These twin windows suddenly look like two holes pierced in a blue mask, revealing shiny black eyes speckled with gold.

"Well. We're missing a book, a key, and a secret passage," David notes, suddenly perspicacious. He shakes his egg, which remains stubbornly empty and silent. "Nothing here." Then he adds, excited: "This is crazy, but..." Bent down, he enters the closet, extends his arm toward the back, and runs his hand along a large wooden panel.

Doris and I watch, perplexed and amused. Suddenly, I feel the fingers of the young woman enlace mine and squeeze tightly. None of this is in the book. I don't know whether the emotion that then leaves me breathless is due to this new gap between the novel and life, or else because of this furtive gesture in which I recognize more than just a passing complicity or a reflex triggered by fear, a sort of fatal mechanism to which Doris and I seemingly want to submit, to abandon ourselves together. When I turn my head toward the young woman, my gaze catches her two gleaming eyes, I feel her trembling fingers squeeze mine even tighter. I think of the Diane Arbus's twin sisters. I think of their hands merged in the center of the photo. I think of our two bodies soon intertwined. The text heralds it, my desire does too.

"What's this?" David says suddenly from the bottom of the closet.

Despite myself I tighten my fingers around Doris's, it's as if each of us were trying to crush the bones of the other. Then my hand brusquely breaks from hers and we turn toward David.

"You found something?" Doris asks in a quivering voice.

I'm on the verge of whispering in her ear: "You," but David catches me off guard:

"A sort of...Yes, that's it, a movable panel. Like a false bottom. There's a hole, a keyhole. But no key. And it sounds hollow..."

As if to prove it to us, he taps against the plank three times, then backs out of the closet. Stands up, faces us:

"We have to find the key. Where could it be? Definitely not in the Easter eggs ... So where?" His eyes suddenly settle on the rag doll that Doris is still holding in her hand. "The puppet! Let me look." He nearly snatches it from Doris's hands, then examines all the puppet's seams. Disinterested in what's to come, I turn my eyes to admire the young woman's hips and waist. "Look," continues David, astonished, "it's like a cesarean scar. Someone opened its stomach and then sewed it back up with large stitches. Can you grab a pair of scissors?"

"How dreadful!" cries Doris.

All the same, she goes to look for scissors in the kitchen while I watch the unfolding of events without intervening. I know what awaits me, I know what awaits us, the book is clear, but I don't know exactly what's in store for Doris and me.

"Give it to me, I'll do it," Doris says to David, returning with a pair of kitchen scissors. "After all, the stomach, pregnancy, cesareans, that's woman business."

David hands her the puppet and she opens its stomach by carefully cutting the beige thread.

When all the stitches have been severed and the threads have fallen on the parquet floor around her shoes, Doris hands the scissors to David and spreads open the two pieces of fabric, then plunges her fingers into the stuffing. First she takes out a small leather-bound book, which she hands to me like a gift.

I open it and read the title page:

"*Fragments épars*, by Boris Matthews." Then I notice a Post-it inside the book cover. "There's a note from Prote," I say, noticing the signature without surprise. I read: "'Bizarrely, I found the French translation of this novel at a secondhand bookseller's not far from your place. I bought it without a second thought. Since I already own a copy of this book in Paris and I have no desire to encumber myself with additional luggage, I selfishly offer it to you. The title suits you very well: you two are nothing but the scattered fragments of an indiscernible whole, of a volatile, vague entity.' Signed: Prote. 'PS: It's not over.'"

"There's more!" Doris suddenly cries out.

Then I see her hand sink into the depths of the puppet's stuffing. Her fist and forearm disappear into the opening, while, face turned toward me, not paying the least attention to David, she stares at me from behind her hummingbird mask, her lips spread into a cruel, voluptuous smile that paralyzes me. Her hand slowly explores the interior of the mannequin, her gleaming gaze stays riveted to me, her smile blooms, trembles, and tenses, her teeth are clenched, there's a slight redness in her cheeks. She seems to be saying to me: "All this is for you, I offer all this to you, please accept it," as if through this hijacked staging she were giving herself to me in advance. Those silent allusions trouble me and curiously numb me, the penetration of the stomach by Doris's fingers, palm, fist, forearm. Soon I think I see her elbow and then her entire arm sink into the opening of the puppet, which suddenly acquires a new rigidity, as if Doris's nude limb supplied the soft rag with a vertebral column it had previously lacked.

My eyes go back and forth between Doris's burning eyes, staring at me, and the penetrated puppet, disemboweled and erected at the same time, stiff for the first time in its marionette existence. Like the arm of the young woman stuffed in the puppet, our gazes are soldered together, and it's that double intimacy—her arm, the stuffing, her golden irises, my eyes, the simulacrum of penetration—that enflames us while excluding David.

A black-and-white photograph suddenly superimposes itself on the scene like a transparent veil: a man with bare butt cheeks, facing me, seems to be plunging the handle of a leather whip into his anus. But it's the gaze of the man, the creator of this pantomime, which is the most troubling: implacably fixed on me, at once to challenge me to look at the image and to force me not to turn away, to face it for as long as possible, to accept this unprecedented and provocative version of a classic pictorial juxtaposition: a face and butt cheeks, usually a woman's, like in Velázquez's *Rokeby Venus*. But here, a man's white butt cheeks and the black handle of the whip, his fixed stare and my worried look.

To my great surprise, beyond that photographic ectoplasm, simultaneously distinct and quivering, I soon distinguish Doris on the other side of the man's made-up face, silently mouthing one word and then another. On her scarlet, moving lips I am then certain of deciphering the words: Ro-bert Ma-pple-thor-pe.

The puppet is aligned with the whip, the naked man's body is covered in tattoos in the form of spirals and orange explosions, his black leather chaps are coated in red. In the foreground is Doris's hand, spreading his pale butt cheeks, she's the one holding the whip, which is her arm.

I am seized once more by the gleaming gaze riveted to my eyes. The two eyespots merge with the made-up eyelids of the man scrutinizing me.

At the edge of my field of vision, I see Doris's shoulder sink into the orifice of the puppet. Her pupils are now dilated, their black discs nearly invade the entire iris, and through these twin holes I think I see her arm disappear into the inside of the wall of the fresco, plumb the plaster and the stone, feel the marine horizon and the blue sky, explore the waves one by one like a vigorous swimmer splashing about, then her hand and her arm, suddenly dry, walk along the shelves of the two closets, sometimes one, sometimes the other, the old massive piece of furniture that nearly obstructs the dark Parisian hallway, then the modern armoire with the open panels covered in mirrors in New York, mirrors that multiply the puppet pregnant with her arm, the yellow dress with the orange spirals and explosions, the madder-red stockings, the jet-black hair, the gleaming and cruel smile, the pupils of the night bird behind the sequined mask, but soon the hand, arm, shoulder are no longer exploring the shelves, nor the painted waves or the blue of the sky on the hallway fresco, but pages striped with uniform lines, strata of words piled on the bottom of the page or wedged at the top of the white rectangle, like superimposed layers of gray clouds or balloons inflated with helium and lined up on the ceiling of a living room. That shoulder, that arm, those fingers grab the words in large bunches to throw them from one page to the next, shuffle them and redistribute them at the whim of a careless coincidence, jostle the order of the text, rework it from top to bottom, juggle the stuffing of language and throw into the air the feathers of the ripped-open pillow to watch them fly through space, weightlessly dance in slow motion, create slow clouds of white starlings, and the angelic hand that grabs the black words delights in this transgression like a child throwing fistfuls of colorful confetti with all their might over their friends and the adults gathered for a party or an anniversary. It's Doris and not me who, in a great burst of laughter and following my own upheaval, incites this vigorous and savage mixing of the text. It's Doris and not me who, hand buried up to the shoulder in the slit of the fabric, swims the breaststroke among the waves of the text and rebuilds the puppet's stuffing, feels, touches, shapes, and reorganizes the internal organs, the path of the words, the rail of the chapters, the symmetry of the novel. She reroutes the promised trajectory, she launches her unexpected game. She is the one I dread, she inspires both fear and delight in me.

"A key!" cries Doris, brandishing a shiny object.

Then I have the rather absurd thought that the puppet must have eaten it, that key, like some miners in South Africa who, while excavating gold or diamonds, discreetly swallow a few nuggets at the bottom of a mine, then, back at home, explore their stool to retrieve the precious stones, hoping the sharp edges of the pebbles haven't ripped their intestines.

"I knew it," says David.

He doesn't seem to have noticed anything of the secret conversation between Doris and me. But perhaps I imagined everything. Indeed, the text does not contain the young woman's suspect gestures, perhaps passionate or obscene, it also does not mention the name she silently articulated, nor her gleaming gaze or our shared emotion. Perhaps I made it all up. And yet, when I look down I still see the imprint of Doris's rings on my fingers, the mark of those jewels that dug into my bones when she squeezed my hand so tightly. All that telepathic hallucination cannot just be a product of my imagination.

"In Paris," David continues, "the key was inside the second egg. Here, it's in the puppet. So that nutcase does allow for variation sometimes. He even organizes it. In any event, I'm sure this key will open the door at the bottom of the armoire. I'll go check right now."

And then, imitating the novel's text to perfection, he squats again in front of the armoire. Once more, I immediately feel Doris's fingers lace through mine, then her hip press against me. Far from shirking away, I push my thigh against the yellow Lurex.

"It fits!" David cries idiotically in a voice muffled by the mass of clothes hanging in the closet. "The key works. Lift the bottom shelf so I can open the door."

Our hands separate, then soon come back together, as if by accident, among the piles of clothes on the lower shelf.

"I know what comes next, it's written in the text," I whisper in Doris's ear while our hands buzz about.

"I know. And I submit to it," she says, before murmuring: "Wholeheartedly."

Our faces draw closer by the second shelf, level with David's T-shirts, button-downs, and colorful sweaters. Our bodies freeze. Our fingers find each other again.

"What are you doing," David suddenly cries from the bottom of the armoire.

"We're coming, we're coming," grumbles Doris, distancing herself from me, but not before planting a quick kiss that misses my lips and slides over my cheek, as I think to myself perversely that David, his body squeezed between the ground and the lower shelf, has now adopted the standard position of the sworn translator, while Doris and I act like living pillars.

We continue to clear the shelf, setting the piles of clothes on the floor near the armoire. Then I raise the plank and lean it against the bedroom wall.

"Done," I say.

"It's about time. I'm sick of being bent over like this. Okay, I'm opening the door."

Doris and I, hands on our knees, which brush at the same time as our fingers, stare at the back of the armoire. David turns the key in the lock, then pulls the panel toward him.

At the back of the armoire, behind the secret door, we see a large plasma screen built into the wall.

Doris and I sit next to each other on the parquet floor. She nearly falls backward and grabs onto my arm, letting out a little amused cry. David backs out of the armoire to join us and sits on the other side of the young woman. Suddenly, without anyone touching a single button or using any remote, the screen turns on.

"Bastard," David says between his teeth.

I jump: has he picked up on the little game between Doris and me? But I quickly understand that the insult is addressed at Prote. David mutters:

"How did that bastard manage to install all of this while I was gone?"

Doris bursts into laughter. Hands damp, I remain silent.

On the plasma screen appears an open door leading to a flight of stairs that descends into shadow.

"But," cries Doris, "that looks like... That's the entrance to Abel's secret passage, in Paris!"

In a slow forward tracking shot, the camera pans the staircase, descends, then bounces along the underground tunnel, its gritty walls, its deplorable lighting. The tracking continues, jerky and silent.

Prote's booming voice then bursts out:

"Congratulations! You should be proud of your ingenuity. I was hoping for a secret passage to appear here, at the bottom of your armoire, David, but I had neither the desire nor the means to demolish the wall behind your awful modern piece of furniture, to barge in on your neighbors in the middle of the rubble, to emerge stumbling from a cloud of fine gray dust, surprise them in bed in the middle of their amorous gymnastics or else gathered with their kids around the lunch table, excuse my unexpected arrival in their home, dust off my pants and jacket, thus raising new gray clouds around my henceforth colorless clothes, before following my progression through their apartment as they look on stupefied, a mallet casually slung over my right shoulder like the seven dwarfs carrying their pickaxes—which one suits me best do you think? Grumpy? Doc? Dopey?—then saunter to the wall opposite the hole recently dug behind the armoire and vigorously attack this second obstacle hoping it's not a load-bearing wall, praying the entire building doesn't collapse on top of me and that innocent family sitting at the table for the family meal. No, this type of exercise is not for me, this athletic prowess is not for someone my age, even if, as you know, the idea of a tunnel or passage has always obsessed me as much as my need for symmetry.

"So in this instance, I'll settle for the image instead of the real thing. The image is less costly. Less risky. Less physical (when we look at it, not when we fabricate it, as you will see). The image is more temporal. More mental. Hypnotic. Minus the sweating, it should remind you of the good old days of your underground romp. I am now filming as I advance shakily through my secret passage. See how the frame sways and trembles. I'm less than an amateur filmmaker: a mere novice."

"What a show-off," murmurs Doris.

"Another thing," Prote continues bitterly: "I am not inviting you on a guided tour. This is not a documentary on the catacombs of Paris. Nor on the underground of a banal historical monument. You are not Japanese tourists. Nor is this a private visit organized by a gallerist for his or her collectors or by the owner of a castle for his or her guests. For you are no longer my guests, you are no longer welcome in my home. This is also not an instructional video like the ones you see on display at hardware stores, flaunting the merits of an extravagant household accessory or a revolutionary drill. It's not a virtual simulation to familiarize the most daring of vacationers with the speleology of a sinkhole or a siphon in the deep Dordogne. No, I am not inviting you on an acrobatic adventure among the seeping grottoes, I am not inviting you to purchase any state-of-the-art equipment, I am not giving you a tour, I am not showing you any tantalizing images. As you will discover, it's more of an exploit or a performance. This video that you are both watching, sitting cross-legged in front of the open armoire—I know, I planned it all, you are still obeying me ("He's got it so wrong, the bastard!")—this video is simply to say 'Go away.' Piss off. For good. Get out of my life. Get off of my cloud! Scram! Adios. So long. Sayonara. Et cetera. This video is my last move on the chessboard, and it's a tour de force! When I'm done, it'll be checkmate."

"Bastard." David lets out again.

I jump despite myself.

On the screen, the camera continues to move through the tunnel, which becomes more and more narrow.

The camera suddenly freezes. Prote's voice goes quiet. Change of scenery. The camera, now on a tripod, is set up almost in the middle of the secret passage. There is no more sound. A dark silhouette appears in the shot and grows distant, its back to us. Prote is prancing about in the tunnel carrying a rather heavy object, which he places carefully on the ground twenty yards in front of the camera, in the middle of the passage. Then he moves mysteriously around the object and comes back to the camera, doubled over and unfurling a large black cable behind him. When he passes in front of the lens, he waves his hand and aims a large smile at the viewer. Despite the very dim light, his face is perfectly recognizable. He looks delighted, overexcited.

"I've never seem him in such a good mood," comments Doris, slightly worried.

He exits the shot. A few seconds later, as if the impulse were stronger than he, as if he were indulging in an irresistible schoolboy prank, Prote comes back in front of the camera to display a grotesque grin, a sort of great silent burst of laughter. Then he disappears once more from the shot.

Several seconds go by during which absolutely nothing happens. The massive object is still placed on the floor, rather far from the camera, in the center of the image. A black cable emerges from it, snakes over the dirt floor and ends at an invisible point behind the tripod. Still nothing happens. None of us talk. A heavy silence prevails.

I grab Doris's hand. I know what's coming.

A deafening explosion suddenly reverberates through David's bedroom. The sound of the home movie, absent for a long minute, comes back with a frightening violence. An orange glow invades the entire plasma screen installed at the bottom of the armoire: Prote's secret passage has been pulverized, a cloud of dust and earth immediately sprays forth, as if on fast-forward, toward the camera. The three spectators, seated cross-legged on the floor of the bedroom, recoil automatically to avoid the gray rush that suddenly masks the blinding ball of fire on the screen and rushes toward them.

The echo of the filmed explosion has not yet dissipated when another resounds, even louder, strangely close. I let myself fall backward and drag Doris in my fall. All three of us cry out. A thick rain of tiny spikes pours down onto us and scratches our hands, necks, faces, as if thousands of killer bees were attacking us at the same time. A wave of heat submerges us. I squeeze Doris against me. She lets out muffled groans. She is terrified. In a state of shock. Perhaps wounded. I wasn't fast enough.

"Checkmate, my lambs!" Prote's voice suddenly roars. "This is my film debut, but for a novice I'm not half bad! And I'm a pretty good pyrotechnist too, no? Okay, the first explosion nearly scorched my hair, my beautiful suit was almost torn to shreds by the stones that suddenly shot through the tunnel. My explosives collapsed the secret passage. I am no longer of an age to dart back to the costume room to return my disguises from the night before and grab others in exchange. And besides, in the absence of any offspring, I don't see what use this secret passage would serve ... But what did you think of my second methane explosion? Not bad, right? I simply installed a sensor inside of this television screen embedded in the wall, linked it to a small bomb and programmed it to light my little bomb and blow up the screen as soon as the sensor felt the reverberation of the first explosion. But without wrecking the speakers, mind you. So that you could hear the voice of its master! I did my research: my sound sensor does not react to the sound of a bottle of champagne popping. So you were able to rinse your throats in peace before appreciating my talent for editing and my final pyrotechnic surprise!

"The symmetry is now perfect. I'm surprised you didn't suspect this ultimate consequence inspired by the principle of Protean reciprocity: an explosion in Paris necessarily engenders another in New York. As naïve as you are, perhaps you believed you would get off easy? That the image would suffice? That it would make up for the real explosion? That the rush of pebbles would be reserved for me alone and that you would be spared? That the retinal delectation would get you out of the test of fire? Though of course the virtual has undeniable qualities, nothing compares to a confrontation with the real.

"And no-ow," continues the voice, getting slower and deeper, "adiosss. I don't want ... I don want ... ever again ... to he-e-e-ar ... aboouuut ..."

Increasing static keeps me from grasping Prote's final words. The home theater's sound system, damaged by the explosion of the screen, shuts down.

"Fuck him!" shouts David.

Next to me, Doris slowly props herself up on an elbow. Her yellow dress is speckled with minuscule slivers of glass, but at first sight intact. I examine her pale face, her black voluminous hair shining with a swarm of stars. Like a city seen at night from an airplane window. Besides a slight scratch on her forehead, Doris doesn't seem hurt.

"Are you okay?" I ask her.

"Mostly…"

"And you, David, are you okay?"

"I hate him, that bastard and his stupid jokes!"

A bit reassured, I sit up in the middle of a deluge of gleaming glass. David, already standing, shakes out his shirt and pants, raining down another shower of small hailstones that clinks on the floor around his sneakers.

When I extend my hand to Doris, she uses it to pull herself back onto her feet.

"Son of a bitch," she says to me with a mean look, "you should have warned us."

I couldn't have warned them. For though the first explosion was written in full in *Translator's Revenge*, the second is missing. Once more, the mere presence of Doris has changed the translation of the text into life, but in an unprecedented way: by addition. Until now it was one thing instead of another—for example, the salt cod in place of the cuttlefish in ink sauce. But now life has unilaterally imposed an additional explosion that does not appear in the text. Because of the confusion reigning in the apartment, I forgot another addition: the appearance of a second, unidentified dessert on the dinner table.

"Sorry," I say pathetically. "But the explosion of the screen is part of what we call life's vicissitudes. The text doesn't mention that bomb attack anywhere. You have a small cut above your eyebrow," I say to Doris, who then brings her hand to her forehead before looking at her bloodied finger and walking hesitantly toward the bathroom. Then I turn toward David.

His black T-shirt is speckled with a myriad of minuscule shining pixels. The fabric is shredded in places, riddled with small tears that, I am certain, did not exist before the explosion. But there is no trace of blood, not on his arms or on his face. David is white as a sheet, he looks into the haze, he cannot believe the spectacle of his devastated bedroom: the bottom of the lacerated armoire is still smoking at the place where there was a plasma screen just a moment ago, now reduced to a carbonized carcass, contorted, unrecognizable; the parquet floor is constellated with slivers of glass that crunch beneath our timid steps, sink into our soles. We're treading carefully, not daring to move.

"More afraid than hurt? *Plus de peur que de mal* ? Do you say that in French?"

"Yes."

Then I notice that the brown slats of the varnished floor are covered in a kind of crystal rug that splays from the armoire to the interior of the room. Our three cross-legged bodies had stood in the way of the almost instantaneous dispersion of the fragments of glass. That sparkling blanket in the shape of a giant frozen hand whose four spindly fingers had brutally slid around our chests, squeezing and perhaps crushing them. Prote had certainly not foreseen the sudden, deafening appearance of that mortal frost flower, that icy sharp hand bursting from the armoire in a flash to crush all three of us. King Kong plunges his hairy paw through the window of a skyscraper to snatch the beautiful blonde from her luxurious sofa. It's neither Zorro the masked avenger nor the man in black from the Sandeman port label, but an uncaged monster, the animal strength of a screen of glass blown up by a bomb: the enormous black fist of a gorilla flattened into a thin blinding rug of quartz crystals, as menacing as a large bucket full of caltrops spread over the flat surface of a bed sheet, of a bathtub, or of a varnished parquet floor.

"That was a close call," David continues in a distracted voice, before adding mechanically: "The bastard." Then: "I need a drink."

"Good idea."

With small careful steps and extending our arms like tight-rope walkers, we go back into the dining room. Our shoes raised on slivers of glass crunch on the parquet floor. We both empty our glasses of Guigal in one go.

David immediately sinks into a chair and begins to repeat like a comatose litany, like a lullaby:

"The bastard. But really, what a bastard. The bastard. That dirty bastard..."

I head toward the bathroom; the door is closed. I approach the two Diane Arbus photos. I knock softly. Three times. Inside, Doris responds, as if from very far away:

"Coming. Just a minute."

The intonation of her voice has changed, but it's the same words that Doris said only two hours earlier, just after my arrival. The words of the novel, the dialogues of our life, are they on a loop now? Or thrown haphazardly into the thread of time like random quotations, involuntary pastiches, unpredictable parodies. In any event, one thing seems sure: with the explosion of the plasma screen, life has abruptly diverged from the text. I no longer know what path it will follow. Perhaps our dialogues have also been blown to smithereens. I am without bearings, I have to improvise, I am afraid.

All of a sudden, the fake Siamese twins jump into my face again, the frozen giant pivots and grows in the blink of an eye, his bespectacled genitor moves as if to strike me, then these slender characters grow slimmer to the point of disappearing, magically replaced by Doris's radiant face, the green-and-gold eyespots around her dilated pupils like two dark twin wells, nose slightly hooked, lips full and red, abundant black hair, and her large convex forehead where I am stunned to no longer discern the least trace of a scratch.

"Where and when?" she whispers to me.

I feel her hot breath on my cheeks and mouth. Doris smiles at me. Her eyes smile at me.

Caught off guard, I don't know how to respond. I see her two eyes leave my face and stare at a point situated above my right shoulder. I extend my arm without thinking, my hand touches the orange spirals and explosions on her hip as if to balance myself, while I turn toward the living room in order to follow Doris's gaze. Behind me, I see not the puppet of the fresco as I almost expected, but David's drooping, inert, seemingly dislocated body seated on a chair. He's still murmuring:

"The bastard. But really, what a bastard. Son of a bitch bastard . . ."

Then I understand and reply in a whisper:

"Tomorrow at six o'clock. My place. My address and telephone number are on the folder containing the two versions of *Translator's Revenge*."

"Okay."

"Read them."

"I will."

Chapter 15

TRAD'S SECRET PASSAGE

Yes. Last night. Everything began last night. The colorful hummingbird on your face and the black-and-white photo of the same mask on the wall, the crown of dried violets, the fabric puppet into which you plunged your hand, then your arm, all the way up to your elbow, all while staring at me, first extracting the book and then the key, as if with you as midwife the homunculus gave birth to those two hard, angular objects, but a few seconds before the delivery of the key, Doris, when you still had your arm buried deep into the stuffing, you and I both saw the whip between the butt cheeks of the man, his gleaming thigh-high boots, his disheveled head turned toward us, his shining eyes staring at us, pushing us toward each other, pressing us to each other, then our fingers interlaced in front of the armoire, our thighs pressed together, I almost kissed you and then, yes, the orange spirals and explosions on your yellow Lurex dress, the ball of fire in Prote's secret passage, my body now riveted to yours, it's still me speaking, for once you keep quiet, you listen to me, like you have been since last night, now you know that I know what you are capable of, your true colors, the words you use to get what you want, you read my book up to the end of the previous chapter, "The Dinner," you know that I know about your disguised soirées with Prote, your amorous delirium in Chapter 9, I'm the one who put those tender words in your mouth, those coarse words, I who ventriloquized you long before sinking myself into your stomach, lending you my voice against your will, but I think that you recognized my music, my rhythm in my words, like your yellow Lurex dress that fits you like a glove, my words meld into you, they are in harmony with your voice, with your breath, your body also suits me like a glove, I have the curious impression of recognizing it and not, as I should, of discovering it for the first time, in a certain way it is already familiar to me, my hands already know it though I don't understand why, for my words could not create the texture or the heat of your skin, your heartbeats, the timbre of your voice, or the pressure of your fingers against my neck.

Doris, I had not foreseen that everything would go so fast, that so soon we would be skin against skin, my breath inhaling yours, your green-and-gold eyes so close to mine that don't lose sight of you even for a second, my cock slid into your silk to probe its niches, its hiding places, the bends and folds, the walls, the crevices, the ravines and inclines, the slopes and passes that you've come here to offer me in my home at the appointed time, thank you for this gift, thank you for that secret agreement last night just before my departure, thank you for this punctual connivance, this kept promise.

Wearing a black dress, simple and sheer, and mid-heel pumps, you came to my home, I wanted to kiss you on the cheek, say hello, serve you a drink, chat a bit, be sure of your desire and of your two recent readings, talk about them with you, know what you thought, what in the two novels surprised you, scared you, seemed to you unclear or incomprehensible, captivating or clumsy, the French version should have imitated the American and yet it diverges savagely, in the end differing from it greatly, only the French title remains faithful to the original, but immediately my mouth changed direction against my will, it slid along your cheek toward your lips, I whispered hello, your body drew nearer to mine and I saw your eyes gleam, for it was what you desired, and immediately, without beating around the bush, what I had not decided, what the novel had not predicted, you always catch me off guard, you're always one step ahead of me, ahead of the cadence of the book, I wasn't planning for it to happen so fast, that proximity, that embrace, even if I was dying for it and for an hour had been waiting for you with my heart racing palms sweaty throat constricted, I still naïvely believed in what the book announced, what it predicted without any ambiguity, which is to say a certain waiting period, a long round of observation, a sharp dialogue, nearly a verbal joust, both of us calmly seated in front of a drink, me leaning forward in my seat, you with your legs crossed modestly, but without a word at the entryway of my apartment you slid your hands beneath my shirt, offering me your lips, and now, tonight, I still have not heard the sound of your voice, I am the one speaking ceaselessly as I pin you beneath crumpled sheets, gripping your arms obligingly raised over the pillow like the large white parentheses of the hummingbird mask, putting all my weight on your star-shaped body, my cock sunk deep inside you, thrust in your pussy, screwing you, and gradually I learn that in a burst of laughter you can topple the most sure projects, shake up life as you see fit, proliferate the unexpected, with great difficulty I realize that you have a crazy talent for disconcerting, catching people off guard, deviating the course of things, overturning the text's predictions, and delighting in it.

You make yourself comfortable, you are unencumbered, as if the mask's large white feathers gave you wings, you are no longer mine now that you are mine, you no longer belong to me at the same time as I possess you, since I met you last night at David's I have noticed your power not only over me but also over the novel, over my version of the novel, over my novel, and yet my author and I fashioned you, created you, pulled you from the void, but now that you are mine you are almost entirely liberated from my text, you are no longer our docile creature but my lover at once unruly and submissive. Despite everything, I don't understand what happened, for the words that I whisper into your ear are not even in my book, your silence, your sighs, and your abandon are not either, or else much later, toward the end of Chapter 15, for this chapter of my novel, the one in which I am speaking to you at present, begins with a long dialogue, perhaps a bit too tortuous, in the living room of my friend's apartment in Brooklyn we cautiously bring up the previous night while drinking a glass of red wine and nibbling on crackers, I ask you what happened after I left, you answer that David slowly recovered from the shock of the explosion, you add with a smile that after a while he stopped repeating "the bastard" like a robot and suddenly decided to go to sleep without even asking you how you felt, whether you were hurt, how the cut on your forehead could have disappeared, no, he quite simply ditched you, then you tell me that the second dessert we never touched was a delicious chocolate mousse dusted with ground Espelette pepper, and when I let out a cry of surprise, you burst into laughter, you make fun of me, say: "I noticed that your book does not mention this dessert on the menu for dinner at David's. Chocolate mousse, if I remember correctly, is also what Prote ate on the plane, isn't that right?

After the salt cod? In Chapter 12, if I remember correctly, when you transform into the Invisible Man and hold his small spoon in the air above his meal tray. I loved how uncomfortable he was. He was truly shocked, poor Abel. But it's still bizarre that that chocolate mousse wound up on our table when it should have remained in the novel," and I reply: "Yes, another deviation. An addition. A discreet invasion. An unexpected translation. Two desserts instead of one. Two explosions instead of one. As soon as you're involved, everything's a mess. Don't take this the wrong way, but as soon as you appear, the boundaries become porous and chaos takes over. But really, where did it come from, that dessert? How did it arrive on the table?" "I have no idea," you reply. "I made the raspberry charlotte, but I didn't know about the mousse until it appeared on the table at the end of the meal. It's a mystery." "I know where it came from. It came straight out of Chapter 12, 'The Flight.' If you want my opinion, it's like someone photocopied certain pages of the novel and then inserted them haphazardly into our lives. And I'm really afraid that this business of copy-pasting has only just begun..."★

★ Chapter 15, which you are reading at this very moment, my reader, predicted this perplexing dialogue between Doris and me, Trad. A dialogue that describes a new disparity between the novel and real life: the unexpected arrival of a large compote dish of chocolate mousse on David's dinner table. No one bought it, this second dessert, no one made it either. Each of the three guests believed that it was one of the other two who was responsible for it. The final sleight of hand of this dialogue that was supposed to unfurl the night Doris came to visit me is like a doubly powerful deviation, the interlocking of two alterations: the subtraction of an addition. *(Aghast Trad's Note)*

You drink a sip of wine and then talk to me about the cut on your forehead from the explosion: "Last night, when I went into the bathroom, my head was spinning. I couldn't see anything clearly anymore. I stood in front of the mirror. I saw the drop of dark red blood dripping from the cut above my right eyebrow. Then I watched, bewildered, as the drop faded, slowly became colorless and clear like water, and then that translucent bead fell onto the back of my hand, gripping the enamel of the sink. I looked down to examine it, rub it between the thumb and index finger of my other hand. It was indeed water, and it quickly dried between my fingers. When I raised my head to look once again at the reflection of my face in the mirror, the cut had disappeared from my forehead. I ran my index finger over the place where it had been: nothing. Not the least rough patch. No trace. The skin of my forehead was perfectly smooth and painless. But I didn't dream that cut. I saw it in the mirror, I'm sure of it. Even you noticed it, right? You said something to me about it. It disappeared the way you sometimes disappear: into thin air. At least that's what David told me. Unless he dreamed it on the plane to New York. Unless I only learned it this morning when I read *Vengeance du traducteur*. I don't know anymore. You don't remember either? After all, is it really that important, to know where things, people, objects, forehead cuts and chocolate mousses, feather masks and Lurex dresses, secret passages and violet crowns, model airplanes and *Fragments épars* come from, to what world they belong, if such and such an event actually took place, whether it's from a dream or a book? You think so? Do you really believe we need to know? Now that I've been confronted with all these anomalies, I'm starting to doubt it, even to laugh about it. What's important to me in this moment is drinking a glass of wine with you, feeling you close to me. It seems to me that you are indeed real, in any case more real than the cut on my forehead. But nevertheless I would still like to touch your hand to be sure. In fact, I need to."

So, still in this beginning of Chapter 15 that has been amputated by real life, according to the written version of our meeting that I did not live even though my novel predicted it, I draw nearer to you, seated with your legs crossed on the sofa, you reach out your hand to grab mine like last night, touch it, squeeze it, slip your ringed fingers between mine, close them against my palm and squeeze, mainly to reassure yourself, I know, of my reality, to convince yourself that I am not going to disappear like the cut on your forehead in the reflection of the mirror or like the plasma screen exploding at the bottom of the armoire, projecting its mortal frost throughout the bedroom. Like Saint Thomas venturing a doubtful index finger into the wound of Christ resurrected, you want to reassure yourself that I am indeed a man of flesh and blood and not a ghost, while I should really point out that you, Doris, are the phantom born of my words, a woman of smoke, a creature without substance, a marionette suspended by my phrases, a motionless puppet that derives its existence from only my breath—it's really me that should be verifying that you, Doris, are a beautiful woman that I could fall in love with without suspecting that you might slip between my fingers like sand. Yesterday, the drop of blood on your forehead nearly convinced me of your reality.

Thus we begin this written soirée that belongs only to the book, thus we progress with careful baby steps as I did last night with David on his glass-covered bedroom floor, thus we get to know each other little by little without ever completely dissipating that intimate and shared doubt that unites us perhaps even more strongly than desire: are you more real than the ephemeral cut on your forehead? Am I more trustworthy and durable than a chocolate mousse fallen from the pages of a book?

In the novel, this dialogue that we did not speak soon makes way for the silence of our two voices. Then another conversation begins, which dispenses with words, filled only with the sighs and muffled cries of our two suddenly chatty bodies.

In this precise moment on the time axis, the connection is made, the written and unlived loop of amorous preludes converges with its starting point and the abrupt trajectory of our desire; the verbose fiction of Chapter 15 catches up to our shared reality: our skins at present pressed one against the other, our gasping breaths, our agile hands, and I begin to talk: "Yes. Last night. Everything began last night. The colorful hummingbird . . .

"I am in you, inside you, with you, Doris, you are a moth, a bird with wings spread to accommodate my body, you know now that I am real as I know that you are real, not subjected to my words even if of your own free will you submit to my desire. In this bedroom in Brooklyn, I go back and forth in you without ever ceasing to speak, but then in your turn you speak up and immediately I recognize your words, for they are the ones I placed in your mouth so long ago, those murmurs that you offered to David in Chapter 9, those tender and coarse words that you employ again here with a few slight variations, and I realize worriedly that it's not just the chocolate mousse that has surged from the past to invade the present, I realize that it's not just Prote's voice that has been recorded. Here is what you whisper to me while I keep quiet and continue to go back and forth in you:

… Here you are at home, Trad, get comfortable, explore the grounds, there, that's perfect, verify that everything is in its place, in order, positioned as it should be, don't forget any corner, any overhang, any hiding place, any niche, inspect all my crevices, be meticulous, be persnickety, rigorous, and meticulous, like with the devil, the pleasure is in the details, yes, do a careful inspection, take out your checklist and check the boxes with your pencil, really check that box, verify that nothing is missing, go over me with a fine-tooth comb, twice not just once, make your nest here and act like a bird, crane your neck, it's your turn to spread your wings, like that, that's good, yes, continue, go, excavate there rummage excavate far, farther, keep going, you're almost there, almost at the quay, your dick wedged up against the mooring, you're there, my love, do you feel how I'm squeezing you tightly, you are, you go, if you keep at it like that you're going to make me come, wait, don't move, yes, there, stay, let me squeeze your iron fist in my velvet glove one more time, now hang on for a bit, the inventory is finished, you checked me, relax, be lethargic but don't fall asleep, no, it's important that you not fall asleep, don't leave me, stay with me, just stop moving, breathe a little, grab a folding chair, here, sit here, relax a minute, the movie will start soon, now it's my turn to move, leave my home, leave the lobby where they sell popcorn and soda, cross the threshold of my room, settle yourself comfortably at the entryway, near the little glass booth where they sell tickets, get some air, fill your two fertile lungs, inhale the breeze, smoke a cigarette, see the thickets still soaked with rain at the edges of me, my multicolored silks, I'm ready, take my emotion, break me entirely, the last lights of day make a crimson fog in the sky stained with sperm, oh yes, like that, keep going like that, continue like that, hold me tight, with me in me outside of me there you are allowed to go back and forth between the printed American text you're translating, inflected modified destroyed, butchered, demolished, and the French version you're creating from beginning to end, fashioning inventing and constructing, this is your own secret passage, your personal sleight of hand, your not very professional to-and-fro, your paid and brazen movements, your certified but rogue work, and all the better if in your new profession as a writer you mix business with pleasure, but here in my net and my silk inside me in me outside me you aren't working or toiling anymore, you're screwing me good, Trad, you come and go without creating anything other than my happiness, yes, come, go, I like your back-and-forth, your back-and-forth ravishes me like a glove, *e la nave va*, I leak, trickle, sluice gates all the way open, I sink faint melt drown, come, your light my life delights me, come, Trad, translate yourself inside me quickly yes, I'm coming

Chapter 16

PROTE RECEIVES A FINAL VISIT

"I don't know why I agreed to meet you in my home. I don't know you. You told me you had met David Grey and Doris Night in New York. I haven't been in touch with those two in a long time now. David is the American translator of my last novel, *(N.d.T.)*. As for Doris Night, she was my secretary for a few months. You also are a translator. Is that right? But, according to your telephone call yesterday, French is your mother tongue and you translate from English. Alright. Apparently you've come from America. How can I be of service?"

I am with Abel Prote in his opulent living room, sinister and opulent, two lamps struggle to dissipate the shadows. And yet the curtains of the large windows are open. Beyond the glass, I see flowerbeds and two enormous plane trees in the courtyard whose dense foliage sieves the light of the sky. I am seated in a madder-red armchair. He is seated opposite me on the sofa, backlit, like a human resources director interviewing a potential employee in his office. He's wearing a bathrobe, though it's three in the afternoon. It's mid-May and it's hot in Paris, but Prote has offered me nothing to drink. Not even a glass of water. I came with my computer. Alone. Doris moved heaven and earth to come with me and I had a hard time convincing her to stay and wait for me at her place in Belleville. I repeated to her that my computer would suffice to keep the French writer under control. Battle weary, she ended up ceding to my arguments.

Without asking Abel Prote's permission, I light an American Spirit. He murmurs an uncomfortable "Hmm..." then, grudgingly and taking his time, he goes to look in the kitchen for a small chipped saucer, which he places carefully on the armrest of my chair.

"Here's what brings me to your home," I say after two or three drags from my cigarette. "I've just finished translating an American novel entitled *Translator's Revenge*. In French, *Vengeance du traducteur*. It turns out you are a character in this novel. Like me, Doris Night, and David Grey. No, let me finish. You can snicker later, if you still want to. *Translator's Revenge* also includes your novel, *(N.d.T.)*. I'm giving you everything all at once. Try to retain and absorb the information. This American novel, by an anonymous author, or rather by an established writer who does not want to reveal his identity, I not only translated it but adapted, modified, reorganized it from top to bottom, I appropriated it, vampirized it for reasons that do not concern you. Then a bizarre thing happened: to my great surprise, I noticed that the entirety of my translation, *Vengeance du traducteur*, had—and still has—the curious habit of transposing itself onto real life. Don't laugh. Listen to me. There are two successive translations: the first is my work as a renegade, indelicate, apostate translator; the second, more mysterious, 'translates' the contents of the book into reality. In other words, all I have to do is write that Doris disguises herself as the Iron Lady for her to immediately be wearing this costume. Do you see? It's a system of communicating vessels. Or rather a contamination. My text is prophetic in a way. But Doris displays a rather peculiar characteristic, in fact she possesses the vexing habit of disrupting the projection of the text into real life. So let's say instead that all I have to do is write that the crown of violets placed on your desk in the adjacent room contains a letter by the young American actress Dolores Haze, a letter written at the end of the 30s, for it to be the case. Have you examined the center of that crown recently?"

"Uh, no."

"I advise you to do so. Right away."

"Are you kidding? Is this a joke?"

"Go get it. It's still on your desk. On the pile of books."

"How do you know that?"

"Go on."

Prote stands up reluctantly, goes to his office, and comes back with the violet crown. His fingers are already foraging through it. He takes out the onionskin folded into sixteen, thirty-two, sixty-four, and unfolds it carefully while I turn on my computer and recite, for I have that page of the text, and all the others, memorized:

"'Maurice, you can call me your Dodo, your Dora, your Dollie, your Lolo, your Lola, your Loli, but never Lolita, it's much too vulgar.' Are you following along? You can finish later."

"But…" Prote protests. "How is this possible? I myself am only just discovering the letter in this very moment. I…"

"You see, you're beginning to understand."

"It's a trick. You, or one of the other two scoundrels, shoved that letter there. You're in cahoots with them to conspire against me."

"Be quiet. I can prove to you right now that your novel is included in mine and that you are nothing but a character of *Vengeance du traducteur.*"

"You're not actually going to try to get me to believe the story of the Chinese king who dreams that he's a butterfly who dreams that it's a king who dreams that he's a butterfly, and so on, ad infinitum? That absurd mise en abyme…"

"Yes. And right now, in fact."

I rapidly skim the text, looking for the passage in which David eagerly examines the large painting hung in Prote's office. I select the entire descriptive paragraph and prepare to press the *Delete* key on the keyboard.

"Go back into your office. That canvas depicting a double-page spread is still hanging on the wall?"

"Uh … yes," replies Prote, who obeys. "Why?"

"Admire it for the last time. I am going to delete the description in the novel. Watch. One, two, three."

I touch the *Delete* key.

In the adjacent room I hear Prote cry:

"My Piffaretti! Give it back! Thief! The painter himself gave it to me, you dirty crook! It's worth a fortune! It's my most prized possession! I demand that you give that painting back to me immediately!"

"You are not in a position to demand anything, Abel Prote. All I have to do is save my text file in its current version for that painting to be gone forever from your office, and from the world. You will never see it again. No one will ever see it again. It will have disappeared into the limbo of my computer, annihilated like the thousands of bytes dragged to the trash that gathers everything into a discreet but gigantic black hole, all the bodies, the images, and the spaces that those bytes represent. On the other hand, if I do not save the modifications to my text, the changes perceived in the real world will be undone.

"Look at your wall instead of screeching like a kid who's just had his rattle taken away. I am going to undo the deletion of the paragraph describing the painting. Are you ready?"

I press a key on my keyboard. An exclamation of surprise springs immediately from the neighboring office:

"Well I never! There it is again. My Piffaretti... Intact. Perfectly identical to the old one. It's as if nothing happened. But how...?"

"Come back here." Suddenly docile, Prote comes back. "Sit down." He sits down. "Listen to me. We have already met. But you couldn't see me, even if you suspected a presence right next to you. I will refresh your memory a bit. On your plane from New York to Paris, two weeks ago, you thought you saw, no, you really did see, a small spoon levitating above your chocolate mousse. You had had quite a bit to drink that night, isn't that right, you immediately called the flight attendant, whom you of course did not succeed in convincing. Then you chased from your mind that unwonted vision, blaming the alcohol, you willfully erased the memory of that levitation even though it was indeed real. Do you remember now, the small spoon? Stop giving me that stupid look and answer me: do you remember?"

"Yes," he trembles with a kind of morbid excitation, "it's coming back to me...Yes, the small spoon above my meal tray. I had managed to forget it. That night on the plane to Paris, it's true, I celebrated leaving New York a bit too much, after settling the final deft details of my best treasure hunt..." Then, after a silence in which he seems to lose himself in recollection, he adds: "But... how could you possibly know the story of the small spoon, the episode that I am the only one to have lived? And how is it that you know so well what went on in my head that night?"

"For starters, I was the one holding your little spoon in the air. But you didn't see me. I was invisible, as invisible as your painting was a minute ago. I had just lost my translator body, I had not yet integrated my author body. I was like a text typed in size 0 font. Ten minutes earlier, I had just jumped from another plane to yours. But that doesn't matter. Secondly, I repeat, you are only a character in my novel. And my memory is infallible."

"I don't believe you," comes Prote's retort, as he gets up, crouches in front of the bar, and takes out a bottle of Black & White whiskey. "It's nonsense, I don't believe a single word of your hogwash. You just want to swindle me."

"Serve me a glass of Sandeman port. I'm a fan of the man in black on the label."

"My word, you've already been here!" Prote says, outraged. "Or else your two repugnant accomplices gave you a very detailed description of my apartment and the three of you are trying to hoodwink me, dispossess me."

"I'll start the demonstration over again. For the last time. Let's see... Yes, that's it, I'll modify your interior again. A brief paragraph of the novel describes the decor of your walls. I'll select it now: 'Drab tapestries—depicting Diana's bath, a hunting scene, the passing of a comet above a bucolic landscape where rural peasants seated on the threshold of their cottages raise their astonished eyes toward the black sky streaked with a thin pale stripe—all these images darkened with time suck even more light out of the rooms and accentuate the feeling of a permanent dusk.' Are you ready? I'm pressing the *Delete* key. Ah, right away we can see better in your living room, don't you think? So about that port, are you going to serve me or do I have to do it myself?"

"Right away, right away, but I beg of you, give me back my tapestries. All those large pale rectangles on the walls...such horror...such vertigo...Atrocious! It was my grandfather on my father's side who..."

"Hurry up. And bring me a glass of water, too, while you're at it. I'm waiting."

"Okay, I won't be long," murmurs Prote, who goes back into the kitchen holding his forehead as if he were suffering from a sudden migraine.

Maybe I should really shut that bastard up, I say to myself, suddenly exasperated by all his phony simpering. I rapidly revisit Chapter 5, select a few phrases, press the *Delete* key. Immediately, I hear Prote hoot pleadingly from the kitchen:

"Excuse me, but ... I can't return to the living room. There's ... there's no more hallway. My apartment has lost its hallway ... I don't dare leave the kitchen. Please ..."

I place the computer on the thick brown carpet, get up, go to the door of the living room and notice with stupefaction that in place of the hallway a uniformly gray space seems to sink into the ground to an unknown depth. The armoire has also disappeared. In a Venetian mirror hung on the opposite wall, I see the inverted reflection of the puppet in the fresco: the marionette now seems to be falling into a bottomless void.

Next to the reflected puppet, Prote with distorted features is frozen in the frame of the kitchen door. Standing on the edge of the chasm, he's holding a tray with a glass of water, a small stemmed glass, and a third, stemless glass.

"Is that enough for you?" I ask. "The violet crown, the painting, the tapestries, the hallway. Are you convinced or would you like me to keep purging your furniture?"

"Yes, yes, yes," my host stutters in a meek voice. "I believe you, but have mercy, put my hallway back in its place."

I return to the living room, grab the computer, undo the most recent modification to the text, and immediately I hear a relieved sigh come from the kitchen. Prote arrives and places the tray on a side table before going to get the two bottles of alcohol still on the bar. He is deathly pale, his hands tremble.

"Thank you, that's enough," I tell him dryly once he's poured two drops of Sandeman port into the small stemmed glass, and almost as much garnet liquid onto the varnished wood of the tray. "Let's proceed to the conclusion of my demonstration: in the same way as any object or space in my novel, I can also select the name of a character of *Vengeance du traducteur*. If I hit the *Delete* key on the keyboard, well, this character disappears like your painting, your tapestries, or your hallway. Do you follow, or would you like for me to repeat myself?"

"No, no ... or rather yes, I understand perfectly."

"For example, I can delete this odious, manipulative, noxious, arrogant, intelligent but egotistical, cultivated but pedantic character who calls himself Abel Prote. I can delete you, by merely erasing your name from my text file. And unlike your painting, which I've just reproduced, your deletion might be definitive, irreversible. Would you like for me to try?"

"No ... Thank you," answers Prote, visibly scared to death. "That won't be necessary. Let's not make any rash decisions. Let's remain calm. I take your word for it. You've already given me enough proof as it is. I am convinced. But what ... what do you want in exchange for my survival? Money? I don't have a lot. My most precious possessions are in fact those three tapestries you've just stolen from me."

"I am not a thief. I am happy to make things vanish and, sometimes but not always, make them reappear. Like an illusionist makes coins disappear, or colorful scarves, his white rabbit, his rings, or his assistant. But I don't want money. Do I need to remind you that your tapestries exist only in the virtual state of my text file, and nowhere else? I can neither sell them, nor hang them on my walls."

"So then what? I beg of you, give them back to me."

"Maybe later."

"What do you want?"

"I want for you to piss off from my novel, to scamper from my prose, I don't want to see your evil oaf face anymore, I want to be definitively rid of your pretentious and contemptuous voice, I don't want to ever hear of you again, Abel Prote."

"I promise to leave you alone, to do no harm to you, or Doris or David Grey. Although, Lord knows they've poisoned my life, those two."

"Be quiet. I paid them a visit in New York, not long after your stay in David's apartment. You who plan everything out, for fear of the least surprise, you who think you anticipate and manipulate the gestures and emotions of everyone you meet, you did not guess—and for good reason—that I would be in New York with my two favorite characters ... There, your little exploding tricks made their mark, believe me. The glass stacked beneath the duvet, the caltrops in the bathtub and the sink, the burnt trash in the oven, the lacerated ties ... Such tact! Such lovely thank you gifts! How thoughtful you are! But most importantly, blowing up the plasma screen nearly killed all three of us—for you did not predict that I would be there with them when David opened the panel hidden at the bottom of the armoire and triggered the start of the video, then the explosion of the screen. You nearly killed me at the same time as David and Doris, I who am the only guarantee of your earthly existence."

"Believe me when I say I'm sorry. I didn't ... "

"Shut up! I've had enough of your hypocrisies, your moronic, malevolent maneuvers. This novel, which you know nothing about but which your life depends on, is called *Vengeance du traducteur*, don't forget it, I have not yet exacted my vengeance. But I know the end of the text, for I've already translated and copiously rewritten the last pages of the present chapter. It's Chapter 16, if you're interested. Here is the end of the book."

I highlight the words *Abel Prote* throughout the entire text and my right index finger lowers toward the *Delete* key on the keyboard. Prote bounds brusquely from the sofa with a vivacity and nimbleness I did not think him capable of. His fingers grip my arm, push it back toward the armrest of the chair. Then his head violently collides with my computer and suddenly I find myself alone in the room. The massive body of my assailant, for a brief moment lolled over mine, has disappeared. Suddenly I gasp. I didn't press the *Delete* key, but Prote's forehead did, while that idiot was trying at any cost to stop my finger from reaching the small black rectangle ... I slowly gather my spirits, then look around me: no cadaver encumbers the living room, there isn't the least trace of blood. On the side table, the three glasses are knocked over in a puddle where the garnet-red port mixes with the golden beige whiskey and the transparent water. That two-tone puddle is bristling with slim luminous fragments: the stemmed glass has shattered. The chipped saucer containing my ashes and my cigarette butt has scattered its contents over the carpet and the oriental rugs. The sofa cushion where, a few seconds earlier, Prote gathered momentum to launch himself at me slowly regains its convex form while emitting a slight hiss, as if no body had ever sat there. An absolute silence soon reigns in the apartment.

I deliberate: will I reverse the arrow of time and go back and resuscitate the French writer, or else enshrine his disappearance with a click?

I hesitate, stand up, stroll through the living room avoiding the dark furniture, then, prey to indecision, I go back into the office. On the desk, next to a pile of books and Prote's computer, is a small block of amber containing a fossilized insect. My fingers mechanically seize this paperweight, from the depths of time or else from the factories of the People's Republic of China, where it was fabricated in a supply chain two months earlier (this is the first time this object appears in the novel, I have no memory of it). Distractedly, I turn it over in my impatient fingers, touching and examining its perfectly smooth sides, the perfectly rectangular edges. Still hesitating, I lower my eyes toward this geometric mass, translucent and yellowish. Suddenly, I come up with an idea.

I return quickly to the living room, take my computer, pull up the end of Chapter 16, then, after the words "Suddenly, I come up with an idea," I feverishly type these few paragraphs:

"I leave Abel Prote's apartment and go back onto the landing. I close the door behind me, and save the most recent version of my text. Then, from the other side of the thick wooden panel, the living room, the office, the bedroom, the entryway and the hallway, the kitchen, the bathroom as well as the entire secret passage situated behind the armoire, are covered instantaneously in fossil resin, in that petrified sap we call amber. In the blink of an eye the hard funereal material climbs up to the ceilings, insinuates itself in every crack, thoroughly molds the objects, encircles the furniture, books, and clothing, the Post-its from the cork board and the ties in the armoire, the gleaming slivers of the stemmed glass recently broken on the side table, the cigarette butt and ashes spread over the living room carpet, the large pale rectangles on the walls designating the places where the tapestries henceforth forever absent still shone this morning, even the little yellow amber paperweight containing the insect embalmed since the Oligocene era, that tiny block encased like a Russian doll, or an Easter egg, in the enormous block of petrified amber.

"Then I turn around, go down the few stairs leading to the courtyard, and stroll onto the street."

Holding the computer between my hands, I leave Abel Prote's apartment and go back onto the landing. I close the door behind me. The bolt clicks in the keeper. I turn around. Then, with a resolute finger, I hit save on the file named *Vengeance du traducteur.* Click. Then, after a slight pause, another click. I suddenly hear behind me the wood of the door creak and split under the pressure of the yellow amber. I pivot to the left, go down the few stairs that lead to the flowery courtyard and to the two majestic plane trees, I turn back to face the large windows with the strangely opaque squares, as if I were in front of a gigantic abandoned aquarium inside of which I can barely distinguish a few vague shapes through the stagnant water: a phantom couch, a little farther back the dark brown hole of an open door, one or two lighter rectangles on the walls that testify to an absence.

Then I cross the courtyard to the dark porch. I hear muffled crunching behind me, like a monstrous grinding. I press the button that opens the door leading out to the sidewalk. Then, without turning around, I'm back on the street and turn right toward the Odéon metro station to take the Line 4 that will bring me underground to Barbès-Rochechouart. Then I will change to take the aboveground metro on the Line 2 which will take me to Belleville and to Doris.

EPILOGUE

In the end, *Vengeance du traducteur* was published in France under only my name, so much did I adulterate the original text with my changes. With the agreement of the enigmatic American author and his publisher, another French translator was chosen to carry out a more faithful version of *Translator's Revenge*. The funniest part is that a publisher in Dallas has just acquired the rights to my novel to have it translated into English and published in the United States. What Doris sometimes jokingly calls a "return to sender," or a "lovely back-and-forth."

I fear that my American translator is none other than David Grey, whom neither Doris nor I have had any news from since that blessed and terrifying night when the plasma screen exploded before our eyes and unleashed its wave of sharp slivers upon us.

Doris and I have been living in a three-room apartment in the 10th arrondissement of Paris for some time now. Every so often I perceive in her gaze a sort of distrust or perplexity, as if she suspected me of having hidden her keys or deceiving her, without any proof. I can't pretend that I don't also sometimes fall prey to that astonishment, that incredulity that suddenly makes me frown and interrupts me in the middle of a sentence, when the cold, implacable logic whispers to me that it's impossible and unreasonable, even dangerous for my mental equilibrium, to believe in the possibility of sharing a life with the character of a novel I've written. I have no desire to reread *Vengeance du traducteur*. Even if I still have not yet managed to forget a single phrase of the book, I do not want to change a word of it.

There was much ado in the press about the disappearance of Abel Prote. On May 22, 2007, *Le Monde* published this brief article in its literary supplement:

A Writer's Mysterious Disappearance

Abel Prote, the author of several daring and remarkable novels—including *La Maison du deuil* and, more recently, the very unique *(N.d.T.)*—had not shown any sign of life for a week in his Parisian home in the Odéon neighborhood. And for good reason. The police, alerted by the building concierge, tried in vain to enter the writer's apartment. Even with the help of a locksmith, the police did not succeed in forcing open the door. After breaking a few windows, they had the unpleasant surprise of immediately running into a compact wall made of a sort of hard resin, yellow and translucent, similar to amber, which filled all the rooms of Abel Prote's apartment up to the ceiling. Investigations are underway to determine the exact nature of this uncommon material. The police now wonder whether they will discover the body of the novelist fixed in this impenetrable mass, like an insect of the Oligocene era fossilized in a block of amber. The inquiry is, as they say, underway.

Doris just went out. She was delighted to hear me tell of the unusual circumstances that allowed me to rid myself of Prote with his own involuntary complicity, then of how I transformed his apartment into a monumental mausoleum for an absent cadaver: a final subtraction, followed by an unexpected addition. A double click and the job was done. It brought us even closer. I think Doris…

Someone's just rung the doorbell. I have a meeting with my American translator, who's visiting Paris. A certain Emma Ramadan. She lives, I'm told, in Providence, Rhode Island. Not New York. We're supposed to work the entire afternoon on the most difficult passages of my novel. To be honest, I sincerely doubt that it's possible to translate *Vengeance du traducteur* into English… First problem that comes to mind, the English title *Translator's Revenge* is already taken. She'll have to find another and then write the American version taking the new title into account. But first she'll have to rethink the embedding of the narrative bearing in mind this unexpected interlocking, this new level of expansion…

This Emma Ramadan seems nice. Enthusiastic, zealous, and nice. She wrote to me that she really likes my novel. She's even translated a few pages already. I truly hope that it's not David Grey using a fake name. But, in addition to this rather understandable apprehension, I harbor another, more insidious fear: that this Emma Ramadan will be like me, that she will not remain humble, enthusiastic and zealous, modest and rigorous. That she will take herself for Zorro, the masked avenger, or for a vampire. Or heaven forbid, that she take herself for a writer.

I get up to open the door. I fear the worst.

BRICE MATTHIEUSSENT is an award-winning translator of over 200 novels from English into French, including the writings of Jim Harrison, for which he was awarded the 2013 Prix Jules Janin from the Académie française. In 2000, he was awarded the UNESCO/Françoise Gallimard Prize for his translation of Robert McLiam Wilson's *Eureka Street*. His other translations include the works of Jack Kerouac, Henry Miller, Annie Dillard, Rudolph Wurlitzer, and Charles Bukowski. He graduated from the École nationale supérieure des Mines de Paris in 1973, and earned his PhD in philosophy in 1977. Matthieussent currently resides in France, where he teaches the history of contemporary art and aesthetics at the École supérieure des beaux-arts in Marseille. *Revenge of the Translator* is his first novel, and was awarded the Prix du style Cultura upon publication in France in 2009.

EMMA RAMADAN is a translator living in Providence, Rhode Island, where she is co-owner of Riffraff bookstore and bar. She is the recipient of a Fulbright grant, an NEA Translation Fellowship, and a PEN/Heim Translation Fund grant. Her translation of Anne Garréta's *Not One Day*, published by Deep Vellum, won the 2018 Albertine Prize, and her translation of Anne Garréta's *Sphinx* was nominated for the PEN Translation Prize and the Best Translated Book Award. Her recent translations include Anne Parian's *Monospace* (La Presse), Oulipian Frédéric Forte's *33 Flat Sonnets* (Mindmade Books), and Fouad Laroui's Prix Goncourt-winning story collection, *The Curious Case of Dassoukine's Trousers* (Deep Vellum).

Thank you all
for your support.
We do this for you,
and could not do
it without you.

DEEP
VELLUM

DEAR SUBSCRIBERS,

We are both proud of and awed by what you've helped us accomplish so far in achieving and growing our mission. Since our founding, with your help, we've been able to reach over 100,000 English-language readers through the translation and publication of 32 award-winning books, from 5 continents, 24 countries, and 14 languages. In addition, we've been able to participate in over 50 programs in Dallas with 17 of our authors and translators and over 100 conversations nationwide reaching thousands of people, and were named Dallas's Best Publisher by *D Magazine*.

Deep Vellum is a 501c3 nonprofit literary arts organization founded in 2013 in Dallas's historic cultural neighborhood of Deep Ellum. Our mission is threefold: to cultivate a more vibrant, engaged literary arts community both locally and nationally; to promote the craft, discussion, and study of literary translation; and to publish award-winning, diverse international literature in English-language translations.

As a nonprofit organization, we rely on your generosity as individual donors, cultural organizations, government institutions, and charitable foundations. Your tax-deductible recurring or one-time donation provides the basis of our operational budget as we seek out and publish exciting literary works from around the globe and continue to build the partnerships that create a vibrant, thriving literary arts community. Deep Vellum offers various donor levels with opportunities to receive personalized benefits at each level, including books and Deep Vellum merchandise, invitations to special events, and recognition in each book and on our website.

In addition to donations, we rely on subscriptions from readers like you to provide the bedrock of our support, through an ongoing investment that demonstrates your commitment to our editorial vision and mission. The support our 5- and 10-book subscribers provide allows us to demonstrate to potential partners, bookstores, and organizations alike the support and demand for Deep Vellum's literature across a broad readership, giving us the ability to grow our mission in ever-new, ever-innovative ways.

It is crucial that English-language readers have access to diverse perspectives on the human experience, perspectives that literature is uniquely positioned to provide. You can keep the conversation going and growing with us by becoming involved as a donor, subscriber, or volunteer. Contact us at deepvellum.org to learn more today. We would love to hear from you.

Thank you all. Enjoy reading.

Will Evans
Founder & Publisher

PARTNERS

SUBSCRIBERS

Ali Bolcakan
Andrew Bowles
Anita Tarar
Anonymous
Ben Nichols
Blair Bullock
Brandye Brown
Caitlin Schmid
Caroline West
Charles Dee Mitchell
Chris Mullikin
Chris Sweet
Christie Tull
Courtney Sheedy
Daniel Kushner
David Bristow
David Travis
Elizabeth Johnson
Ellen Miller
Erin Crossett
Farley Houston
Florence Lopez
Hannah McGinty
Holly LaFon
Jason Shaver
Jeff Goldberg
Joe Maceda

John Winkelman
Joshua Edwin
Kenneth McClain
Kevin Winter
Lesley Conzelman
Lytton Smith
Mario Sifuentez
Marisa Bhargava
Martha Gifford
Mary Brockson
Matt Cheney
Michael Aguilar
Michael Elliott
Mies de Vries
Nathan Wey
Neal Chuang
Nicholas R. Theis
Patrick Shirak
Robert Keefe
Ronald Morton
Shelby Vincent
Stephanie Barr
Steve Jansen
Todd Crocken
Todd Jailer
Will Pepple
William Fletcher

John Schmerein